# YELLOW ROOM

# YELLOW ROOM

## Shelan Rodger

THE
DOME
PRESS

Published by The Dome Press, 2017

A CIP catalogue record for this book is available from the British Library
ISBN 978-0-9956723-7-6
[eBook ISBN 978-0-9956723-8-3]

The Dome Press
23 Cecil Court
London WC2N 4EZ

www.thedomepress.com

Printed and bound in Great Britain by Clays., St. Ives PLC
Typeset in Garamond by Elaine Sharples

For Mum

# PART ONE

# CHAPTER 1

Buttercup-yellow walls shine in the warm, late afternoon sunlight that spills into the room and through the slats in Emma's cot. Emma and her four-year-old sister are lying side by side, playing babies. Chala pretends to be asleep, even trying to produce the funny, spluttering sound that comes from her father's open mouth when he snoozes in front of the television. Then she rolls over suddenly and gently shakes or tickles her baby sister to show that she is really awake. Of course, Emma has been watching her all the time. She knows perfectly well that her sister is pretending, but this doesn't stop her delight every time Chala pounces on her. She looks at her big sister with her brown-dog eyes that haven't yet learnt fear. There is no one else in the room.

The game gathers momentum and, each time she pounces, Chala's movements are a little stronger and Emma's giggles a little louder, but it is Chala who grows bored first and looks around for something else to play with. The only toy in the cot is a rag doll, called Rosie.

'Now Rosie can be your sister,' says Chala. 'You go to sleep next to Emma,' she says gently, lifting the small pillow so that Rosie and

3

Emma can lie more or less side by side. Emma gurgles with pleasure, while Rosie stares up at Chala with unblinking, black-cloth eyes.

'Go to sleep, Rosie,' says Chala, covering Rosie's eyes with the pillow. She lifts the pillow, but Rosie's eyes still stare at her. 'I said close your eyes,' she says more roughly, forcing the pillow back down over the two baby faces. Emma's gurgles have changed key and suddenly she is crying.

'Shh-shh—' says Chala, growing distraught and pushing the pillow down harder to muffle the sound of her sister's cries. 'Stop crying, Emma. Stop!' Emma struggles and splutters, and Chala pushes harder and harder, and suddenly the crying stops.

When Chala lifts the pillow, her sister's eyes are wide open.

\* \* \*

'Chala! Food's ready!' She jumped. After three years of marriage, Paul's voice could still make her jump. There never seemed to be any warning. He was either there, in your face, loud and utterly present, or simply not there, no background clatter to give him away. The same was true of his moods, which flashed inexplicably from playful optimism to gruff despondency, with no apparent transition from one state to the other.

'Are you coming or not?'

Paul's voice again, rising and impatient. Sometimes Chala wondered how he was able to deal in the subtleties of colour on canvas when his words were so often black and white. But maybe that was what made the canvas so important; perhaps it was the one place in his universe where contradiction was allowed to flourish and the decisiveness he projected to the world became blurred.

'I'm there!'

She raced downstairs to the kitchen and remembered why she loved him. Paul was standing by the table, an open bottle of wine in his hand and a tea towel draped across his arm. He removed a rose from her glass and poured, beckoning her to sit. Candlelight, soft jazz and an avocado mousse for starters. The seductive pull of black and white.

'What—'

'No reason,' he cut her short. 'It's good to have you back, that's all.'

'But I've only been away a week,' she protested softly, defensive.

'I don't resent the fact that you've been away,' he cut in again, looking straight at her. 'I just think life's too short and it's important to remember what's good about it every now and then. Sorry if that's too romantic for you, but I'm genuinely happy to see you!' Paul was laughing now, but serious.

'I'm sorry. What an ungrateful old cow you married! I didn't mean—'

'Forget it.'

There was an edge now. She felt chastised, guilty for not giving him the benefit of the doubt. And yet Paul's spontaneity had been one of the things that had attracted her to him. When they first got together he was constantly staging small surprises. He would insist on packing her things for a weekend away, so she would have no idea where they were going. He would send her a text, saying meet me at such and such a place in an hour, which might turn out to be a comedy club or just a walk on the beach.

But when she had first been introduced to his parents and affectionately told an anecdote about turning up to one of his surprises in totally inappropriate clothing, she had seen Paul's face cloud and his mother had talked over the end of her story. Chala had been disconcerted to realise that her open admiration for their son was a source of embarrassment to them. Their hallway was filled with signs of his achievements – a star pupil certificate, a rowing trophy, a class portrait and then another with the New College, Oxford crest, a framed law school certificate. Their only son's stepping stones to success were on proud display, but there were no smiling photos and – most shockingly to Chala – no clue to his passion for art.

Surely, she had said to him later that evening, you must have been good at art at school? Yes, Paul had sighed, I loved art, but Mum and Dad didn't. In that moment a sense of purpose was born in her; the resolve, come what may, to stand by his art, to fill in the cracks his parents had left and help make it part of his life.

'So, tell me about your week away,' said Paul into the silence forming between them.

Over avocado mousse and a Jamie Oliver special of pasta with chorizo and fennel, she talked. She told him about the chaos of bicycles on the street, about the delicacy of the food and the earnestness of the people, their desire to welcome and please. She described the hotel in the centre of Ho Chi Minh, long hours talking behind closed doors that could have been anywhere in the world, and then stepping out at night into a feast of light and warmth. The humour of animal noises in different languages, which served them so well over dinner one evening with their Vietnamese hosts, and how this gentle congeniality clashed with the sex trade that lurked so close to view all around the city. But Vietnam was a place she would like to return to, a place to add to the must-visit-one-day-with-Paul list.

What she didn't tell him was that a colleague had made a pass at her one night. She hadn't responded, hadn't even been tempted, but she had been flattered. So why didn't she mention this? The question gnawed at her.

'Paul,' she said suddenly, changing the subject, 'the words we used at our wedding, do you remember? Kahlil Gibran – "Let there be spaces in our togetherness" – something about two trees growing side by side with their roots reaching toward each other, but without obscuring each other's light?'

'Mmm …' Poor Paul. He had that look. Caught suddenly in a conversation he hadn't chosen, knowing that he was about to be asked to talk about the dreaded 'f-word' – feelings. The place for these was in his paintings, not in conversation. He tensed almost imperceptibly, but Chala reacted to his body language.

'Don't panic. I'm not going to ask if you still love me. But—' She saw him for a second with a stranger's eyes – permanently tanned, healthy from the time he spent outdoors, with none of the pallor of the commuters who poured back into their Sussex village at the end of each day, his boyish, blue-eyed, square-featured looks radiating self-confidence. She knew it hadn't always been the case, but the cliché was made for him: he was comfortable in his own skin.

She grasped for the thread of what she had been about to say.

'But what does any of that really mean? Does it mean we *shouldn't* be totally honest with each other? Should I keep things from you if they're hurtful or insignificant? Do you keep stuff from me?'

For a moment Paul looked trapped, but then he relaxed again.

'Yes, I "keep stuff" from you. I mean, I don't tell you every time I have a wet dream about Cameron Diaz.' He was laughing, trying to coax her back to the easy exchange of anecdotes and impressions.

'What if it's a dream about someone we know?'

7

'No. I don't see the point in that.' More serious now. 'Chala, what's this about? Where is this going?'

'Please, Paul, don't be defensive. If we are "two trees" then it's good to talk about this kind of thing, isn't it?' Chala didn't really know where she was going. She paused and looked into her wine – and suddenly, inexplicably, emotion was rising in her throat. 'It's just … I don't know. I think it must be different for you. The only thing you can think of to mention is wet dreams, for God's sake! It's just that … sometimes …' There were quiet tears on her face now. 'Sometimes, I'm afraid of myself.'

A gentle weariness dragged at the lines around Paul's eyes. He had always wanted Chala to be open. As their trust in each other had grown he had encouraged her to dig into the black holes of her memory, thinking she would be able to move on. He respected her darkness, loved it at some level, but the pull was always there and increasingly he found himself reaching deeper and deeper for the strength to draw her back.

'Che, my lovely, what's brought this up all of a sudden? Don't do this to yourself. This is just your imagination talking. Come on, let's leave all this. Let's go to bed.'

As he drew her up from the chair and into his arms, she felt equal tugs of gratitude and fear: gratitude for his ability to paint away the bubbles from her past, for his faith in their future, and fear that she didn't deserve it.

# CHAPTER 2

'Phiwip! Where are you?'

Chala's screams bring Philip to the room in seconds. He sits on the edge of her bed, pulling her out from under the covers, wiping the sweat from her brow and stroking away her fear. 'It's OK, my sweet. You were just having a bad dream, that's all. You're OK now.'

'Where's Rosie? Is she still there?' 'Of course she is, my sweet.'

'Where? Where is she? I need to see her, Phiwip.'

Philip responds to the fear on her face. 'She's where you left her, in the toy trunk. Look, I'll bring her to you.'

Chala backs up against the wall as Philip walks across the room with the doll in his hands. 'Has she got two eyes?'

'Of course she has,' he says, sitting down and noticing Chala flinch as he holds Rosie up to her. 'What happened? What did you dream?'

'We were playing a game, and—' Chala takes a gulp of air and races through the memory. 'And then it was my turn to sing "Twinkle, Twinkle", but I forgot the words and she started laughing, and—'

'Who started laughing?' Philip struggles to keep up with her. 'Rosie, of course. She was laughing and laughing and then I got angry and I pulled her eye off her face and then she was crying and—' Chala is sobbing again. 'And I think she's dead, Phiwip.'

'Listen, my sweet, she's absolutely fine. It was just a bad dream.'

The next question catches him in the stomach.

'When is Emma coming home?'

Philip frowns and holds her small shoulders in his hands. 'Emma can't come home, my sweet. She had an accident and died. It's very sad, but sometimes that happens to babies. She's gone now. It's just you and me and Denise now.'

'And Rosie.'

'And Rosie.'

'Will you stay here for a bit?'

'Of course I will, my sweet. I'll stay here until you get to sleep again.' And Chala snuggles up against him and feels his beard brushing her face and finally feels safe again.

* * *

'Chala, are you deaf? It's Philip on the phone!'

Chala came to with a start at Paul shouting again. She had been working on a report, but her words were long since tucked up behind the screen saver of Rudolph, their pet hamster. She had no idea how long she'd been staring at him.

'I'll take it in the bedroom,' she called. She shut down the computer and hauled herself back into the present.

'Chala, my sweet, how are you?' Philip sounded more tired than usual.

She struggled with the juxtaposition between past and present that still swam in her head. 'I'm fine, Philip.'

10

'You sound tired.'

'So do you, actually. Are you OK?'

There was a moment's hesitation and then he filled it. 'Yes, my sweet, I'm absolutely fine.'

'So, what have you been up to?' Still, she sensed a reticence.

'Well, a lot of gardening and sitting looking.' This was a piece of family vocabulary Chala had grown up with. Philip had once been to Cuba and marvelled at the way people sat nonchalantly watching the street or a view without a trace of hurry or boredom. He used to say that we in the West had lost the ability to sit and look, and Chala always made a point on her travels of noticing those that still could.

'And I'm finally going to start some general sorting out.'

'You mean you're actually going to tackle that heap of old boxes in the attic?' Chala tried to make light of the fact that, as far as she knew, these mementos of a past long buried had lain untouched since Denise's departure over twenty-five years ago.

'Well, I can't leave it for you to sort out when I'm gone, can I?' He, too, was playing it down.

'Not that you're going anywhere soon, are you?' There was the tiniest edge to her teasing – that sliver of nervousness that creeps in when we joke about the death of a loved one.

'No way – not until you've learnt to beat me at chess anyway.'

'Good. Then I'll come down for the weekend when I get back from Australia. I told you, didn't I, the company is sending me to Australia?'

'Yes – what a dreadful waste of money! Enjoy yourself, my sweet, and ring me when you're back.'

'OK, I'll see you in a couple of weeks, then.' She hesitated, acutely aware of the emotional significance of what he planned to do. 'You be careful in that attic … I love you.'

She put the phone down gently, a moment of stillness around their conversation.

Then Paul's voice broke in, 'Che, we're leaving in fifteen minutes!'

She dived into the shower without answering. Eight minutes later three outfits lay discarded on the floor as she lunged for a green velvet skirt and a bright orange crinkly top that clashed with the red in her hair. When they'd first met, Paul used to say that her looks were perfect for an artist. Her dark skin and long red hair were an unusual combination, and there was an air of mystery and impenetrability about her which sometimes frightened those who knew her history but fascinated those who didn't. She had gone through phases in her life of trying to hide the elements that drew attention to her – cropping her hair like a schoolboy, avoiding make-up or colour in her clothes – but the starkness had, if anything, been even more striking, and in the end she had resorted to bright clothes and long hair as easier to hide behind. Wet hair, no make-up. Oh well, this is about Paul, not me, she thought, and fled downstairs.

He was ready and waiting, in jeans and a faded blue shirt.

'Aren't you going to dress up?' she teased.

For the briefest of seconds he looked like a small child, almost hurt. Chala realised he must be nervous and reached out to ruffle his hair, but he caught her hand in the air.

'Don't,' he said, and she swallowed the impulse to take it personally, knowing this was just his way of feeling strong. The elephant shadow of his parents' disapproval hung briefly between them and she wished he could let her stroke it away for ever.

\* \* \*

Chala was standing in front of a black-and-white photo that had been partially coloured in – and battling the desire to find the child responsible and make them clean it up. The photo itself, she quite liked. It was a dusk view of woodland with white light filtering through the trees, but she couldn't see that the vibrant red bush or bright yellow flower added anything. To her literal eye, it just looked silly. She didn't like all of Paul's work, but at least his paintings were – what – real? Vital? Intense? Vivid? Chala bit her lip at the clichés she reached for whenever she tried to think about a piece of art and thanked God that at least she wasn't an art critic. Sitting looking – that's what people should be doing, Philip would have said. Too much talking, talking, talking …

'So, what do you think? Do you like it?' Oh no, not the artist, please no. 'Don't worry, it's not mine – you can say what you like!' Chala looked gratefully at the woman in front of her, but still didn't speak. The woman was clad in some kind of checked material which was doubtless very trendy, though it made Chala think of golf, but her face was open and slightly flushed.

'Well, it's not really—'

'Your thing?' She laughed. 'No, I don't like it either. I don't really get it. I mean I wish it would just be a photo without the attempt to, I don't know, art it up.'

Chala wished for confidence like that. She knew that her own looks were often a hurdle. Even if she wasn't conventionally beautiful, the fact that she was striking meant people assumed she was self-assured, too.

'Come on, you look like you could do with a drink. I'm Nicola.'

Chala followed Nicola to the bar, hoping no one else could see through her, but they had only just got into a conversation about something unrelated to art when Paul sauntered into the middle of it with a corduroy-clad stranger at his side.

'Che, I want you to meet a friend of mine – Daniel.' Mmm, thought Chala, such a good friend that I've never heard of you before. And then, 'Daniel, this is my wife.'

'Chala Hutchings,' she said. She hated it when Paul called her 'Che' in public. As for 'my wife', she had loved the sound of that when they first got married, but now it smacked of a sense of possession that had nothing to do with the content of their wedding vows. It made her feel like an accessory, and she didn't know how an accessory was supposed to behave.

'This is Nicola,' she added, 'a friend of mine.' Nicola caught the irony – though Paul didn't – and laughed.

On the way home Paul was driving and they both seemed content to let silence wash through them after the twitter of endless sound bites. Chala's thoughts drifted back to the phone call with Philip, trying to put her finger on what had bothered her about him. The resolve to rake through those boxes in the attic must be weighing on him much more heavily than he was prepared to admit, but it was no use talking on the phone. She knew he hated talking on the phone. When she went to visit him on her return from Australia, they would go walking on the moor – their safety net for conversation. Then she would be able to make sure that he was really OK.

Paul cut into her thoughts. 'So what the fuck's wrong with you tonight?'

Chala jolted back to the evening they'd just left behind, aware that she had lapsed into a half-presence after Nicola had left them, unable for the life of her to think of anything to say to Daniel or any of the others who had joined them. How she wished for Nicola's easy confidence. How she wished she could be the person Paul so obviously wanted on his arm.

'Nothing's wrong. It's just … I don't know … I'm sorry if I let you down.' She didn't know how to talk to him when he was like this.

'No you're not.'

'Not what?'

'Sorry.'

'I am. I *am* sorry.'

'No you're not. It's always the same. "Oh, how fantastic, you've got an exhibition, I'll be there for you."' His high-pitched imitation of her voice made her feel as if she had been winded. 'And then when it happens, you're never fucking there.'

She slumped into silence, defenceless.

She knew she wasn't good at these events, not good at parties or social functions. And yet there were other – less public – ways of being there for him. Had Paul forgotten the slow exorcism of insecurities that had made it possible for him to leave a safe career in pursuit of a dream? The days when Chala had slowly inched into the raw place inside him that had been carved out by his parents? She had seen through the comfortable skin he offered to the world, stunned by and yet sensitive to the lack of self-belief that had kept him in a job he hated. She had believed in him. She still believed in him.

When they got home, he walked in ahead of her and went straight upstairs to bed. She climbed in beside him a few minutes later, careful not to touch him, and lay spooned away, staring in the dark. Nobody prepares you for this, she thought, nobody tells you that loving someone is not enough.

She scrolled back through the years to the first time they had met. It was at a mutual friend's wedding in Andalucía. Guests had poured in and occupied the entire village, with seasonal bars opening in June just for them. She had noticed Paul the day he arrived, the day before the wedding, and felt bashful. At the reception their shared status as members of the unattached minority had thrown them together at the same table. What she only realised in retrospect was that they had talked about things they wanted to do in life rather than the things they actually did. Paul had talked to her about painting. She had only learnt from someone else that he was a lawyer and it had instantly struck her as a misfit. She had talked to him about Africa and travel and an undefined yearning to 'do something worthwhile'. They had danced together and he had touched her hair and she had calmed the tremble in her hands behind his neck, but then they had drifted to different parts of the room and nothing more had happened.

Back in the UK, six months later, they had still not slept together and yet they were spending more and more time with each other, and had already begun the process of sifting back through the incubation period of their relationship, turning it into a story. One day, sitting on the crimson sofa in her bedsit after an evening at a comedy club and remembering the Spanish wedding, she told him that she had longed for him to dance with her again.

'What!' he had said with a stage slap of his palm against his forehead. 'Why didn't you give me any clues? Why didn't you ask *me* to dance?'

'Too shy,' she had said, feeling even now the rush of blood to her face.

'With your looks? You shouldn't be.' And he had stopped more words with his mouth on hers, and then she had seen his eyes glance

16

towards the bed in the corner of the room, and suddenly he was leading her to it, saying 'May I? I want to see more of you. I want to look at you. I want to paint you. I want to fuck you senseless.'

And she had felt the blood not just in her face but all through her body.

Afterwards, she had picked up the story again, teasing him. 'So, why didn't you ask me to dance again? Why didn't you come near me again?'

'You were too scary, too beautiful.'

'I'm neither of those things. Go on, what was it?' She had rolled over to face him and was looking for answers in his eyes.

'No, really, you seemed distant and I wasn't sure that you were interested. And ...'

'And?' She was like every other woman in the world at this moment, poised for the next delicious detail in the story they were making about their discovery of each other. But what he said next had shocked her.

'I didn't want to frighten you away. Claire warned me about you—'

'Warned you?' She was stiff then. 'About what?'

'Bad choice of words – I didn't mean it like that. I mean she told me what happened when you were a kid and that you were wary of relationships, and for the first time in my life I didn't want to blow it by rushing in and spoiling everything.'

She had drawn the sheets up around her in an involuntary movement to cover herself and then started to pull towards the edge of the bed, to move away, but he had grabbed her by the wrist and forced her to look at him.

'Chala, I realise this is a big deal for you, but it isn't for me. Just remember that. Don't ever forget that.' Something about the way he

17

said 'ever' made her feel safe. She had melted back into the bed beside him and tried to convince herself that it wasn't important.

# CHAPTER 3

Somewhere in the blur of the weeks that follow, Chala is standing behind Denise in a check-out queue at their local supermarket. Denise has a slightly wild, unkempt look about her. Her hair, chestnut brown and usually pulled back neatly into a ponytail at the back of her head, hangs loose and wiry over her shoulders. Her face has the grey stamp of insomnia and even the tiniest act seems to require enormous reserves of concentration. At this moment, she pours intense effort into the simple business of piling the items from her shopping trolley onto the counter, unaware that she has duplicated certain things and forgotten others. She registers with a pang the approach of a mother and pushchair at the end of the short queue, and then concentrates even more fiercely on her shopping.

She doesn't notice Chala's involuntary wince as the baby in the pushchair joins their queue. Chala steps closer to Denise and concentrates on the pattern on her jeans pocket as she bends over to take out the last tins from the trolley. It's just a baby, silly. You don't even have to look at it. And anyway, it's not even looking at you.

But then something awful happens. The lady immediately behind them suddenly remembers something she has forgotten and disappears, muttering, to fetch it, and the mother pushes her baby forward so that it is now right next to Chala. Delighted by the sight of a little girl almost at eye level, the baby starts to gurgle, gazing at Chala as if it has known her all its life. A proud smile is already breaking out on the mother's face – the smile of a million mothers worldwide, so besotted with their own child they assume others feel the same. But what happens next converts the smile into an expression of horror.

Chala loses concentration, looks up from the pattern on Denise's jeans pocket, accidentally makes eye contact with the baby and screams. Denise jumps and drops a jar of marmalade, which shatters on the floor and Chala, still screaming, clings to her leg, trying to hide from the baby ghost that is looking and looking at her. The mother with the baby pulls the pushchair backwards, away from the queue, and, with a parting glare at Denise, crouches to comfort her own baby, who has now started to cry. Everyone is staring at Denise, but she barely registers this as she tries to separate Chala from her leg. Sorry, she mutters to the cashier, who looks if anything a little frightened, and Denise bends down to try and calm Chala. But Chala is clinging and sobbing into her leg and she is forced to pull her away quite roughly, at which point Chala screams again. For an awful second it looks as though Denise might hit her, but then she too starts to cry, picks Chala up and holds her tight, and everyone looks away, embarrassed, as a kind of normality slowly returns.

When they get home, Philip is already back and Chala rushes straight into his open arms. Philip doesn't notice that his wife says nothing. He doesn't notice the weariness on her face or in her step as she brings in the shopping. After all, the limpness in her movements has become normal over the last few weeks. She has almost finished unpacking when it occurs to him to leave Chala for a minute and go to greet her. He walks around the bar into the kitchen area of their recently fitted open-plan living area and approaches her from behind to peck her on the cheek. He doesn't feel her stiffen.

Later, Chala wakes up to the sound of Philip and Denise arguing. She can't really hear or understand what is being said, but Denise's voice gets louder and louder. Chala tries to shrink under the covers, but every time she closes her eyes it is as if Denise is standing there beside the bed, screaming at her.

And sometimes, very late at night, Emma's ghost comes back to visit, but it isn't Chala she comes to see, it is Rosie. She comes to make sure that Chala hasn't hurt her. Chala woke up screaming the other night, because they were making such a noise playing together in the drawer where she had packed Rosie away, out of view. Philip came running in and hugged her, and listened to her explain that Emma and Rosie were making too much noise.

'Where are they, my sweet? Where did you hear them?' And he had followed her frightened little finger and opened the drawer, and told her that it was OK, Emma had gone now. 'Do you want me to take Rosie away somewhere?' He had sensed her revulsion at the sight of the cloth doll. I don't know why we don't just throw it out, Denise had said once in a moment of irritation after another nightmare had broken their sleep, but Philip had caught the look of alarm on Chala's face and understood it.

'Shall I take her away?' he had gently offered again.

'No, no, no, she mustn't go away. She will be angry, Phiwip.'

'OK, I tell you what, how about we put her in a new place, somewhere nice and comfy, where she can rest without being disturbed?'

'But where, Phiwip?'

21

'What about on the top of the cupboard, with your spare blanket?'

'OK. And then you kiss me goodnight?'

'And then I'll kiss you goodnight, my sweet.'

But it never worked, Emma always found her sooner or later and then Chala would wake up screaming again.

* * *

The battery was running low on Chala's laptop, so she shut it down with a double edge of reluctance and relief. She could finish the presentation later and anyway she had drifted off again. She packed away the laptop and settled back into her seat to contemplate the hours left. The first leg had been quite painless – a meal, a film and sleep of sorts. A brisk walk and a foot massage at Bangkok airport, and now the time-travelling had really begun. When the flight landed in Sydney she would have lost a day over the ocean.

Chala toyed with the concept of time and wondered whether it is ever really possible to recapture the past. All memories are reconstructions. How much could she honestly claim to remember of her early childhood? So many early memories had a textbook quality about them, details learnt from photos or the repetition of anecdotes. Even she and Paul had been together long enough to dispute the detail of shared memories. Did she really, truly, actually remember what had happened that day in the yellow room? She had worked out a kind of explanation that made it possible to live with herself, but how much of it was true? Every now and then some detail would force itself onto centre stage of a memory, so irrelevant or intimate that she felt it couldn't have come from someone else's story, something that just felt irrefutable. But how could so much of the past that defined her exist beyond her grasp? She blinked, hauling herself back into the present.

'What are you planning to do in Australia, then?'

Shit. She had been remotely aware that her unchosen companion on the flight from Bangkok had been itching patiently for an opportunity to start a conversation, despite the empty seat between them. She hated talking about herself.

'The company I work for has just bought an Australian company and I'm going over to visit their schools.'

'Oh, what sort of company is that then?'

She looked at him for a moment. Did it really matter what sort of company it was? Then he would ask her exactly what her job was. He was English. He would need this information to open the gates to further conversation. Then she would have to ask him what he did. Something to do with the City she thought, but not too senior, otherwise he would be travelling business class. And then – God forbid – they could get on to more personal questions about each other's partners and marital status.

'We have a number of schools for international students in the UK, the US and now Australia. We offer language and academic preparation programmes for universities and I'm working on product development across the group, so I need to see how the schools work in Australia.' This would surely bore him into silence. 'I also have a husband, I don't want children and I don't want an affair,' was what she felt like adding. Just in case.

'Oh, interesting.'

Result, she thought. He's bored. Now all I need to do is not ask him what he does and then there will be a few moments' uncomfortable silence before we can both retreat back into the space of our own privacy.

'So, what do you do then?' She kicked herself mentally under the seat in front of her, convention winning the battle.

'Do you really want to know?'

Whoops. And suddenly – now – she did.

'I didn't, but I do now!' The words took her by surprise. She laughed and the ice was broken.

His name was Bruce, which had nothing to do with going to Australia. He had walked out of a City job and a relationship, which were both strangling him – that explained why he was in cattle class – and he was off to spend the paid leave he had negotiated travelling round the world, first stop Sydney. Despite the conversation opener, he was interesting, didn't waffle, and laughed easily. Actually, she thought, with an obscure sense of guilt that seemed unrelated to the situation, those words could describe Paul, and yet she was sure these two men were very different.

'Have you ever slept with an Aussie?' Her neighbour was looking at her slightly quizzically.

'No,' she laughed nervously. 'Why?'

'I don't know, I just wanted to make sure you were still here. You seem to spend a lot of time in a daze, that's all. Like when you were working on the laptop, I don't think you would have noticed if a bomb had gone off.'

'So you were spying on me, then?'

'Just looking … I like the way you look.'

Chala switched away from his eyes and noticed his hands. They looked like the hands of a guitar player, almost feminine, and the thought of them touching her shot through her. She blushed and opened her mouth to say something quickly.

'Do you play the guitar?' she asked, and looked back at his face.

He hadn't struck her as good-looking in the peremptory glance she had given him as she sat down, but the intensity in his eyes as he regarded her now did nothing to relieve the blush she could feel spreading across her neck. She noticed that his hair was thick and straight and slightly spiky and made you want to stroke it.

'No. Why? Do you?'

And so went the ping-pong of conversation between them. She answered his questions quickly, unthinkingly, as if silence were some kind of threat. Despite the empty seat, he felt too close.

They had dinner and then more wine, watched the same film and then agreed to meet at the same place for breakfast.

'Why don't you raise the arm? You can have those two seats to sleep on. I can rest my head against the window,' he offered gallantly.

'Sure, thank you,' she replied immediately, grateful that the lights were dimmed. But what if her feet poked into his legs? She felt foolishly self-conscious. It wasn't as if she hadn't done this before! You simply shrink and create a protective layer around you that tucks you into your own tiny space. So she drew up her legs, tucking them in tightly at the knees, wondering if it wouldn't be better to move into the seat in the middle and keep her legs on the side of the aisle. God no, her head might flop over onto his shoulder!

She nestled slightly further into the space between them, acutely conscious in the semi-darkness of the tiny gap between her foot and his thigh, and tried in vain to sleep.

After a few minutes, he shifted in his seat and she felt a flood of static as he touched her accidentally with his thigh.

'Sorry,' she muttered, feeling immediately stupid.

'Don't mind me,' he countered sleepily, sinking further against the window.

Chala battled through the night against the unsought intimacy of their proximity and her own restlessness, which only highlighted the electricity of each accidental brush against each other. Once she woke up to the feel of him pushing gently past her to visit the loo. Her body moved to let him through.

When breakfast came at last it was a relief to be able to start talking again, but Chala was annoyed with herself. Why in so much conversation had they steered so clear of personal circumstances and, specifically, why had she failed to mention Paul? Yet if she did so now it would sound out of place and much more important than it was, like an acknowledgment of something that needed to be held in check, and if that something were all in her imagination, she would just look silly. What would Paul have done in her place, she wondered. He would have spilled his personal situation in black and white right from the start, she was sure.

In a rush of guilt, she suddenly gabbled out a CV to Bruce, which included the fact that she had met Paul five years ago and they had been married for three. He looked up from his congealed omelette with a smirk on his face that made her want to either hit him or ruffle his hair. Paul hardly ever let her ruffle his hair.

'No worries, Sheila,' countered Bruce with a mock Australian accent, and then, apparently serious, 'I knew there had to be a good reason.'

'For what?'

'For not having sex with me on the first night.'

'You arrogant—' And she did hit him, with a mock slap across the cheek.

'OK, look,' he said, serious this time. 'I am running away from boxes and locked doors, and I have no desire to get myself – or you

– into trouble before I even get off the plane, so relax. No pressure, OK? I'll give you my mobile and if you feel like a drink on land, then call me.'

Chala's immediate impulse was distrust. This was real cool-speak – much too cool for her. And there was something about the unsought chemistry of the night that flashed on and off inside her. But she took the number.

# CHAPTER 4

By the age of six, Chala has burnt off some of the toddler fat of her early years, but her rosy-cheeked, full-moon face retains a chubbiness that keeps her puppy-like. Her red hair is always too long, even days after it has just been cut, and stray curls across her face are in almost every photo ever taken of her. She has grown into a rather shy, nervous little girl, capable of spending hours playing on her own, but when she smiles, and two puckered dimples pierce her roly-poly cheeks, she looks like an angel straight from a da Vinci painting. In morbid, introspective moments, the Chala of later years will look back at photos of herself and strain to see some sign of what lies beyond the sham of innocence.

Today, she sits expectantly on the chequered rug that has been laid out in their little walled garden on a spring Sunday afternoon. Ever since Denise left, Philip makes a point of doing something special on a Sunday. They go for excursions to the beach, play hide-and-seek in the woods on the edge of the moor, pick blackberries or bake bread together – and they discover an effortless companionability with none of the edge that so often accompanied the attempt at family outings with Denise. Chala doesn't know where Denise has gone and Philip doesn't talk about it. Today he is making her favourite picnic lunch: marmite sandwiches with banana.

At last Philip appears at the glass door that opens straight from his study into the garden. He is carrying the expected tray, piled high with sandwiches, juice, beer, raspberries and cream. There is something of the absent-minded professor stereotype about Philip. With his soft beard, longish, prematurely greying hair and glasses he is forever losing, he is perfectly in context in his primary school classroom full of eager or unruly young faces. Elsewhere there is a gentle clumsiness about him; an awkwardness that Denise used to find endearing when she first met him, but struggled with over time. In the kitchen he looks quite out of place, and most women if they see him there cannot contain an impulse to wave him aside and take over. The mess behind him now belies the outcome – he must surely have cooked a three-course meal, not a few rounds of sandwiches!

They tuck into their picnic with shared relish and then lie back on the rug and look for shapes in the clouds. Philip sees trees and rivers and mountains. Chala sees mostly dogs and horses, and Philip makes a private resolution to buy her a dog. A dog will be a distraction and good company for both of them.

'Phiwip?' Chala says, still looking up at the sky above them, and he tunes into the sudden childish earnestness in her voice. 'Why did Neece leave us?'

Philip thinks hard about how to present reality to a six-year-old but, impatient, she fills the pause with another question. 'Was it my fault?'

'Of course it wasn't, my sweet. Why would you think that?' Philip is glad that they are staring at the sky and that she doesn't see the tears in his eyes. He launches into a simple, adult explanation. 'Sometimes things go wrong between a man and a woman. It's nobody's fault, but sometimes it just happens and they can no longer live together, and then one of them has to leave.'

'Has she gone to look for Emma?' Chala is still woken up by occasional nightmares about Rosie, although Emma hasn't been to check on Rosie for a while now. Once Chala ripped Rosie's arm off and hid it in the rubbish, another time she buried her alive in the garden, but these things happen less often and during the day she finds that she can even let Rosie sit on her bed sometimes.

Philip swallows hard. 'In a way, yes, I think she has sort of gone to look for Emma. You know, my sweet, she doesn't blame us, it's just that, well, I suppose in a way, we both remind her too much of Emma not being there.' Chala says nothing and Philip decides to give her more adult information. 'You know, Chala, before Denise and me, you had another mother and father. Your real mother was my sister—'

This is too much for six-year-old Chala. 'Don't be silly, Phiwip, you don't have a sister.'

'Not now, no, but I used to have one and she was your mother. Her name was Sarah Bryan – you see, she had the same surname as you and me – and your father's name was Robert Walsh. When you were two years old, they had an accident and ... and they died, so you came to live with us.'

'Look at that cloud there, what can you see?'

Philip wonders if he was wrong to tell her, but when is it the right time to tell a child that you aren't her real parent? 'Um, I can see ... I can see ... a giant fish,' he offers with a proud jolt of his imagination.

'Don't be silly, it's not a fish, Phiwip,' she chastises him.

'Well, what is it then?' he says, almost put out.

'It's your sister!' And Chala starts to giggle at her own joke.

Philip laughs too and comforts himself with the hope that he has done the right thing. Over the months that follow, his sister and brother-in-law become figures in a story for Chala, good ghosts to crowd out the bad ones. Philip is always reticent, but gradually, over the years, Chala will coax out the story of what happened and what they were like. She will look at old photos and play imaginary games with them. When she becomes a teenager she will love the tragedy of the way they died, in a climbing accident on Mount Kenya during their honeymoon. She will love the knowledge that her own birth parents were unconventional enough to wait until she was two to get married, at a time when this was hardly the norm, and the fact that they were adventurous and young, and that this will never, ever change. Mount Kenya will become a legend in her imagination … honeymoon mountain.

But when she talks about her birth mother to Philip, she never says 'my mother', it's always 'your sister'. 'Tell me more about your sister, Phiwip.'

At school, some of the kids laugh at her and ask why she calls her daddy by his first name, but she shies away from a direct answer. Her stories are private and she doesn't want to share them with her classmates.

The day of her eighth birthday is one that she will never forget. Philip drives her to her school on the way to his own, just like any other day. Having himself suffered the stigma of being a student in his father's class, he was determined not to let that happen to Chala and applied for a teaching job outside their primary school catchment area. By now, they have developed a comfortable routine around their day. Chala goes home with her best friend, Amanda, who lives down the road. Philip picks her up an hour or so later, with Rusty, their gorgeous springer spaniel puppy, and they walk him home together. On long summer evenings, they walk past their converted cottage into the woods and watch Rusty chase butterflies through the ferns, but on cold, dark winter nights, they march straight back to the house and warm their cold noses by an open fire. Like a retired couple who have slowly grown to resemble each other in old age, sharing and acquiring each other's habits, Philip and Chala have both discovered something safe in the act of walking and talking. It's a time they both savour, when the distractions of Rusty and the weather and the view around them make intimacy less intense.

On her eighth birthday, which falls in July, they are to have an after-school picnic in the woods with Amanda and her family. Chala is excited, but she makes Amanda promise not to tell the other children that it's her birthday. She hates being the centre of attention and yet, in the playground during break, a tiny incident will launch her centre stage with a force that will ensure she needs to take beta blockers before any form of public speaking for the rest of her life.

She and Amanda are part of a group of girls who have formed a circle. In the middle, two girls are rotating a skipping rope. A girl called Louise, with rolls of fat and lots of freckles, is the leader. Chala is a little bit afraid of Louise, but all her friends are Louise's friends and everyone does what she says. 'One, two, three,' chants Louise, 'tell us about your brother' – or your mother or your favourite game or the boy you'd like to kiss. And the girl whose turn it is to skip has to shout out things on cue to the rhythm of her skipping.

'Tell us about your father' is the cue when it is Chala's turn.

'Philip is a teacher … Philip's got a beard … Philip's …'

And then she trips with the concentration of thinking of more things to say and everyone laughs and suddenly someone is saying, 'Why do you call your daddy Philip?' And others chime in, 'Yes, Chala, why do you do that?' And Louise says, 'I know why,' and everyone crowds round her expectantly and the skipping rope lies forgotten underfoot.

'He's not her daddy, he's her uncle. It was on TV. My mummy told me about it, but said I mustn't tell.'

'Tell, tell, tell,' chant the little girls.

'She killed her baby sister with a pillow when she was four.'

There is a moment of complete silence as the girls absorb this shockingly delicious revelation about their classmate.

Chala's face is stone-still. What does Louise mean? She can't really remember what happened, but she knows that baby Emma disappeared one day and never came back. It was an accident – that's what everyone had always said.

But then she feels the eyes around her, bursts into tears and runs indoors, followed only by Amanda. And the rest close ranks to invent more detail in the story of Chala's crime.

From this moment on Chala will find herself the twin butt of their revulsion and their fascination. No one except Amanda will want to be on the same side as her when they are asked to form teams for PE. Only Amanda will sit next to her in class. And yet they will not be able to stop looking at her. Her entry into a room will never go unnoticed again.

\* \* \*

Chala rubbed her eyes and wondered how many years it would take to undo the damage of who she was. Despite her resolve to master jetlag and stay awake through the day, she had drifted to sleep and woken up in the grip of some kind of half memory to do with being taunted at school. It was probably all just a matter of nerves, because she had to give a presentation the next day. Pathetic, she added to the list of taunts for herself. Get over it.

She went into the bathroom and took one of the Valium she reserved for moments like this. She thought about calling Paul, but it would be too early in the morning there and, anyway, what was the point? Why burden him with something so ridiculous, so far away? She tried to look away from Paul's presence in her mind, to look inside herself for strength, as if conscious of a need to break the habit that had formed so seductively between them, the black and white cushions of his arms around her. She climbed back onto the hotel bed, dragged her laptop out of its case and opened the unfinished presentation with a slow and deliberate deep breath.

By eight o'clock in the evening the pill had done its work. She had finished the presentation and felt a soft white wave of calm wash through her. Now she found she no longer felt tired and realised she would probably pay for the failure to stay awake through the day. Still, there was nowhere she needed to be until the following afternoon when she would visit the Sydney campus. She flicked through the room service menu and then thought, with an uncharacteristic flash of spontaneity, sod it, I'm in the gourmet capital of Australia. I'm going to a restaurant.

She spent the next fifteen minutes consulting the hotel guide and reception staff about where to go and how to get there, which meant that it took her longer to think about where to eat than it took her to do something utterly uncharacteristic that would change her life. She phoned Bruce.

* * *

'So how was your day?' The question was deliberately ironic.

'Fine. How was yours?'

'Not bad. So … what's new?'

They were sitting in the top-floor restaurant of a building that appeared to be made only of glass, with an intoxicating view of lights all around them, sipping very cold and very dry white wine. This wasn't fair, thought Chala. Why were they imitating a married couple? But Bruce was smiling warmly at her and she smiled back.

'Right. Time to introduce me to your husband. Come on. Let's get him out into the open!'

'Does your arrogance really work that well with women?' Chala countered, genuinely shocked by his absolute air of self-assurance.

'Bad call,' Bruce fired. 'Not arrogance. Just fed up of hiding shit beneath the surface. Did too much of that with the job – and with Janie.' The subjects had dropped from his sentences. This made him sound like a character from a very bad western and it made Chala giggle, despite herself.

'Sorry,' she explained to the momentary look of hurt on his face. 'It's the way you're talking. You sound like a poor imitation of Clint Eastwood, that's all!'

'Well, you can be pretty direct when you want to be, can't you?' Bruce raised his glass to hers.

'No … not normally, no.' Chala chinked her glass against his and looked away from his eyes. 'You never told me if you've actually been to Australia before.'

This was the way Chala worked. She needed to put spaces between intimacies. And neither of them realised that the subject of husbands and ex-girlfriends had been sidelined. They shared impressions of their travels and talked about safe dreams; dreams for him of living somewhere different, somewhere a million miles away from the City; dreams for her of doing something worthwhile, perhaps some kind of voluntary work in Africa, something that might 'help', if only she could define what that meant ...

'But what you do now is all to do with educating international students. Isn't that worthwhile?' Bruce asked her.

She sipped more wine and plunged into a subject she was not used to talking about. 'That's how I justify it to myself, but if I'm honest it's not really about helping people, it's about making money.'

'Tell me about it – you want to do a job swap?'

'I just wish I had something valuable to offer. I mean can you imagine how it must feel to be a surgeon or ... or a lifeguard?'

They both laughed and she took another sip of wine. Chala knew that she was drinking more than she should. She knew two other things. One was almost subliminal: a gentle lapping of guilt beneath the surface. Surely she was crossing a line. Or was this just space in their togetherness? But the second was more powerful, more present: she was enjoying herself, enjoying the freedom of anonymity, enjoying this man who knew nothing about her. With him she had no past. She did not need to be anything or anyone – she was free to imagine being a lifeguard, for goodness' sake, free from the fear of failure to live up to expectations – and this made her feel as though she were finding a new part of herself that she hadn't known existed.

They talked on over coffee and brandy, moving onto the open terrace, and then their conversation slowed. With the bill already paid, the empty glasses drew attention to the dilemma gathering momentum in the sudden silence between them. Chala felt dizzy and was not at all sure that it had anything to do with the wine and the brandy.

'Time to go,' she said, and was at once relieved and disappointed when he raised no objection.

'You're the boss,' he said, and followed her out into the lift that would take them back to normality.

What happened next took Chala by surprise and showed her another part of herself that she hadn't known existed. They were alone in the lift when, in one simple movement, Bruce put his hands against the wall on either side of her and kissed her deeply. Her mouth responded. There no longer seemed to be any connection with her brain. Her body ached for his to come close to hers, but he stayed where he was with arms outstretched either side of her, hands against the wall, and only their faces touching. His tongue searched inside her for an answer to the unspoken question and he got it.

They took a taxi back to his hotel and he led her to his bed. He kept her eyes his prisoner as he removed her clothes and then his, and she blocked out everything except her heartbeat. She pulled his head to her breast and he, too, heard the desire in her. Not a word passed between them. Their bodies didn't need words. Her consciousness couldn't form them. And afterwards, they fell asleep immediately.

Chala woke a few hours later with semen spilling out of her and a stranger's arm around her. In the first few seconds, before the inevitable tide of self-condemnation that would come, what she felt was: bliss. She would hate herself for it, but there was no other word to describe it – an extreme she had never achieved with Paul or the only other man she had ever slept with. She felt as if she had just done a bungee jump and overdosed on Valium at the same time.

'Hey, gorgeous.' Bruce stirred and pulled her to him.

And because she knew that the damage was done and that this had to be the last time she would ever see him, she squashed the tide down into a deeper part of herself and they made love again. And again they talked only with their bodies, but slowly, so much more slowly this time. He looked at her, and into her, and she felt intensely female. And everywhere he looked he followed with his hands. And when they came, she was just a split second ahead of him and he was holding her face and looking into her eyes … and it felt like a part of her was either dying or being born.

# CHAPTER 5

The birthday picnic happens, but newly eight-year-old Chala doesn't smile. Amanda's two-years-previously widowed mother, Julie, Amanda and her two younger brothers, Danny and Justin, are all there. They have brought rucksacks stuffed with sandwiches, pasties, orange juice and lemonade. There is even a chocolate cake, neatly packaged in the box that Philip bought it in. Their dog, Rusty, has found the perfect spot to lay down the blankets and the food, a small clearing in the wood next to the stream. The ground is soft and springy beneath them, and there is still a pleasant tang of wild garlic in the air.

The boys disappear as soon as they have unloaded their rucksacks and the girls organise their picnic feast in the middle of one of the blankets, while Philip uncorks wine for the adults. Chala is quiet and Amanda is fidgety, but Philip, perhaps shy in Julie's company, doesn't appear to notice anything. When Julie asks Chala to go with her to round up the boys, who have disappeared into the woods, Amanda corners Philip with precocious determination. She gives a rapid summary of what happened at school that day, wary of the others coming back too quickly.

'What does it mean?' She follows up her brief explanation with the question that has been plaguing her all day. 'Why are they saying all those things?'

Philip wishes Denise were at his side. 'Listen, Amanda, you're going to hear lots and lots of nasty things and most of them will not be true. The truth is there was a terrible accident and Chala's baby sister died. Chala was only four at the time and she was there when it happened, but she didn't do anything wrong. It wasn't her fault.' He pauses to weigh the impact of his words on the eager little face in front of him. 'And now she is going to need a really good friend at school.'

'I am her best friend,' Amanda says proudly, and Philip hopes desperately that this is enough. She ponders something for a moment and then asks, 'What was the baby's name?'

Philip marvels at the human thirst for detail, already manifest at the age of eight. 'Emma,' he says slowly, and the name seems full of sadness on his lips.

'But she wasn't Chala's sister really, was she?'

'Well, they were just like sisters, but no, you're right, by birth she was really Emma's cousin. Chala's mother was my sister.'

'OK, I understand.' And this is enough for Amanda.

Chala has another nightmare that night. She and Rosie are playing babies and she is bathing baby Rosie when suddenly she finds herself pushing Rosie underwater. Rosie screams and screams until there is no energy left inside her and her body is limp and wet in Chala's hands.

Over the days and weeks that follow the revelation in the school playground, she begins to make private sense of these dreams about Rosie. She begins to understand that it was never Rosie she killed, it was Emma. This knowledge will settle inside her like worms inside a dog; slowly, slowly invading her organs, pervading her emerging sense of self over the years to come.

Philip tries to tell her that it was an accident, that she did nothing wrong, that she shouldn't listen to the things people say, but grown-up little Chala knows he is just trying to protect her. It's the same with Father Christmas. People don't like to tell you that he doesn't exist because they don't want you to get upset, but Chala knows there is no Father Christmas and now she knows that she killed her baby sister when she was only four.

Over the coming months, Philip spends even more time with Chala. They take Rusty on a camping and walking holiday, just the three of them. They go on another holiday with Amanda and her mother and brothers, and Amanda and Chala hatch a plan in private and make a public proposal to the adults that they get married, so that they can all become brothers and sisters. Julie blushes harder than Philip.

Philip quietly watches Chala, carefully assessing her mood at the beginning and end of each school day. He never asks her a direct question, but he gives her harmless detail about his own day to see what she will offer him back. At first she is sullen and offers him nothing, and then gradually snippets filter through and begin to grow.

'We've started learning netball,' she tells him one day, clearly bursting to say more.

'And?'

'The teacher said I'm such a good runner I should be centre!'

'That's fabulous!' He realises there is still more. 'And?'

'And Louise wanted to be on my team.'

Philip wishes it were easier for men to cry. He knows what a huge milestone this is. Something that has been tense inside him for months slowly relaxes. He lets himself believe that he made the right decision not to pull Chala out of the school and away from her one staunch ally, Amanda.

When Chala is eleven and has just started secondary school, and begun to have tentative daydreams about what it might be like to kiss under the mistletoe, there is a day when she and Philip are on their way back from Sunday lunch at a local country pub. They both spot a furry shape in the middle of the road at the same time and, as Philip veers sideways to avoid it, they catch sight of it twitching. Philip immediately stops the car and reverses back to check if the fox has any chance of making it. He pulls up close to the hedge, so that there is plenty of room for other vehicles to get by, and both of them step out. As they do this, the poor fox pulls itself up and limps in pain and terror into the undergrowth of the hedge. Afraid of losing the chance to save it, Philip beckons Chala and they follow the blood, but just as they draw near, it forces itself further into the thick mesh of leaves and sticks. Philip is distraught and Chala doesn't know if she is more frightened for the fox or for him. She is not used to seeing him like this.

'We've got to do something or it'll die.'

'Well, why don't you go and get help, and I'll stay here and watch it.'

Philip hesitates a moment and then almost shouts. 'No, no – are you mad? Of course I can't leave you here on your own. Anything could happen.' Chala is silent. It's almost as if he is angry with her and that isn't fair, not something within her experience.

Another car draws up and Chala keeps watch on the fox, while Philip talks and gestures through the driver's window. Then this man disappears and returns, after twenty long minutes, with someone in gloves from the RSPCA, who catches the fox with a blanket and takes it away in a cage. Chala feels vaguely embarrassed to see tears in Philip's eyes and know that hers are still dry.

When they get home, Philip pours himself a larger than usual whisky and is exceptionally quiet. Chala looks around for a distraction and asks him if she can have a glass of whisky too. He seems about to say no and then changes his mind.

'OK, just a tiny tot. Why not?' He fills her glass so full of ice it's like licking whisky rather than drinking it. Chala won't realise until much later the extent to which Philip fails to subscribe to convention on how to bring up a child. Philip's basic premise in life is that everyone's view is valid. This makes him either wet or tolerant, weak or perceptive, brave or a coward, according to the outlook of those who come into contact with him. Whether as a teacher or a parent, he simply refuses to be judgmental, and young minds are forced to make their own choices.

It is not until she's fifteen that Chala feels a vague surge of rebellion. Without warning, and outside the comfort zone of their walking-talking time, she catches him off guard one day after a Wimbledon semi-final in their living room.

'Philip, tell me what really happened.' Just like that. She expects Philip to know immediately what she means. He shifts in his armchair and looks desperate.

'I have a right to know,' Chala continues, but she already feels bad about putting him on the spot, already less sure of herself. 'Don't you think?'

'Why, Chala? What good will it do? Why torture yourself? It was an accident, my sweet. If anyone was guilty it was me for not being there.'

'You weren't the one who did it, Philip. You're not the one who has to live with this for the rest of your life.' Her voice is pleading, not angry.

After what seems an absurdly long pause, Philip speaks, but Chala feels cheated; it's as if he is speaking past her, beyond her, through her, not to her.

'We'd run out of loo roll … I thought I would just pop out to the corner shop, so that Denise wouldn't have to go out again when she got home. I thought about taking you both with me, but it was getting late and I needed to do your supper and it would all take too long, so I decided to just nip out. I … thought no harm could come to anyone in just five minutes. When I got back, I had no idea there was anything wrong at first …' His voice is faltering.

'Enough. That's enough. It's OK.' She can see him trembling and she feels cruel for stirring all this up for him. At least she was young enough not to remember it clearly. Maybe it was worse for him. For a moment Philip looks set to continue, but suddenly Chala is jumping up and hugging him and saying sorry, and he holds her close to him and nothing more is said.

But there must have been more. What he saw when he walked into the yellow room must live on inside him for ever. Perhaps Philip was not always so inert and inscrutable. Perhaps it was what he saw in the yellow room that did this to him.

* * *

The noise in Chala's head was deafening. It was a fabulously crisp early morning and she could have spent it, fresh and rested, wandering along Sydney harbour and contemplating the world around her with easy detachment. Instead, her head was pounding, she was wearing the same dress as the night before and the smell of him was still on her. She veered into a moment of reverie and felt him warm inside her … and then veered back into the reality of what she had done.

'Why? Why did I do it? How could I? What is wrong with me?' Beneath the words in her head lurked an unvoiced association between what she did as a child and what she had just done to Paul: a hollow recognition of something dysfunctional.

But then a less dramatic piece of her mind retaliated. 'Oh for God's sake, people do it all the time. It's called passion, and it's what you lose after you've been sleeping with the same man for a few years. Some people just give in.'

'But not me. I've never been unfaithful to Paul. I love him. I love our marriage.'

'Oh no, you're so pure, aren't you? You, of all people! What's amazing is that it's never happened before.'

'No, no, you don't understand. I'd never do that to Paul.'

'But you just did!'

'But I didn't mean to. It doesn't mean anything, does it? What does it mean? Paul would say it could only happen if there's something wrong in the relationship, otherwise why go outside it?' And suddenly there were pieces of anger flying at Paul – as if he too were in her head. 'You and your fucking black and white, Paul! Maybe I needed some colour, some bright, shocking, life-affirming red in my life.'

'So, what are you saying? That our marriage is dull?'

'No, no, no, that's not what I meant.'

'So, you let a stranger put his dick inside you and that made you feel good, did it?'

'Oh … shit. Shit, shit, shit.' The anger shattered and she faced herself again. 'What if I'm pregnant? No, no, I don't think it's the right time of the month for that and it's not as if Paul and I haven't had unprotected sex ourselves, is it? I panicked the first time but Paul said my period had just finished so I should stop worrying. And anyway, even if you're doing it on the right days, it usually takes ages for a couple to get pregnant, everybody knows that, and I'm in my thirties now. But – shit – I could have picked up HIV for all I know. I can't believe I didn't even use a condom. Oh my God, why would I do that, I've never done it before, I've never understood how anyone can get 'so carried away'. But at least he didn't seem like the kind of bloke who would have unprotected sex if he was HIV positive.'

'Oh, so you're suddenly quite the expert are you?'

'And statistically,' she groped for reassurance beyond the taunts, 'statistically, the odds are all in my favour. I only did it once … twice …'

She wanted to scream out to drown the turmoil in her head, and yet no one watching would have known. All they would have seen was a young woman in her early thirties walking serenely through the early morning in a pale turquoise cotton dress, a colour that almost clashed with the red in her hair.

By the time she had finished the brisk walk back to her own hotel, the noise had dropped to a slow whine and she decided to have a coffee to steady herself before going up to her room. She walked past the occasional turned head and briefly relished the anonymity that allowed her to have breakfast in the clothes she was wearing the night before with impunity. She tortured herself momentarily with the consciousness of his smell still clinging to her and the notion that she was delaying washing him away. And, as she stared through the glass at Sydney's workforce waking up, she fought to turn scarlet and crimson into black and white.

But there was no colour in the line she had drawn under the possibility of meeting Bruce again. That, at least, had been very clear. 'You know we can't do this again, don't you?' she had said to his neck as he lay spooned away from her and she stroked his back. He had turned to look at her – he was always looking at her – and said, 'Yes, I know. I felt it too.' It was said with tenderness, not arrogance, and neither of them had said anything more.

Actually, there was colour there, she mused, over her coffee. Green – it was a green goodbye. Not green in the sense of traffic- light green, God no, but green in the sense of gentle.

And then the violent reds were upon her again. Should she tell Paul? Was this about spaces in their togetherness? No, don't go there, she reprimanded herself. Space, you need space for perspective. Paul always said that about painting, and Chala already knew it was true for real life too. So she clung to a strategy from a crisis management workshop she'd once been to, resolving to break the day into manageable chunks, like a smoker trying to give up cigarettes.

But the chunk that came next was not manageable. It was the wrong size.

# CHAPTER 6

Chala is so used to Philip's relativism that he shocks her one Sunday afternoon. They are crossing a peat bog on the moor and Rusty is racing ahead. Chala has just told Philip that Amanda's mother got pregnant accidentally thirteen years after the last of her three children was born, and had an abortion. Because they are walking and the boggy tufts underfoot require more concentration than most terrains, she doesn't notice the long pause. But then he suddenly blurts out, 'Chala, whatever you do in life, don't have an abortion.'

'Why not?' she asks, taken aback. Philip doesn't deal in thou shalts and thou shalt nots. And besides, she knows he thinks there is a place for suicide and euthanasia, so why should abortion be any different? She can sense him beside her, struggling for words.

'I just think it would be very hard to live with the knowledge—'

'Of what?' she cuts in, also uncharacteristically. 'The knowledge of having killed a foetus? I don't think that would be so hard.'

The rest remains unsaid, but Philip picks it up anyway. 'Chala, my sweet, do you really still blame yourself?' She looks down at her sixteen-year-old feet walking in front of her. 'It wasn't your fault.'

She raises her eyes and snatches a sidelong glance at Philip. What she catches is a look of concentration that she cannot make sense of. She can see him searching for words, words that she assumes are meant to comfort her, but she knows that no words can undo what is done, and as the words fail to come, she feels as if he is her prisoner, marching beside her. She feels sorry for him then and releases him.

'Hey, look at Rusty. What on earth has he found?' Sheep shit. There is nothing Rusty loves more than a good old roll in some, ideally still warm, animal manure.

Years later, she will have another conversation about abortion, this time with Paul. It is their first holiday together and they are sitting at a café in a Greek village square full of the noise and the play of children. Something about the way that Paul is looking at them makes Chala say, as gently as she can, 'Paul, you know that I don't ever want children.' She hopes desperately that he will understand without the need for her to attempt to articulate why.

But he looks suddenly childlike himself, as if someone has just broken his favourite toy. 'Please don't say never.' He tries to put his arm around her, but this is too big for Chala. She pushes him away softly. It's not fair to let him have any false hopes about this.

'No, Paul, really – I do mean never. I just ...' She searches for words that will seem less vehement, but finds none. 'I just don't think I am capable of it.'

'So if you ever got pregnant by mistake you would have an abortion – just like that? How can you know how you would react in that situation?' Paul's voice is almost angry and she realises what a very raw place this is, in different ways, for both of them.

'Do you really want children, Paul? Is it very important to you?' She says it very softly, wishing there were a way to paint away the knowledge of who she is, a way to be everything she longs to be for Paul.

'Well, not yet, but one day.' He looks away and she can tell he is looking into his own childhood. 'I'd like to be a different kind of parent, to bring up a child with the freedom just to be a child and let them discover what they want to become in their own time.' Chala understands why Paul and Philip get on so well. 'I just don't think anyone can say they would have an abortion with certainty. Things change – why shouldn't we end up with a family of our own?'

'Paul,' she forces herself to speak. 'I know it must seem extreme and I wish I could hold your hand and say I'm sure it will be OK, but I'm not sure. And I just don't think it's fair to let you have any illusions about this. You need to be able to make your choices now, before it's too late, and ...' She breathes in and wills herself to continue. 'And if that means you want out of what we have I understand that, but if you want to stay then you also have to know what you're staying for.'

The look on Paul's face is immeasurably sad and she feels bad for denting his optimism.

* * *

Her mobile flashed on the bedside table, where her subconscious had abandoned it. Last night she'd realised too late, and too drunk, that she'd forgotten it. Chala knew she should have rung Paul, that he'd probably called her and would be wondering why she hadn't called back, but she needed to shower before she could bring herself to speak to him. She let the hot water turn her red, wrapped herself in the standard fluffy white dressing gown – if I had a hotel, she thought, they would be all the colours of a rainbow –and picked up the phone with a sigh, a final glimmer of the green goodbye. She flinched, realising there were seven missed calls and three voicemail messages.

Message one: 'Che, it's me.' Paul's pet name had grown out of a mocking reference to Che Guevara in their first days of getting to know each other. 'Hope you're OK. You're probably out for dinner and can't hear the phone. Listen, I need to talk to you. Can you ring me as soon as you get this message? It doesn't matter what time, just call.' There was something overly solicitous in his tone of voice.

Message two: 'Chala, where are you? It must be two in the morning there. I need you to call. Ring me please.' This one sounded angry, but also desperate.

Message three: 'Chala, I don't know what the hell is going on or where you are. I didn't want to have to say this on voicemail, but I don't know where the fuck you are. Listen, you need to call me. Something really bad has happened. Call me, Che.'

When she got through, the need for explanations had disintegrated.

'Che, thank God you're OK. Listen, there's no easy way to tell you this …'

Please don't tell me to sit down, thought Chala, from inside a tunnel.

'Are you sitting down? It's Philip. There's been an accident. He's dead. Che, I'm so sorry, my love. Are you still there? Just talk, say anything. I wish I was there to hold you. Che, speak to me …' Paul was breaking up as he tried to control his sobs. Chala felt as if her spirit was leaving her body and she was taking one last look at herself before drifting off into a white sky.

'You need to come home, Che,' he said. 'We'll get your ticket changed. Do you want me to come over and get you?'

Chala forced herself to speak. Or at least she tried. What came out was an animal noise, a kind of whimper. She remembered the day that their dog had died. Rusty had made that kind of sound when Philip brought him back from the vet. He just wasn't strong enough to get over the anaesthetic. Philip had been there to hold her hand.

'Che, my lovely Che, I'm so sorry. Speak to me.' Paul's voice reminded her that he was there for her now, but his voice sounded so very far away. As Chala watched herself from above, she had the sense of her body shrinking and collapsing inwards; as if the energy that kept her alive had left her body and there was now too much space inside her skin. In this slow-motion moment, Paul became a stranger to her. Maybe if he had been there it would have been different; she could have cried in his arms and he could have helped her through the awful journey that lay ahead. But his physical distance suddenly felt more than physical and the cavern that was opening up inside her had nothing in it …

As Paul tried to coax sound from the other end of the telephone line, Chala carried on watching herself. The Chala that was still holding the phone did nothing, said nothing. The Chala that was watching was obscurely aware of a growing sense of distance. The Chala on the phone had also become a stranger.

The stranger spoke – in slow, monotone words that felt like nothing more than a bodily function. Her blood continued to circulate, her nails continued to grow, her eyes continued to blink and she continued to speak. 'I'm OK, Paul. Thank you. It must be awful having to do this on the phone. I'm just a bit … shocked.' The word sounded so utterly inadequate and unrelated to her. 'I think I just need to lie down for a bit and then I'll ring you back.'

'Do you want to know what happened?'

'Not now. I'll ring you back in a few minutes.'

'OK, but don't leave the hotel without ringing me back.'

Oh yes, of course, she was in a hotel on the other side of the world.

Poor Paul, poor Chala, thought the Chala that was watching. Horrible Chala, thought another part of the Chala that was watching. Philip, Philip, Philip, thought the Chala that lay back on the bed and stared through the ceiling into a place that didn't exist.

# CHAPTER 7

The volcanic lake below them is a deep ominous green, as if it's populated by shadowy, seaweedy creatures who twist and turn just beneath the smooth surface, waiting for unsuspecting little boys and girls to play too close to the edge.

Chala shudders involuntarily at the knowledge that she has just been in that water. There is something oily about it, and its cloying touch against her skin had been at once sensual and disconcerting. She has no idea how deep it is. It's fine to swim in, they had told her at the lodge at the top of the crater rim, the minerals are good for you, but she had been the only one in the water. A confident swimmer, she had set off towards the centre of the lake, with Philip looking on over his beer from the top of the rim, but as she had forged a passage through the thick, still water, her mind had plunged away from the sunlight above into the unseen depths beneath her and she had felt a surge of irrational fear. She was alone, utterly alone. Philip was watching, but what could he do if she needed him now? It had taken her ten minutes to scramble down the hillside to the water's edge. What if there was an unexpected current that pulled her down into its depths – or crocodiles? She willed calm into her movements and fixed her eyes on Philip's small figure above. If she panicked, he would panic. She looked at him and drew strength. She forced herself to breathe deeply and counted her strokes back to him.

By the time she reaches him at his table on the edge of the veranda overlooking the lake she is flushed red from the effort of the climb and the relief.

'That didn't last long. How was it?' Philip teases her. She had been adamant about swimming in it.

'Well, at least I did it! I wonder if your sister went in when they were here.'

'Oh, I'm sure she did. I'm sure that's where you get it from!'

'Get what from?'

'Your stubbornness.'

'I am *not* stubborn.'

'Could you put a little more emphasis on the not?'

Philip is happy. The lines on his face are comfortable, his eyes are alive. Chala relaxes into the warmth of their conversation and lets a cold beer wash away the memory of the lake on her skin.

The thatched wooden lodge sits almost dangerously close to the crater rim and swathes of bougainvillea flow over the edge. Beyond the water looms the rocky presence of Mount Mawenzi, sister peak of Africa's most famous mountain. Kibo, the highest of Kilimanjaro's two peaks, sits discreetly, snow-capped and quiet, in the background. The border of two countries – Kenya and Tanzania – runs, invisible, through the middle of Lake Chala.

For many years it has been a private dream of Philip's to make this journey with Chala to her namesake lake in Africa, and her recent graduation has provided the perfect occasion. They drove for hours through harsh, dry land to get here, penetrating the deepest and most unvisited corner of Tsavo National Park, chancing upon lion prints in the dirt road and a small herd of elephants spouting red water over each other in a shallow mud pool that would turn into a river when the rains came. Exhausted and thirsty, they had finally found the lodge and been amazed by this jewel of a lake hiding in a remote crater in the centre of East Africa.

'So, come on, spill the beans. Why was I named after a lake?'

'All I know is what I told you. Your mother came here with Robert shortly after they met and they loved the place. Sarah fell in love with the name Chala and decided if she ever had a daughter that's what she would call her.'

'And then I came along before they got married. Maybe I was conceived here!'

'I've never really thought about that. I suppose you might have been! The timing would be about right.' His enthusiasm is infectious and Chala looks away in her mind from the feeling she got in the water.

'But they didn't come back here on honeymoon?'

'No, Sarah had a thing about going back to certain places. If there was something very special about a place or a time in her life, she always wanted to leave it intact. She never wanted to repeat the same thing again. She was never very good at reunions and that sort of thing.'

'She sounds a real romantic. What a nightmare for Robert!'

'You're more like her than you know. You remind me of her a lot sometimes.'

'So they decided to climb Mount Kenya. That's a pretty bizarre honeymoon choice.' Chala shies away from comparisons and back to the story. 'Was it Sarah's idea or Robert's?'

'I think it was Sarah's. She was pretty headstrong, but Robert wanted to do it too.'

As Philip talks, Chala drifts. She tries to imagine Sarah and Robert here. They step out of the photos she has got to know, wearing the same clothes and made of paper. For all Philip's reminiscences, there is nothing to draw on, nothing to make them real. She looks at this man of flesh and blood in front of her and she cannot imagine that any daughter's love for her father can be more real than what she feels for this man who has been with her all her life.

And now he is gone.

* * *

The effort of thinking was therapeutic and gave Chala a sense that there was still energy inside her, but the collision with the present emptied her instantly and she snapped into a sitting position on her hotel bed.

She had done all the practical things there were to do, watching herself all the while with a kind of morbid fascination. She had rung Paul back and asked him in a matter-of-fact voice to speak to her boss in the UK. The Sydney staff had been fantastic and even sorted out her ticket. They had offered to keep her company, but she had lied about having a close friend in Sydney. The earliest she could travel was the following night. That left her with twenty-three hours to kill. Her boss in the UK had phoned her after Paul's call and told her she shouldn't even think of contacting work for the next couple of weeks.

She had taken her last Valium and lain down on the bed, willing it to kick in quickly. Memories came flooding into her body: tiny flashes like torn photos; vague half-memories like plots reconstructed from a forgotten novel; and full-bodied recollections with the vivid sharpness of the present. They crowded her consciousness, these memories, battling for attention, battling to keep her away from the slow journey that would turn Philip into a ghost, pleading for reassurance that these things were not gone for ever.

Paul phoned again and she sank into a deeper part of herself. 'Don't you want to know what happened?' His question sounded odd, like someone asking if you want to know the end of a film before you've had a chance to see it. She said nothing. 'It was an accident, it—'

'No ...' She felt suddenly sick again. 'I don't think I can ...'

'OK. It's OK. It can wait. Just try and get some sleep. Have you got any pills to help you sleep? Listen, Che, try and sleep, OK? But phone me whenever you want to.' Paul's voice was shaky, trying to be strong.

Time seemed to move backwards and forwards and stay still with an abrupt, irregular motion that added to her sense of dislocation. She was surprised to discover it was two in the morning and that meant only seventeen hours to go before her taxi, already booked, for the airport. And then the next hour seemed to leak like a broken tap. She fell asleep eventually, dreamt about stabbing a fox and woke up shivering at eight in the morning. Only eleven hours to go, but to what? To a 24-hour journey that would take her backwards to relive the whole of the previous day. Yet her blood kept flowing, her nails kept growing, time kept passing.

It was only when she was on the plane and out of contact that the full impact of her ignorance dawned on her: she knew nothing about how Philip had actually died. An accident, Paul had said, but she hadn't trusted herself to deal with the detail yet. Somehow it seemed irrelevant. The isolated fact of his simply no longer being there was enough. She couldn't face the knowledge that would make this any more real.

She had grown up with blurred edges around the detail of that other 'accident' at the core of her existence, learnt to live with the void, and now her life had turned a corner and here was a new one. What do you mean, I can't come and play chess with you anymore? What do you mean we can't go walking and talking on the moors? What do you mean, never again? She dug deeper and deeper inside herself and all she could find was a rock face.

# CHAPTER 8

They are sitting on the beach in spring, surrounded by sausage rolls, lemonade and fresh Devon cider. Just Philip, Amanda and Chala – oh, and Rusty, of course. Amanda and Chala are gearing up for their exams, and one of the books they have to read is Camus' *L'Étranger*.

'Do you think suicide is wrong, Philip?' Amanda waits in vain for a judgement from Philip to make her own. He bats the question back.

'What do you mean by wrong, Amanda? Wrong by whose standards?'

'Well, most religions condemn it, don't they? But is it necessarily wrong?'

Chala lies back on her beach mat, content to listen to the discussion without needing to partake. She loves the fact that Amanda thinks her uncle is so cool. Amanda's own mother, Julie, would be horrified at this kind of conversation. The sun laps at the bare patches of skin around Chala's ankles and arms, and she feels a warm glow of anticipation at the long summer that will follow their exams. Philip's voice drifts over her.

'Just suppose that someone you loved had a terrible accident and became paralysed. They have all their mental faculties about them, but they cannot bear the crushing disability that life has dealt them. Would you hold it against them if they wanted to die?'

Amanda takes up the thread. 'Or someone in a concentration camp who thinks they will never escape. Or someone who murders their lover under the influence of drugs and cannot bear to live with what they've done. Or—'

'Bloody hell, Amanda,' Chala offers to the sky above.

'Well, I think you've answered your own question, Amanda,' says Philip with a smile.

'But,' Amanda is on a roll now, 'the truth is that lots of suicide attempts are just that: attempts. You wonder if someone who slashes their wrists or takes a load of aspirin really, really wants to die or if it's just a desperate cry for attention or help. I mean, if I was going to commit suicide I would make sure that it couldn't fail. I mean, don't you think it says a lot about you, the way you choose to kill yourself? Can you imagine jumping off a building?'

'I don't know,' Chala sits up, unable to stay out of the conversation any longer. 'I think jumping off a building is quite romantic. At least it's dramatic and quick and the outcome is pretty certain.'

'But what if you happen to land on top of someone and kill them too?' Amanda and Chala are both giggling now. 'What about you, Philip? How would you do it?'

Philip looks suddenly serious. 'I don't think I've got it in me to do it.'

'Oh come on, that's another question entirely.' Touché, Amanda! Philip would approve of her reasoning. 'But just suppose you did, how would you do it?'

He looks out at the waves washing the sand.

'I know, I know.' Chala cuts in. 'You'd just walk out to sea, wouldn't you? No fuss, no drama. Wouldn't you?' she coaxes, pleased with herself, proud of her uncle.

'Yes, I think you're right. That would be a good way to do it.' Philip, too, is laughing now. 'Come on, that's enough existentialism for one afternoon. Let's go and find Rusty.'

\* \* \*

'Oh, my God … Paul!' The memory had flooded her half-sleep with sudden and absolute clarity and she came to, screaming for Paul. Searching, and finding only empty space in the bed beside her, she remembered it was still afternoon. She'd been back about thirty hours and slept dismally the first night. Paul had treated her carefully, as if she were made of eggshell. It almost made her want to laugh. If only she were that easy to break. If only her body would stop working. He had refused to speak to her about what had happened until they were home and she had stepped in and out of the hot bath he ran for her and she had made a token gesture of nibbling at a croissant with thick, hot, strong coffee. Finally, she had snapped.

'Paul, just tell me what happened. Please!'

'A policewoman came round, asking for you—'

'Don't give me context,' she said with growing urgency. 'Just tell me what they know.'

'He had gone for a walk along the cliff. The tide was up and it was a foul day. They think he slipped and fell and the sea pulled him away …'

'Go on.'

'His body was washed up a bit further along the shore. You know, where the proper beach starts.'

'But how did they know he had gone for a walk?' Even though Rusty had never been replaced by another dog, Chala knew her uncle had stubbornly kept to his habit of walking, regardless of the weather, and yet she looked for holes in the story, as if that might bring him back.

'He mentioned where he was going at the village store. When the police asked questions, old Mrs – what's her name?'

'Mrs Vale?'

'Yes, she said she'd told him he was incorrigible, going out for a walk on a day like this.'

'But what if he was murdered?' Chala was struggling with a notion that she would not allow into the active part of her brain.

'Che, the police have no reason to suspect murder. There's no evidence of anything except an accident. They even …' Paul hesitated for a second and Chala's fear filled her head. 'They don't think it was suicide, Chala. They searched the house. There was nothing – no note, nothing out of the ordinary. Of course, they want to talk to you, but they are treating it as an accident.'

Chala stared at Paul. He could smell her fear. 'Che, it was an accident.'

Of course. Just like the pillow in the yellow room. No, Chala reasoned, this was a *real* accident. How could the police be wrong? They had experience of stuff like this. They had even done a post-mortem. It was a shitty, pointless, accident. Philip had been expecting her to go and play chess with him on her return from Australia. Everything had been normal. He had simply lost his footing on a blustery day.

# CHAPTER 9

There is no crying now, just still, yellow silence. When Chala lifts the pillow up, her sister's eyes look a little like Rosie's, as if they are made of cloth. She prods her sister, trying to nudge her flesh back to life with an animal-like intensity, but Emma seems closer to Rosie now. They stare back at her, both of them, as if in possession of a secret from which Chala is excluded.

At this moment, Philip walks into the room. Chala is kneeling beside Emma, holding a pillow and staring. As he approaches the cot, Philip sees the open eyes of his baby. This is the image that will haunt him for the rest of his life. Poor Philip. Sound breaks through the barrier of shock around Chala. She screams. Philip starts to reach out to her, but his legs give way underneath him and he drops to his knees in front of the cot, as if he has been playing musical statues and got stuck in a funny position.

Suddenly Denise is tumbling into the room. No one had realised she was back, but she heard the screams as she opened the front door. She tries to take in the meaning of the picture in front of her: Chala sobbing wildly and Philip inert on his knees in front of the cot. But the picture doesn't make sense. Philip doesn't look at her as she sweeps past him to the other side of the cot. She is about to scoop Chala into the kangaroo pouch of her mother's arms when she stops short. What's wrong with Emma? She's too still, and pale, and her eyes are open. What is wrong with her baby? Her face sets into grooves she has yet to grow into: a pinched mouth with tiny symmetrical lines pulling the lips taut beneath her nostrils, a deep furrow in the middle of her forehead contracting her eyes inwards into their sockets, so that the gently emerging crow's feet seem more pronounced. Then, in a split second the lines melt and her face contorts unnaturally.

'Emma! What have you done to Emma? What have you done?'

* * *

Chala stared at the plate of pasta in front of her as if she didn't know how to eat it. In the past, she had made vain attempts to summon up some kind of authentic memory of the events that had shaped her life. She had even visited a psychotherapist briefly, but had given this up, feeling a vague sense of guilt and abhorrence at the sense of being centre stage.

Paul had been good for her, had grounded her, made any attempt to reconstruct her past seem rather pointless and irrelevant. But now, as she grappled with the fear that her childhood act had driven Philip to a belated suicide, the essence of what had really happened seemed to matter in a more urgent way than it ever had. No wonder Denise had left. How could she possibly bring Chala up as her daughter when her own baby had died because of Chala? And Philip, oh yes, she must surely have blamed Philip too – the one who wasn't watching.

And yet Philip had been there for Chala, had managed to accept her as his own daughter despite what had happened. This was such a fundamental facet of her existence that Chala had never thought to question it. But maybe it had taken its toll after all. As if, with Chala finally settled in the world, married and confident enough to travel across the globe for her work, he was released at last from a duty that was his penance for his own share of guilt in what had happened.

Chala felt a surge of anger flush through her and looked up at Paul sitting opposite. 'He did it, you know. He fucking committed suicide.' She saw the impact of her words, the deep frown as his pupils shrank. She knew he had grown fond of Philip, that somewhere inside, he too was grieving, and one of the chorus of Chalas watching in her head felt obscurely, helplessly, sorry for him.

'Che, why are you doing this to yourself?' Paul couldn't keep the edge out of his voice. 'You've spoken to the police, you've spoken to the coroner, you've seen the report. It was an accident.'

Chala looked for patterns in her uneaten spaghetti. She had grown up with this statement. Slowly, words materialised. 'But they didn't know Philip. I knew him better than anyone else in the world. You don't know what it did to him.'

'So, of course it's all your fault, is it? After thirty years, he suddenly can't live with it any longer and trots off to commit suicide without telling anyone? Look, I'm sorry, Che.' Paul's voice was softer now. 'I know this is devastating for you, but you need to let yourself grieve for his death and not wind yourself up into a frenzy of blame over some imagined plot in your own head. You've got to keep a sense of—'

Don't, thought Chala, don't say perspective.

'—perspective.' He reached out across the table to touch her hair, but she recoiled.

'Fuck your perspective, Paul! Have you lost a mother or a father? Do you have to figure out a way to live with yourself, knowing that the one person who's been there for you all your life has killed himself because of an act that *you* committed?'

'It was a fucking accident, Chala!'

She didn't know whether he meant the death of Emma or the death of Philip, but a part of her hardened like a stone inside a piece of dried fruit. She said nothing. She got up, threw her uneaten meal into the bin and walked out of the kitchen.

Paul rose slowly, put his own half-eaten plate of spaghetti into a plastic container, washed the dishes, sat back down at the kitchen table and put his head in his hands.

After a while, he got up again, boiled the kettle, stared through the window at the back garden and made two cups of tea, which he carried upstairs, guessing that Chala would be lying on the bed.

She was curled up in a foetal position, facing away from the door, and she didn't move when he entered the room. Paul wished that life was a canvas and that he could simply paint over the words that had passed between them downstairs. He approached slowly, put the cups down on the bedside table and gently lowered himself onto the edge of the bed. He turned her slowly towards him and buried his face against her wet cheeks.

'I'm sorry, Che, I'm sorry. That wasn't fair.'

She put her arms around his neck. She knew that sorry was not a word that came easily to Paul. 'It's OK. I know I'm not easy to live with at the moment.' She held him still. 'Why can't we just be there for each other?'

Paul sat up and took her head in his hands. 'We are there for each other, Che. I am there for you. I will always be there for you.'

An image of herself naked under Bruce shot through her and she pulled Paul closer to shut it out.

'If only …' She was speaking into Paul's ear. Her voice was low and trembling and she didn't know what she was going to say. 'If only … I had been there. If only I had been able to talk to him, it might have been OK. I knew he sounded odd when I spoke to him on the phone before I went to Australia. I should have pushed him to find out what was wrong. I should have gone to him. I should have—'

'Enough, Che. Enough.' Paul's voice was soothing now. He held her to him and let her sob.

# CHAPTER 10

Chala is dressed in cream silk, her face is tanned and her hair is on fire. Inside she is nervous – she has told no one, not even Philip, that she has taken a beta blocker – but to the rest of the world right now she is serene.

Paul Hutchings is waiting on the grassy slope above the cliff to give her his name. When he sees her step out of the car and walk across to him through the long, soft sunlight of a summer afternoon on Philip's arm, he feels as if he is inside a painting. He is overcome by how beautiful she looks and by the surreal feeling that a few words spoken in public on the edge of a Devon cliff are going to change his life. They have already done the registry office this morning, so technically they are already married, but this is the part that matters. A few carefully chosen words in front of a small group of family and friends and the sea.

Chala walks towards the man she has decided to share her life with. He looks nervous, but happy. She feels calm, as if she is moving in water, and side-steps the notion that while her nerves are all hidden on the inside, Paul's are on his sleeve, brandished honestly for all to see. Philip is by her side and they walk hand in hand. He, too, is nervous and smiling. She can feel the light sweat in his palm.

Paul Hutchings and Chala Bryan stand face to face and offer the words of Kahlil Gibran to each other and the universe. Paul's parents look on with barely concealed awkwardness. Chala knows that, for all their strained politeness, she is a disappointment to them. They would have chosen some high-achieving, power-dressing woman who would have propelled their son further into the limelight of success and gone on to multi-task and produce a bunch of perfect children. Not someone who would tempt their son with the promise of a future in painting; not someone who would choose to get married on the edge of a cliff.

After the vows, Philip reads a poem and Amanda sings a short Irish ballad in a pristine, soulful voice that raises the hair on people's arms. The couple kiss and it is done. Champagne bottles are popped to hide the tears in people's eyes.

Later, as the sun is setting and barbecue coals are finally glowing, Chala notices Philip standing at the edge of the cliff looking out to sea. She goes up to join him and links her arm through his.

'Are you happy, Philip?'

'I am happy for you, Chala. Paul is a good man. He's good for you.'

'Gosh, that sounds a bit solemn.'

'It's not meant to be.' He hesitates and then puts his arm around her shoulders, pulling her close to his side, so that they are both facing towards the sea. 'I just think you need to hold on to what you've got and I'm glad that it's someone like Paul.'

'Do you still miss Denise?' This is not a question Chala would ever normally ask, but it slips out, responding to the moment.

Philip looks suddenly old and wise. 'Miss her? No, not really, not after all these years. I got used to being without her a long time ago, but sometimes I just wish she'd given us all more of a chance.'

'Why did she go? I mean, really. Was it all about Emma? Why could you cope and she couldn't? And why didn't you ever meet anyone else?'

'That's an awful lot of whys in one go ...'

Chala can almost feel him drifting away beside her, his gaze travelling out to meet the sun on the watery horizon. She wonders fleetingly what kind of a woman Denise had been and had become. 'Come on, Philip,' she says, tweaking his beard affectionately. 'Why don't we have another glass of champagne?'

'Now, there's a why that's easy to answer.' And they turn away from the sea, smiling, to join the crowd.

* * *

Why, why, why? Chala strained to see through the tears that blurred her view of the road. Amanda had offered to come with her, but Chala was adamant. She needed to do this alone, to have the chance to simply be in his house, around his things, without needing to care about how she looked or behaved. She didn't want to be observed in the sanctuary of the home she had grown up in, even by Paul or Amanda.

She ached at the memory of the words that came back to her from the cliff top of her wedding. 'You need to hold on to what you've got.' Was he trying to warn her even then? Did he already know that he wouldn't always be there? Is that why it was so important to him that she was with Paul? So many unanswered questions. There had always been unanswered and unasked questions between them, but now ...

now there would never be an opportunity to ask him anything else ever again. That simple fact thudded and thudded inside her. She remembered the fox on the side of the road and how desperate Philip had been to save it. That's how people should live their lives, being faithful to themselves and never passive, never letting a moment pass that might turn into a regret. Always ask the question that's inside you.

The blurred hedges gave way to open fields and Chala swung the car into the lane that led past the big farmhouse and on to their little cottage. It was not all that long since she had last been there, but she paused to take it in before getting out of the car, as if some change must surely have taken place on the outside to reflect the change inside. Ivy scuttled up the walls and the magnolia tree was sprouting tiny, eager spring shoots. No, of course nothing had changed.

She got out of the car, firmly wiping her nose dry, and marched up to the front door. Unable to rid herself of the sense of being observed, she let herself into the house and moved quickly, almost theatrically, from room to room, as if her physical appearance in each would banish whatever karma lay in wait for her. Her face had a set look about it. She had stopped crying and her eyes darted this way and that, assessing, taking in everything around her as if for an exam. To an outsider at this moment, she would have looked more like a policewoman at a crime scene than a bereaved daughter.

Everything around her looked normal, no more or less tidy than normal, nothing to indicate that the person who walked out of this house had any idea that he would never return. This is exactly what the police had said. They had looked in every room, in every drawer and, finding nothing, left everything as they found it. Now, oddly, all this belonged to Chala. How could there be so little of him in it?

There were slippers by his bed, an unfinished novel on the bedside table, pictures on the walls, a few photos on a mantelpiece, impersonal paperwork on a desk, a Ray Charles CD in the CD player, a few scattered newspapers on the living room floor, but all this seemed to belong to the house rather than to him. How could a man be so self-effacing as to leave no real trace of himself after a life on this earth?

Chala rifled through drawers and cupboards, even jacket pockets, in the frantic hope of finding some clue to his departure. Then it hit her. Of course. Their phone conversation just before she went to Australia. He had said he was going to sort out the old boxes in the attic. She had no idea what was in those boxes, but whatever past he had chosen to save would be there. And if he hadn't gone through the boxes, then perhaps the police were right after all. The only way into the attic was to use the ladder in the shed, so perhaps the police hadn't even thought of looking there.

A few minutes later, armed with a torch, she hauled herself up the soiled ladder and pushed open the hatch to hoist herself in. What she saw didn't answer any questions. There was an old shop dummy, draped in orange. God, what was that – something to do with Denise? There were cobwebs, bare floorboards with old rolls of insulation spilling over them – and one box. Just one box. Did that mean he'd cleared the rest out? Or was there only ever one box? She was the one who'd referred to that heap of old boxes in the attic and she strained to remember what Philip had said about what was really there. Shit, he was already a ghost.

So, with the help of a torch and the light filtering up through the open hatch, she sat and worked her way through the contents of the one and only box. There was a picture of Denise, beautifully framed, and Chala looked at this long and hard, holding it to the daylight from below. She was young in the picture, younger than Chala now, and there was a ripe glow about her. Her thick, chestnut hair bounced around her face, her lips were red and almost parted in a smile, her eyes were long-lashed and soft, greeny brown. So he did still miss her after all this time; he couldn't bring himself to throw this one out.

'Fuck you,' she said aloud to the picture. 'Why did you walk out on him? Why didn't you support him? Why weren't you there when he needed you?' A faded half-recollection of the woman whom she had once assumed to be her mother stirred in some distant part of her brain – and was then displaced by a twinge of panic at the thought of their imminent reunion. The police had located her, and Chala had agonised over whether to invite her to the funeral. In the end she had bowed to convention, but Amanda had been the one who phoned her. So, suddenly, impossibly, as the father figure in her life retreated, the spectre she had thought she would never see again was to appear before her in the flesh. She had less than a week to prepare herself, but how did you prepare yourself for a thing like that?

Now she was crying again and on the verge of giving up on the anonymous contents of the box, when her hands found an unopened envelope. She peered at the front of the envelope. It was Philip's handwriting and it was addressed to Denise. Chala was about to rip it open, but then decided to get out of the attic first. She let herself down through the hatch slowly and shakily.

Half an hour later she was sitting in the armchair by the fireplace, staring at the unopened envelope, but still her fingers did not act. She thought of the fox in distress on the side of the road and of what Philip would have done. She thought of Paul and knew what he would have done. Amanda – Amanda would have snatched the envelope from her there and then. She saw herself wading through shit and trying in vain to shake off the failures that clung to her: the accidental murder, her inadequacy and infidelity as a wife, failure to be there for the father figure who had nurtured her all her life in his moment of need. And now she was about to open a private letter, addressed to a woman whose relationship with Philip began before she was born, a relationship that had nothing to do with her. Didn't she owe it to Denise, whatever her own feelings, to pass on this letter unopened? How could she condemn Denise after what she herself had done or failed to do?

Her fingers folded the letter away and the image of herself in shit receded. This was a fox she could save.

# CHAPTER 11

Colour and laughter. Babies and small children sprawled across blankets on the lawn, surrounded by tiny slices of pizza and juice packets with straws. Adults clustered around the makeshift drinks table, some of them mothers holding glasses of Pimm's and lemonade, keeping half an eye on their children, and a group of men gravitating towards the barbecue near the walled edge of the garden, where Philip slaves uncomfortably over the coals. Denise floats from person to person, touching someone lightly on the elbow or the shoulder as she passes, making sure they've got everything they need, the perfect hostess. She is dressed in some sort of sequined, floaty material, a bright green that brings out the fire in her eyes. Her mouth is painted orange and smiling. She catches sight of Philip and chuckles gently to herself at his awkwardness, grateful for the effort he is making, a wave of almost maternal warmth washing over her as she drifts through the smoke to his side. She reaches up to give him a quick, secret kiss and he looks up from the fire into her eyes. Click – someone has caught a perfect paparazzi moment on camera. Their third anniversary eternalised.

The photo is beautiful. It sits in the small family gallery on the top of a bookcase in the living room. There is another photo of Denise in a green polo-necked sweater and jeans, holding baby Emma up to the sky on a sunny winter day and laughing. And another of the whole family, a slightly self-conscious Philip, one hand on Chala's shoulder as she crouches in front of him, the other arm pulling Denise towards him. In this one Denise wears bright orange and the ready smile of someone happy to be photographed. Only Emma is too small to realise that she should be looking at the camera. She gazes straight up at her big sister, reaching out to clutch her curly hair.

When Denise leaves, the photos do too. There must have been more than these three, some must surely have gone with her, but these and the one of Denise when they first met have been packed away in a box for twenty-five years.

* * *

Chala sat with the photos spread in front of her on the kitchen table and stared relentlessly at them.

'You're not still looking at those bloody photos, are you?' Paul swept past her towards the sink with the kettle in his hand. 'Coffee? We've got half an hour before we need to leave.'

'Do you think I should take them and show them to Denise?' It was only a half-formed thought.

'Why? To stir things up for her like you've done for yourself?' Paul meant this protectively, Chala knew that, but it grated, this niggling implication that she was making her own suffering worse, as if it was a matter of choice.

'But they might mean more to her – be more real for her.'

'I know,' Paul cut in, with his back to her, pouring the water. 'You can't relate to the image of Denise in these photos, your memories are too blurred, too marred by what came after.'

Chala looked at her husband's shoulders, hunched away from her as if in resignation, and smarted. 'Oh, I'm sorry if you've heard all this before.'

'Well, I have, haven't I?' He was walking over to her now, bringing two mugs of coffee, and smiling warmly in an attempt to lift her, keep things calm before the journey ahead.

Something in her softened and she felt sorry for this man who was trying so hard to help her through the minefield she had entered. Fingers of guilt clutched at her insides. 'I'm sorry, Paul.'

'Shh—' He put his arms around her from behind the chair and his head against her ear. 'You've got enough on your plate for now – coffee and a funeral to go to.'

She laughed weakly and felt protected and wished that she could somehow capture the love she felt for Paul in this moment and keep it alive for ever – like one of the photos that still stared at her from the table. But then, that was the whole problem, wasn't it? They were just photos, arbitrary moments, there was nothing *real* about them. She simply could not reconcile the image of this woman in the photos with the haggard, screaming half-memory that lurked in her own mind.

* * *

Amanda was the staunch friend she had always been. Not only had she been the one to call Denise and the few others invited to the ceremony, but it was Amanda who was hosting the gathering after the cremation in her ramshackle family house overlooking the moor, not far from Philip's own house. She and Chala had talked late into the nights when Chala had made the visit to Philip's house and batted around the awful question of what to do about the funeral. At first Chala refused to talk about it, couldn't think about it, but Amanda just kept talking patiently herself, slowly coaxing and forcing her friend to start processing what was happening. Amanda's husband, Richard, a rather rugged, mountaineering type, who was easy to talk to but difficult to get to know, kept the two-year-old twins at bay and gave the girls as much space as he could.

The screaming inside Chala softened and slowly she found herself talking through tears about what Philip would have chosen. Chala knew he would have hated to be buried, a prisoner for duty visits and pointless flowers over years to come, but she recoiled from the notion of some morbid ritual around an urn full of ashes.

'What about the cliff where you got married? We could go there after the cremation and you could throw the ashes into the sea. Wouldn't that somehow feel like the right sort of thing to do?' Amanda shared none of Chala's suspicions about suicide, so there was no irony in her suggestion. Each time Chala had raised her fears, Amanda had simply smoothed them down, like the mother she was.

But Chala was acutely aware of the irony. 'How could you even think of that?'

Amanda indulged her, made other suggestions, none of them palatable, and then tentatively hinted that maybe she should give the ashes to Denise.

'Fuck Denise. She wasn't there for him in life. Why should she have him in death?'

Amanda flinched at the vehemence in Chala's voice. Chala saw it and wished for her friend's serenity.

'You don't know how it was for her, Chala.'

Chala looked up at her friend. It might have been Philip talking. She realised suddenly what a powerful influence Philip must have been in Amanda's own life, how much she too must be grieving, and she put her arms around her friend.

In the end Amanda had persuaded Chala that they needed a certain amount of ritual to help them through and they had sketched out a plan, but the ashes were something that Chala would decide on later, something she was not yet prepared to part with.

And so Paul and Chala had left their coffee mugs in the sink, done the long drive down to Devon and spent a restless night at Amanda's house before the cremation at eleven on a Friday morning.

Everyone was ready to go – everyone except Chala. She had insisted that Paul leave her to be alone for a few moments before she joined them all. She looked at the appalling rings under her eyes in the mirror, pulled the rebellious red curls into a knot at the back of her head and flinched at the sight of herself, dressed up to witness the burning of a body in a box. Then she started to shake, and fumbled through her bag for a beta blocker. She was just about to pop the pill when Amanda strode into the room.

'Don't Chala. Not if you can help it.'

'Don't what?'

'You know what – that pill. I just think it would actually be better for you to allow yourself to feel what you feel. This is not—'

'Not what, Amanda?' Suddenly Chala felt that no one really knew her, knew the worthless core of her. 'I even took one of these for my own wedding!' She lashed out, wanting to shock her friend into some kind of realisation of the distance between them.

'I know that.' Amanda's voice was gentle.

'You knew?'

'Chala, I've known you for ever. I guessed.'

Chala felt the salt in her eyes and put the pill down. 'Oh Amanda, you are the best friend in the world.' She moved over to Amanda and hugged her. Finally, both shaken, they let go of each other and Chala took a deep breath.

'Come on then. Let's do this thing.'

* * *

There were already people there when they arrived at the crematorium. Chala fought back the sensation that she was attending some sort of wedding ceremony. Men in suits were standing under a magnolia tree whose petals were already starting to open. Women, chic in black, fussed with neat handbags. Their eyes lifted towards the small entourage walking along the path from the car park: Richard pushing a twin pushchair; Amanda on one side of Chala, holding an immaculate bouquet of wild flowers she had picked before anyone else got up; and Paul on the other side, holding Chala's hand, seeming to carry her along above the ground, as Philip had done on the day of their wedding.

As they drew near the figures that hovered outside the doorway into the crematorium, one figure separated itself and stepped towards them. Chala stopped walking and felt the flesh of Paul's hand around her nails. When she thought about it afterwards the most incredible thing about that moment was the fact that she recognised Denise. She didn't deduce that it must have been her or find her oddly familiar or see traces of the photos she had studied, she simply and irrefutably recognised her – it was strange. It was only much later that she would be able to take stock of what Denise looked like now, but there was a poised elegance about her, an air of self-sufficiency, which was inviting rather than intimidating. She wore strong dark orange lipstick, and the faded green of her eyes still shone. Her hair, now streaked with grey, was cut almost in a bob, and the deep lines around her eyes and her smile betrayed only the fact that she had lived.

Chala didn't move. It was Denise who broke the silence.

'Chala.'

She said nothing else, simply stood in front of her and looked straight at her.

The men cracked. Richard bent over the pushchair to pointlessly adjust some item of clothing on the sleeping twins; Paul put his arm around Chala's waist and opened his mouth to speak.

'It's OK,' said Chala first, looking at Denise, still shocked at knowing this woman.

And then suddenly there were people pouring out of the crematorium and it was their turn to go in and the two groups mingled unwittingly for a few moments as people milled past each other. Amanda took charge and indicated where people should sit. There were skylights in the wooden roof and sunshine poured through, illuminating the floral arrangements on the raised decking at the end of the room. People took their places on wooden benches facing the podium and Chala was vaguely conscious of Denise on the other side of the aisle, also in the front row, just to the right of her range of vision. She sat, mutely aware of her hand, lifeless in Paul's, and unable to take her eyes away from the curtained hatch that loomed ominously behind the flowers, the tunnel that would deliver the man she had grown up with to eternity. Except there was no such place as eternity, and everything happening now was for the benefit of people left behind.

Afterwards, she found it difficult to remember the exact sequence of events. The coffin had been carried down the aisle like a bride, to the sound of Jacqueline du Pré. Then there were a few words and a song sung by Amanda. Chala had been surprised and almost angry to catch sight of Denise with tears streaming down her face, oblivious to all around her, but beyond that there was nothing really, just a numbness.

Back at her house, Amanda had plied everyone with cava and olives and sausage rolls in an attempt to lighten the atmosphere and encourage people to comfort each other with gentle memories. Chala had the sensation of circling, cat-like, padding in and out of conversations just long enough to ensure that they only skimmed the surface of her consciousness, always aware of Denise in another part of the room. They had not spoken yet and Chala realised she was biding her time, gathering strength for the moment they would face each other. She thought about taking the beta blocker in her bag, but it would take an hour to work properly and she wasn't sure she could postpone the moment for that long.

* * *

When it happened, it caught her off guard. Paul had just taken Chala's empty glass to refill. Chala looked quickly around the room, unable to see Denise and suddenly alarmed that she might have left already. Then, turning back, she found that Denise was approaching her, had sought her out, obviously waiting for a moment when she was on her own. She fought with conflicting emotions: a feeling of being trapped, of curiosity, and again, this deep, disconcerting sense of recognition.

'You're a brave woman, Chala. This must be desperately hard for you.' It didn't sound patronising or like a platitude. Chala felt a flood of questions gasping for air inside her and yet no words formed on her lips. Denise looked as though she didn't expect her to speak. 'You must have been tortured by questions over the years, and now this … I wouldn't blame you if you had no desire to see me after so long, but I want to thank you for being brave enough to let me come to the funeral.'

'It was Amanda who persuaded me.' Chala was struggling to put some distance between them. There was too much empathy. 'But I'm glad you came. I'm glad you still cared enough to come.' Chala tried to hide the accusation in her voice.

'Me too.' Denise's response was strangely ambivalent. Yet she hardly looked racked with remorse. The lines on her face had a softness; there was no bitterness there and she seemed at ease with herself. Chala longed to cut through the caution between them and articulate the questions that had lain latent inside her for so many years, but suddenly she felt nauseous and weak.

'Are you OK, Chala? Listen, this is all too much. We shouldn't try and talk here. I'm leaving now. I just wanted to say thank you personally and' – she reached inside her handbag and handed Chala a handwritten card with her contact details on it – 'if you want to meet up I would love to see you. Just give me a call if you feel like it.'

For the first time she looked awkward and Chala was vaguely aware of an impulse for some kind of physical contact, but then she remembered the fox in her own handbag. 'Wait. Hold on a moment. I've got something I need to give you.' And she dashed into the hallway, grateful for the diversion. She opened her bag and picked out two envelopes – one held the photos that she had contemplated giving to Denise, but this she put back. Suddenly she wanted to keep those photos. The other was the envelope addressed to Denise.

She returned, breathless, to Denise's side. 'I found this in a box in the attic. I haven't opened it.'

Denise took the letter and stared down at it, slowly registering Philip's handwriting after all these years. Chala waited for the shock to settle. When Denise looked up, her eyes were wet.

'You really are very brave – much braver than I ever was.' And they placed their hands on each other's shoulders lightly for a second, before Denise pulled away and Chala turned to look for somewhere to sit.

# CHAPTER 12

Her feet sink in the impossibly fine white sand. She is panting as she climbs, each footprint feeling sacrilegious, hollowing out another shelf in the side of the dune. She can feel him getting closer, hear him panting too. She looks for the top of the dune, but distances are deceptive; the white knife-ridge against the blue sky looks as far away now as it did when she started. She braces herself, dragging her right foot up to get a hold in the sand, but suddenly he is upon her, grabbing her left foot and pulling her down beside him. They lie at an angle against the side of the dune, letting the adrenalin subside, gazing at the expanse of white and blue all around them.

'If you could build a house anywhere in the world, where would it be?' This is one of those places that brings out what Paul affectionately calls her lottery obsession: the temptation of the second conditional.

'Well, it wouldn't be half-way up a bloody sand dune, that's for sure.' He rolls over on top of her, refusing to indulge her this time, planting his lips on hers to shut her up.

Later on the same day, they sit on a tree trunk by the small *brai* that Paul has lit and watch the chops start to sizzle in the late evening light. Their little igloo-shaped tent is pitched a few feet away. Amazingly, there is no one else at this campsite on the edge of the sand dunes. People must be put off by the fact that, apart from the neat little concrete barbecues in each plot and the occasional tap, there are no amenities here and you have to bring absolutely everything, including drinking water, with you. Chala jumped at the idea when Paul suggested it and so they had left the comfort of the quirky little B & Bs around Cape Town to come and camp for a couple of nights.

Chala is tucking into her third lamb chop, her fingers oily with animal fat, her hair still sticky with sand that she has been unable to wash off, when Paul laughs suddenly.

'What?'

'You! Look at you – you're strangely gorgeous!'

'You mean simply gorgeous.'

'No, definitely strangely. You know what I'd like to do tomorrow?'

'Close the doors to the rest of the world and live for ever and ever with me in De Hoop?' He looks at her oddly for a moment and Chala feels embarrassed, but what he says next takes her completely by surprise.

'I'd like to draw you – out there on the sand, naked.' He is looking at her intensely and she feels a sexual thrill flush through her, mixed with horror at the idea of such exposure and scrutiny. But then he looks away sharply and she wonders if she has somehow disappointed him. What would she say, she asks herself quietly, if he were to ask her to marry him. Her lottery obsession again.

* * *

He had drawn her, Chala remembered, and yes, it had been oddly sexual and excruciating all at once. Her hatred of being the centre of attention was so ingrained that it took Paul a good while just to relax her. He fooled around and made her laugh and was patient. Eventually she stopped thinking about herself and watched him instead, the patient intensity in his face and his hands as he turned her into an idea on his sketchpad.

That afternoon she had insisted on him boiling water so that she could wash away the sand that had stuck to her inner thighs. That night, they had made love with more abandon than usual.

Chala bit back the memory of a different night's abandon. She rarely thought consciously about Bruce, but every now and again the feel of him would grip her unawares. And then remorse would take over and she would try and banish the memory, as if she could persuade herself that it had never really happened. Once, she'd wondered cynically if Philip's death was an excuse to avoid confronting the consequences of what she had done. Yet the question taunted her: did Paul have a right to know about a single night with no meaning? Sometimes she wished there was someone she could talk to, but it would feel like another betrayal to tell Amanda, and the loneliness of her guilt felt like a fitting punishment.

She closed the photo album on their South African holiday and put it to one side of the bed, hugging a mug of hot chocolate to her knees. Paul couldn't understand her need to rake up the past. She knew he was getting increasingly irritated by it and yet she was just responding to an impulse, attempting to create some semblance of order out of chaos. Like sorting a deck of cards into suits. As if the cards falling into place might provide the answers to the questions that burnt holes in her grief. Should she tell Paul about that night? Had Philip chosen to die?

They had returned from Devon a week ago now and a small wooden box of ashes nestled in the bottom drawer of Chala's bedside table. For the first few days after the funeral Chala had busied herself frantically with the business of sorting out the will, stung by the sad irony of the real-life lottery question she was now facing: if you inherited a house with no mortgage and about £50,000 in shares, what would you do with it?

She had made one decision, not altogether supported by Paul – to resign from her job. His words still rang in her ears.

'I just think you need a sense of normality. Going back to work will be good for you. You've already had change forced upon you, so why create more change when you don't need to?'

'Do you remember how you felt when you gave up being a lawyer?'

'Yes, but that was different. There was a reason for it, something to replace it.'

'Look, maybe there's a reason for this too. Maybe this is the moment to do something different. I don't know – get involved in some voluntary work or something, feel I'm doing something that means something. You're an artist, and art makes a difference to people's lives. Philip had a huge impact on people's lives. What I do feels so … so worthless.'

'Well, I just don't think it's the right time.'

'Perhaps there is never a right time.' She wondered in a tiny, judgmental part of herself whether this was all about making amends. She wanted to reach across the space that was swelling like a river in the rain between them, yet the shadow of a new wrong hung in her way.

\* \* \*

When she phoned her boss about her resignation, he refused to accept it, insisting that she took another week's leave and gave herself time to think about it, but the resistance her decision met at home and at work hardened her resolve. She thought fondly of Philip's refusal to judge. He had never tried to steer her path through life. And yet he had judged in the end; he had judged his own existence – of which she was a part – and rejected it.

Chala opened another of the photo albums on the bed. This one had pictures of a windswept Irish coast with pink houses. There had only been one day warm and dry enough to remove their coats, Chala remembered, and yet it had been a wonderful week, with one evening Chala would never forget. After a day in the wind they were sitting around a pub fireplace with pints of Guinness and Chala had drifted into a conversation about other people's marriages.

'What about Amanda and Richard – do you think they're happy?' They had got married just a couple of months previously and Chala had never been sure about Richard, but she couldn't put her finger on what it was that bothered her about him.

'Yeah, they seem happy enough to me.' Sometimes Chala succeeded in engaging Paul in this kind of conversation and sometimes he just didn't seem to get it – she guessed this was a man thing.

She tried again. 'But I wonder how much she actually tells him about herself. How well he really knows her.' What was it that bugged her about Richard?

'Maybe that's not important.'

Chala was about to give up the conversation, assuming that Paul was just doing the man thing again, but then he continued.

'Do two people have to bare their souls to each other to be happy together? Can anyone ever really know another human being? If you love someone and want to make a life together, isn't that enough?'

'So, if you and I were to get married one day,' – the lottery obsession slipped out without her meaning it to – 'that would be it – no more exploration, just your paintings downstairs, television dinners upstairs and a shag on Sundays?' She was laughing and their knees were touching under the table.

'You missed out the slippers and the blowjob when I get home from work.'

'But you don't work! Whoops, I mean you don't go to work.'

'Every time I come upstairs, then. In fact, I think that should be a new house rule!' They were already living together.

'OK, but supposing one of us had an affair?'

'Then it would be over.' Black and white. Sometimes he seemed complex and yet sometimes he would slip into certainty with no warning. It always jarred slightly for Chala. She was too used to Philip's lack of absolutes.

'How do you know that? What if it wasn't important? Something totally out of character? Something meaningless?' Chala couldn't know how ironically these words would echo in her own head three years later.

'It couldn't be unimportant. If something happened, it would happen for a reason. But—' Paul looked pensive all of a sudden, reconsidering his own reasoning. 'I suppose, in the end, that would be up to you to decide. You would be the one who would have to live with it. I would only stay with you as long as I knew I wanted to and I would expect the same from you. So, yes,' Paul looked self-conscious all of a sudden, 'two individuals, living our lives together, but separately.'

Chala caught the use of the word 'you' in the pit of her stomach and felt herself blushing, but Paul continued.

'I could only marry someone I trusted.' He lifted her chin and stroked the red blush on her neck. 'And I trust you.'

He looked nervous now, and she realised that the lottery question coming was for real and it all felt ridiculously like a fairy tale as he produced a ring rather bashfully from under the table and they sealed their commitment to each other, oblivious to the cosy hum of voices around them. She had never doubted her decision. In black moments she had doubted his, wondering if she was good enough for him, but the only time she had tried to voice this he had laughed it off. He was so optimistic. Chala loved his optimism and it made her stronger.

Her eyes were wet as she closed the album on the conversation that had marked a turning point in her life. How could she tell him about what had happened in Australia? What right did she have to inflict her guilt on him or expect him to forgive her? Why should she ask him to live with what she had done? A single, meaningless night – was it such a high price to suffer this alone? Look at what Philip had suffered alone. But, in the end, had the price been too high for him?

The questions came and went. In silence.

# CHAPTER 13

'Now, stand in line, all of you!'

The order is barked by a sweaty man in a green uniform holding a rifle. Women of all ages, sizes and colour grit their teeth and stand side by side in the white sand.

'You!' The man strides up the line, stopping to look a thin Asian woman up and down. He prods her in the stomach with the butt of his rifle and smiles as she flinches. 'Like a good prod, do we?' And he pushes her so that she falls backwards into the sand. A gasp of fear rattles through the women. Who is this man? What is he going to do? What does he want of them? They were just women, walking along a beach.

Now he comes face to face with Chala. She lowers her eyes, wishing for Philip. Where did she lose him?

'Step forward. Let me look at you.' His tone is almost gentle. She steps forward, but doesn't look up. He reaches out and grips her chin. 'You're a bad one.' He says it quietly, and tears sting her eyes. 'We don't want people like you on our beach.' He pauses, looking up and smiling at the row of women. 'Do we, ladies?'

There is a sound of muted acquiescence and Chala feels as if she is back at school. All eyes are on her. How do they know? What was it that gave her away? Why did he single her out?

'Take off your clothes.' The words are barked again. She looks at him now with panic in her eyes and he laughs back at her. 'Don't tell me you're shy all of a sudden. Ladies,' he makes a sweeping gesture as if they are all on the same side against her, 'your friend is shy on the outside.' Then he pushes her roughly with the butt of the rifle, like he did to the Asian woman. She recoils but doesn't fall, and she feels the rifle again, almost winding her. 'Take them off!' His eyes are deep in their sockets now, the pupils tight and unforgiving. His flesh strains inside his uniform.

She trembles as she unbuttons her shirt, trips over as she tries to pull off her jeans. There is no desire in his eyes as he watches her, just vague disgust. She realises that for him this is all about power. In front of the women, her sense of humiliation is worse. She does not blame them for keeping their distance. She is not like them, and the man in the green uniform saw it straight away.

In her underwear now, and backed up to the water's edge, she looks at him pleadingly for a second as he makes another jerking movement with his rifle. His face is fleshy and hot and something inside her shudders. Shaking, she pulls off her knickers and turns away from him to unclip her bra.

'Turn around,' he barks. 'Face me!'

But she keeps her back to him and looks out at the sea. And suddenly she understands its pull. This is what Philip wanted. There is a sharp crack in the air as the man in uniform fires a warning shot. She flinches, but keeps walking. Another shot is fired and still she keeps walking.

Then she looks back for a second over her shoulder. The women have gone. It is just the man in the green uniform now, but his rifle has gone too. And then she sees that his posture is different, pleading, and his uniform hangs on him now. The jolt of recognition is like another shot in the air around her head. It is Paul. He is standing at the water's edge, calling her name, but she keeps walking, further and further into the cool sea. She starts swimming towards the horizon. Paul's cries are gone now. She is alone. The water laps at her body and she feels her nipples tingle as she gives herself to the sea. She floats and closes her eyes, feels warm sunshine on her skin.

And now there are hands caressing her and she opens her eyes to see a man's form above her, about to enter her. His head is silhouetted against the sun. She cannot make out his features, but she recognises him through the sense of longing that flares up suddenly, unashamedly, in the closed-off core of her being. Bruce. For a second she remembers the man with the rifle who turned into Paul, but the water has softened her and she opens herself to this other man without a face, drawing him down inside her, into the sea.

* * *

Chala woke slowly, still wet from an unremembered dream. Something in the way that her body moved against Paul as she went to hold him must have given his own sleepy body a message. For once his morning erection had somewhere to go! He had been careful, wary of sexual contact since Philip's death. They had made love once, surprisingly, just after her return from Australia – a tender moment of reunion in the midst of her heartache – but it had made her cry. She had cried and cried and just wanted to be held and he felt a little frightened of going through that again. They had both drifted away from sexual contact after that, and the longer it went on, the harder the distance was to cross.

Their sleep-aided lovemaking was a relief to both of them, she realised. She closed her eyes as he entered her. She knew his eyes would still be open, taking her in. She used to hate that and love it at the same time, her eyes seeking his out, trying to hold them in hers and keep them from her body. But now it was too much, and she hoped that he would forgive her, offering herself deeply in return. It was over quickly and then he was the one to close his eyes and she held him to her, laughing and stroking his head, the only time she could ruffle his hair, his defences post-coitally gentle.

'I love you, Paul. You do know that, don't you?' Chala suddenly wanted to do more and more to please him. She prodded him. 'Fried egg and bacon for breakfast?'

'Thought you'd never ask!' He was smiling at her now, eyes open, warm, satisfied.

She sang in the shower and felt more cheerful than she had done in what felt like a very long time.

While she was patting out potato cakes from leftover mash, an odd image floated into her head of a fleshy man in a green uniform pointing a rifle at her as she stood in a row of women on a beach. She laughed – that TV programme about the Spanish Civil War must have got into her dreams.

Over breakfast, they found themselves talking about subjects that weren't personally loaded for the first time in ages – the latest news headlines, the latest diet and celebrity fads. Paul was laughing and Chala felt light-headed. This is what normal couples are like, she thought, oblivious to the irony of thinking in those terms.

'What are you working on at the moment?' she asked.

'At last!'

'At last what?'

'You said working!'

'Well, obviously I didn't mean literally. Can I see?' She was tentative, childlike all of a sudden. It wasn't taboo, exactly, but there was an unspoken agreement between them that she never went uninvited to his studio. He liked to finish a painting before he showed it to her, as if the risk of exposure was just too great.

'OK.' He pulled her over to him and she sat on his lap, straddling him, facing him, loving him, happy. 'But don't expect too much. I haven't done a lot lately.'

When she saw the half-finished painting, she blanched. It was a woman standing between two mirrors, looking at her own reflection. Because of the way the two mirrors faced each other, the images of the woman created a domino effect of ever-smaller mirrors. In the first reflected mirror a young, red-haired woman stared back – Chala noticed the likeness to herself; Paul often sought inspiration from her untamed looks – but the next reflection showed the same woman with lines under her eyes and the beginnings of sagging cheeks, and the next the same woman with deeper lines and grey in her hair, and in the one after that her neck had begun to gather empty folds of skin, and there were still unfinished diminishing mirrors receding into the shadows of the background. The effect was shocking. She stood still, not knowing what to say.

'Do you like it?' It was Paul who was childlike now, like a boy showing his mother something he'd done at school, eager for approval.

'I don't know if I *like* it.' She struggled to put her reaction into words. 'But it's powerful, shocking, incredible. I don't think I could bear to have it in my living room, but it's the kind of thing I'd go back to see again and again in a gallery. There's something haunting about it, like staring into a fire.'

'You see why I love you.' Paul was full of her, delighted with her response.

Chala ached suddenly. Ached with the knowledge of the wrong she had done him, and she felt Philip's absence slice through her. It came in waves, a shooting pain that would come and go, leaving her feeling empty and vaguely angry. She wondered if the memory of Philip would grow old, like the woman in the mirrors.

'Do you think I should contact Denise?' The question caught her as much by surprise as it did Paul. She had mentioned their exchange at the funeral, but they had not talked any more about it.

His eyes dropped for a second and when he looked back into her face, the inevitable frown was tender and weary at once. 'You don't think that's just going to stir things up again too much?'

Chala thought about the fox that Philip had saved. About how long Paul had avoided stirring things up with his parents. About how much, for all his apparent spontaneity, he clung to the status quo. Was their marriage like a fox that could be saved by maintaining the status quo?

# CHAPTER 14

'Get a fucking life, will you!'

Chala feels winded. Paul's face is taut and ugly and she thinks she sees hatred there. She feels like walking out – out of the room, out of the house – but she doesn't trust herself. What if he's not there when she comes back? He walked out on her once and disappeared for six hours. When he came back – refreshed, renewed, with a sense of perspective about the pointless argument that had prompted him to walk out in the first place – he was shocked by the state of her. For every inch of perspective that he had found, she had lost two.

So she cannot do it to him now. She tries bleakly to work out in her mind how they got here. The argument seemed to come out of nowhere. She tries to reconstruct their words in her mind to make sense of them, to give her some kind of clue of how to behave now.

'Hey, get off. That's my toast!' They had been having a leisurely Sunday breakfast, reading the papers, when he had reached across and snatched a piece of toast from her plate. Her reaction was simple reflex.

'My God, look at you!' His reaction seemed out of proportion.

'What? You took my last piece of toast.' She knew she sounded a bit like a spoilt child, but it was true, he had taken her toast.

'Mine, mine, mine!' He was imitating the seagulls in *Finding Nemo*, but there was no humour in his face, just a look of vague disgust.

And then it spiralled.

'What is *wrong* with you?'

'Me! Oh, it's always me isn't it, never you. Poor Chala. She's always the victim, isn't she? Always the one who's been misunderstood and punished all her life.'

Chala hated him then. She felt bullied. He was sticking the knife in exactly where he knew it would hurt. Why? Where did his anger come from?

'Why are you so angry with me? What have I done? You were the one who took the toast.' She meant it reasonably, not sulkily. She simply wanted to explain herself, find out why he'd reacted so sharply.

'Get a fucking life, will you!'

He has picked up his paper now, cutting her out. Her eyes blur and part of her wishes that she could simply disappear.

Like Philip did.

* * *

Chala was sitting on a train to London. Paul was still asleep and she had left the house with a bitter taste from the night before, forcing herself not to wake him and ask if they were OK. Now, in the warm fug of the train on a bright, chilly, early summer morning, she sifted through memories of arguments they'd had before, as if to reassure herself that there was nothing wrong or different now. Even before her trip to Australia and everything that had followed, their occasional arguments had been vehement, but had always subsided. Like the one with the toast. They had sought refuge as far away from each other as possible and when they had come together again later in the day, he had been especially nice – no mention of the morning's anger.

At some level, in the quiet that followed these arguments, Chala understood that his flashes of anger were something he could not control. Perhaps there were moments when the weight of his childhood was simply too much. Or the toll of living with her simply too high. She could hardly blame him for that.

Denise was waiting for her at Victoria station. Chala saw her first, noticed the tight frown on her forehead as she searched faces over the barrier, but the frown disappeared when she saw Chala, and her smile was warm and disarming. They touched hands awkwardly and Denise turned quickly, saying, 'Let's get out of here. There's a place we can go for a coffee just round the corner.'

Chala stole the opportunity to look at her as she ordered cappuccinos and sticky oat slices from the waiter. She was dressed in pale green linen trousers with a loose white shirt and a stone pendant necklace with matching earrings. Chala registered inwardly that she had made an effort, cared what Chala thought of her. In her late fifties, she was still attractive. Chala thought of Paul's mirror painting and realised that she must have been stunning in her youth, even more so than the photos gave away. What had brought her and Philip together? They seemed such an unlikely couple. She realised how little she knew about this woman and her relationship with Philip. She felt hollow.

'So, how are you coping?' Denise broke into the silence that had settled since the waiter's departure. Chala pursed her lips. What right had she to ask a question like that? She looked down at the table and said nothing, wondering why she had come.

'I'm sorry, I don't mean to be insensitive, it's just ... a little hard to know where to start. But I'm so pleased you decided to come,' she rushed on and Chala felt a shot of empathy. 'I wouldn't have blamed you if you hadn't, but to me it's a gift ... a sad gift after so many years.' There was a faraway look in her eyes, and Chala thought: she loved him, she did love him after all.

'Why don't we start with you? I mean, with ...' Chala looked for the right words in her head. 'After ...' She faltered, but Denise understood.

'Well, I moved in with a girlfriend in London and temped for a while until I found my feet, and then I decided I needed to do something completely different. I wanted to train as something tangible, learn a skill that meant something – something I could offer other people.'

So, there *was* guilt, thought Chala, wishing she could stop judging her. And yet she felt a flood of empathy again. I know exactly what you mean, she wanted to cry out.

'So, I trained as a speech therapist,' continued Denise. 'It was hard. I had to do an M.Sc., but I loved it.'

'You're lucky to find something you love professionally. I still don't know what I want to do.' Chala was surprised at her own revelation. There was something so straightforward and comfortable about the way Denise talked, but, she reminded herself, they had chosen safe ground. She wondered what the letter from Philip had said, how Denise had reacted after so many years. Would she be so open and comfortable talking about that? Chala realised Denise was talking again.

'Well, what do you do at the moment?'

'Nothing. I'm in limbo. I resigned from my old job.'

'And what was your old job?'

'Well, it wasn't really me ...' And she gave a potted summary of what she'd done and the company she'd worked for and the words echoed a faraway conversation on a plane to Australia, the last time she'd tried to explain her work to a stranger. But this time she found herself adding tentatively, 'I would also like to do something valuable. I mean something that would make a difference, like you do.'

Denise looked thoughtful, remaining silent.

'So, when did you know? I mean what made you realise that speech therapy was your thing?' However effortless Denise made it seem, Chala shied away from the exposure of talking at length about herself. All her life, she had always turned conversations with strangers around.

'Oh, I didn't know straight away. It took time – a long time, actually. And there was no lightning bolt,' Denise laughed. 'I just came to understand slowly that my work was the most fulfilling part of my life.'

Chala looked down, embarrassed, but there was no self-pity in Denise's voice, just a very gentle sadness. She longed to ask how Denise had been able to leave Philip.

'One day, maybe I will be able to talk to you about why I left.'

Chala blushed fiercely. 'Oh no, it's OK. It's none of my business,' she floundered.

'Oh, but it is in a way, of course it is. I never stopped missing him, you know. It wasn't that I didn't love him, but we just couldn't cope together any more.'

Because of me, Chala thought, because of what I had done.

'And it wasn't just the accident either. It had started before that.'

Chala felt tears pricking her eyes and bit them back, hating herself for her weakness, hating herself for coming here. The 'accident' – so this was a piece of vocabulary that had stuck. In their family dictionary, Chala thought sourly, grasping for something to stop the tears, 'accident' was a word used to describe the unintentional murder of a baby by her four-year-old sister. 'Accident' was also a word used to describe either the death or suicide of an uncle thirty years later.

'Do you think he committed suicide?' Chala's words came out softly, unexpectedly.

'What makes you say that?' There was something sharp in Denise's tone for the first time.

'I don't know. I just don't believe it was an accident.'

Denise put her hand lightly on Chala's arm across the table, as if to steady her. 'Chala, I loved Philip' – it was the first time that his name had been spoken out loud – 'but he was a very weak man in many ways. I don't think he would have been able to commit suicide even if he had wanted to.'

Chala found her words strangely comforting. She had not offered platitudes about him loving Chala too much to do a thing like that or it not being her fault. She simply thought he didn't have it in him. That did more to calm her than any of the police reports had done, but the effort of talking about this openly was too much for her.

'So … so, you just sort of drifted apart? Did you argue much?' Last night with Paul was still on her mind.

'No, it wasn't really that we argued. Philip hated confrontation—'

'I know. I think he gave that to me, too.'

'Yes, I can sense that. There's quite a lot of him in you, I think.' Her words trailed off slightly. 'The best parts of him …'

'Philip used to say I reminded him of his sister.' She couldn't believe how easy Denise made it to talk about herself.

'Well, if I were you I'd take that as a compliment. I liked her.'

It was strange to imagine that Denise had known her mother, a woman who existed for Chala only in stories. She wanted to bring the conversation back to the present.

'Can I ask you something? Do you think if a couple have awful arguments it means they are incompatible?'

Denise looked at her for a moment, hesitating. 'Not necessarily—'

'Now *you* sound like Philip!' Chala was amazed to hear herself laughing. She realised that since his death she hadn't really been able to talk about Philip in a positive way. Even her private thoughts about him had been so loaded, tormented by the question of whether he had committed suicide. It was comforting to simply remember him, without digging too deep, and suddenly she didn't want to draw Denise on the letter and the reasons she had left.

'Is this about you and Paul? It's hardly surprising if the situation has taken its toll.'

Chala found herself tentatively opening up to Denise about her fears. She longed suddenly to tell her about Bruce, but this would be too much of a betrayal, would only add to the harm she had already done.

'You know, I went to Kenya once with Philip. He took me to Lake Chala. It was beautiful but there was something creepy about it. I swam in the lake and I almost panicked, but the thought and sight of Philip sitting at the top of the crater kept me calm and I swam through my fear and just kept going until I got to the shore again. Philip was a father to me. But isn't that the way a woman should feel about her husband? Shouldn't the thought of him keep you safe in the same way? I'm just not sure that I feel like that about Paul.'

To Chala's surprise Denise laughed. 'Now you really do sound like your mother – a true romantic at heart! Well, I don't think you need to feel like that about your partner. In fact, I think it might be a little bit unhealthy if you did feel like that about a partner. I never felt like that about Philip.'

'But you didn't last together.' The words left a sour taste in her mouth. She hadn't meant to be cruel. 'I'm sorry, I didn't mean that the way it sounded.'

'No, it's a fair point.' She hesitated, and Chala felt uncomfortable, wanting to switch off the spotlight she had inadvertently shone on the past again, but the next thing Denise said was as surprising as her laughter. 'Why don't you go back there?'

'Where? You mean Lake Chala?'

'Not to the lake, necessarily, but to Kenya. You said you're in a state of limbo at the moment, you want to do something worthwhile, and Kenya obviously holds an emotional significance for you. Why don't you go there for a bit, find something to do, some voluntary work or something, and just take some time out, a little bit of distance from everything that's happened? It might do you good.'

'It wouldn't work. I even suggested something like that to Paul. Not Africa, I'm not sure why I didn't think of Africa, but I saw an ad for VSO in India and suggested we go for it. We've got enough money, and Paul could still have done his art, so I thought it might have been inspirational for him, too.'

'And, what did he say?' Denise asked carefully.

'He just got angry.'

'You know something?'

'What?' said Chala, unable to read the measured look on Denise's face.

'I didn't mean with Paul. I meant on your own.'

'But—' Chala started, unsure of herself.

'It might do you good, you know. It might do you both good.'

And so the idea was born.

# CHAPTER 15

*A young German tourist lost her life last Friday in an incident on the border between Kenya and Tanzania.*

*Her family had stopped for a picnic at an old lodge, beside a volcanic crater lake, near the twin peaks of Kilimanjaro in Tsavo National Park. Petra Schmidt, 16, and her two younger brothers went into the lake, which is said to be safe to swim in, and their parents watched in horror as a crocodile surfaced from nowhere and dragged the young woman underwater. The two boys escaped unharmed. The Kenya Wildlife Service (KWS) searched the lake, but found only a severed arm.*

*When the lodge was still open, it was common for tourists to swim here and locals have continued to do so. This is the first time that a crocodile has ever been sighted in the lake. The KWS believe that it may have reached the lake through an underwater channel from a nearby river.*

\* \* \*

Chala let go of the newspaper as if it might burn her. The article was tucked away in the back pages and it was the word 'accident' rather than 'crocodile' in the headline that had grabbed her attention. She had developed an almost macabre fixation with the notion of accidents in people's lives, wondering what percentage of cases in emergency wards are the result of accidents. If a couple have a bitter argument and he breaks his arm as he smashes it down on a sideboard to underline a point, is that an accident? As soon as you start to look, there are accidents everywhere, literally waiting to happen. What could possibly be more arbitrary and unlucky than being killed by a crocodile in a lake that contained *no crocodiles*? She shuddered at the memory of that same water around her skin, at the irrational panic that had seized her. There was no doubt that it was the same lake – her lake, Lake Chala, now marred by death. She knew it was crazy, but she felt a twinge of guilt, as if she were somehow responsible. How would this poor girl's mother feel if she were to tell her that she had swum in the same lake years ago and had been frightened too, but she hadn't told anyone, because she thought she was just being silly?

Chala got up and filled the kettle again to make more coffee. She was being ridiculous, she reprimanded herself, but a small voice chirped away inside her brain. Maybe this is a sign. Maybe you should keep away from Kenya, it said. Her birth mother and father had died on Mount Kenya during their honeymoon. Philip's sister had hated to go back to a place she had loved. If a place held beautiful memories, it felt like tempting fate to go back; she preferred to keep them intact and alive in her imagination, and if a place held bad memories, then why stir them up?

Paul walked into her Sunday morning then, dishevelled and cheerful.

'God, you look like you've seen a ghost. More bad news?' He gestured at the papers, half smirking.

Chala swung from one extreme to another when it came to news consumption. There would be weary phases of going out of her way to avoid contact with the news or avid phases when she couldn't seem to get enough of it. Since Philip's death, she had seemed unable to focus on anything, so Paul welcomed the sight of newspapers sprawled across the table. Chala didn't mention the crocodile accident. They bantered over other items in the news and she carried on a silent dialogue with herself beyond the spoken words.

'Paul,' she broached finally. 'You know I mentioned the idea of us going off and doing VSO or something?'

Paul looked strained, but she continued. 'Are you absolutely sure that isn't something we can consider? I mean, it wouldn't have to be VSO. We could just do something for a couple of months or so, something,' – she hesitated – 'to break the pattern we're creating—'

'*You're* creating. Don't bring me into this.'

She looked down at her lap.

'I've already told you what I think, Chala. You need to get a sense of normality back and this is not helping.'

She said nothing and his voice rose.

'Fuck this, I've had enough, I can't do this anymore!'

She heard the door slam behind him.

On an evening two days later, Chala sat in front of her computer screen, engrossed in a site about voluntary work in some of Kenya's orphanages. A hand on her shoulder made her jump.

'What are you looking at?' asked Paul.

'Listen, can we talk downstairs?' She half-expected him to lash out, but he was quiet, almost sullen.

Chala walked in front of him, biting her lip, wondering if she was really ready for the conversation they were about to have. 'Hold on to what you've got,' Philip had said at their wedding. She poured them both a glass of wine.

'Paul, I don't know whether you can understand this or whether it's even reasonable of me to ask you to understand, but with everything that's happened I think it might do us both good if we had a break from each other. I thought maybe if we could both go away and do something different together, that that would be enough, but you don't want that. You want us to be able to move on without changing anything, but I'm not sure I can. Not here. Not like this. I want to do something, something that makes me feel good about who I am, something that will help me get beyond Philip's death ...' She looked at Paul, waiting for him to speak, but he was silent. 'I know you think it's all bullshit, but I can't help it. I can't help feeling that he committed suicide.'

'And you blame yourself?' Paul's voice was cold.

'In a way, yes ...'

'So, you want to go to Kenya, is that it?' The words were sharp. Chala looked down at her wine glass.

'I saw the website you were looking at.'

'I'm sorry Paul, it's just—'

'Don't say fucking sorry! If you feel so sorry all the bloody time why don't you do something about it? I'm not a Catholic fucking priest, you know. I'm not going to wave a hand and absolve you every time you say sorry!'

Chala braced herself for more words.

'So what about our marriage? That just gets thrown out, does it? A piece of rubbish Chala's had enough of!'

'Paul.' She reached out to touch him, but he snatched his hand away. 'I just think that the best chance we've got for a future that isn't like this is for us to have a break from each other.'

Paul stared at her and she felt raw and wanted to say sorry, but knew she couldn't.

'I'm not stupid,' she continued. 'I know I'm putting everything at risk, but I also know that those words on the cliff were said for a reason and I want our marriage to be about what we wanted it to be. I know it's been hard for you since Philip died, and I know you've done everything you can to help me get over it, but I feel that I've got to do something to break out of the place I'm in. Space and perspective go together, right? That's what you always say and ...' – she struggled – 'maybe the space will do you good too.'

Paul was still staring at her and she took the step beyond the point of no return.

'I've found an organisation that arranges voluntary placements. There's one now in a children's shelter in the Rift Valley. Two months ...' She stopped and looked up at him, but his pupils had shrunk inside his eyes.

'Would that be OK, Paul? Two months isn't so long, is it?' And when he said nothing: 'I know what the stakes are, Paul. I'm not suggesting this lightly. What do you think? Paul?' She reached out to touch him again, but he caught her arm mid-air and held it between them. She felt the tightness of his grip and braced herself for his anger, but when his response came, it was just one word, almost breathed.

'Go.' He looked at her long and hard, letting her arm drop at last. 'I want the woman I married back again. Maybe you can find her in Kenya.'

# PART TWO

# CHAPTER 16

The smell of human skin hit her the moment she entered the airport building. It brought Philip's ghost to her as clearly as if he were walking beside her. The flashback from ten years before was so acute it made her want to cry. No wonder Philip's sister had shied away from going back. But at least we're spared flash- forwards, thought Chala – imagine a world in which a certain smell or tune conjured up with the same intensity an experience yet to be lived. Imagine how the Chala of ten years ago would have felt walking through Nairobi airport if she'd been able to see herself now, moving through the unchanged space, without Philip by her side, with just his ashes in her luggage. Ignorance of the future is what makes us strong, she thought; hope is only possible because of it.

And despite the appalling sense of loss she felt as she queued at immigration, there was something appealing and earthy in this smell she recognised. The customs official checked her visa and smiled her through. *Karibu Kenya*. The buzz in the baggage hall, already within view of those waiting to meet the early-morning arrivals, was one of muffled excitement; the excitement of tourists coming for adventure or people returning to a country they obviously loved. Chala felt caught up in it.

She spotted the placard with her name almost immediately. The placement organisation had arranged for a driver to take her straight to Naivasha, two hours away, where she would settle into her hotel and meet the person who ran the shelter project. Her driver's name was Chege and his smile might have been for a long-lost friend.

They drove past the life-size elephants in rusty scrap metal that guard the entrance to the airport and off along the potholed road into the city. Lane discipline didn't seem to exist here. Trucks travelled in the outside lane; cars swerved from one lane to another, overtaking wherever there was a space; and when the minibus taxis hit a traffic jam they simply created a new lane between the others or on the dusty verge beside the road. The word for these prolific minibuses, and a memory of them painted in vivid colours and cartoons, came back to her. Now they were uniform white with a yellow line along their sides and relatively subdued announcements painted over the back windscreen: 'We love Nicolas Cage' or 'Fear God'. The last time she was here human limbs (and the odd goat or chicken) had spilled out of open doors and windows. Now they looked like tour buses, with individuals neatly seat-belted in, reading papers.

'What's happened to the *matatus*?' she asked Chege.

'This is one of the good things our new government has done,' he told her. 'By now they are regulated.'

Chala loved the quirky word combinations that crept into Kenyan English; she remembered a Kenyan saying to Philip over a game of chess at one of the lodges, '*Bwana*, you have me beaten. I am really in the bush with this one.'

As they made their way through Nairobi's rush hour and finally emerged onto the open road leading to Naivasha, she realised that all the regulation in the world could not change a culture overnight: the *matatus* might move slower, but they still overtook without hesitation on blind corners. Life was cheap, and trust in God ran deep.

Despite the driving, Chala found herself falling asleep, drifting in and out of a pleasant, woozy state, between the occasional jolt of brakes that would bring her to abruptly. On one of those jolts she opened her eyes to a sight that she would take with her when she left Kenya. 'Third World View Point' read the hand-painted board on the side of the escarpment. A few makeshift, wooden shopfronts, painted in zebra stripes and decked out with carvings and red, checked Maasai blankets, stood like beach huts on scaffolding, clinging to the sheer drop by the edge of the road. And beyond these huts, filling every inch of her peripheral vision, the huge vista of Kenya's Rift Valley poured away into the distance. They stopped, and Chala breathed in the vast landscape and the clean, sharp highland air. She felt bizarrely hopeful, wondering what the future would bring, trusting, for now, the instinct that had brought her here.

# CHAPTER 17

Chala sat on the veranda of Naivasha's rather rundown, old colonial hotel, sipping her first Tusker and waiting nervously for Winnie.

The drama of the view had continued to unfold around her as they drove down the escarpment, past the volcanic nipple of Mount Longonot and into the plains, with Lake Naivasha shining before them, framed by mountain ridges folded back against themselves. The drive into Naivasha town had brought her back to reality. Colour and rubbish competed for attention. There were people everywhere. Entire buildings were painted with the colours and logos of different brands: Nescafé red, Omo washing powder blue, Safaricom mobile network green. Flies and women with children strapped on their backs swarmed around Peter's Butchery, with whole sides of a cow strung up in the open, unrefrigerated shop window. *Matatus* and motorbikes swung around each other, blowing dust from the huge open potholes in the middle of the road. Dusty, tattered pieces of plastic littered the dirt pavements. A young boy lashed out viciously at the skinny donkey that pulled his cart. People wove in and out of the traffic on foot, and occasional shops blasted out the cheerful twang of Swahili guitar.

The overall effect was overwhelming, and Chala was glad of the cold beer. She had dumped her bags in the sparse but clean room that was to be hers for the next two months, showered in a thin jet of lukewarm water and come out to the veranda, where she had sat at the only free table, feeling mildly self-conscious and hoping that no one would talk to her before Winnie arrived. She realised that she didn't even know whether Winnie would be white or black – a 'larger than life Kenyan woman' was all she'd been told. She registered, without eye contact, the mix of people seated on the veranda: whites, blacks, Asians, sometimes at the same table, and Swahili words slipped in and out of the English sentences she overheard.

A tall, heavily built black woman with braided hair, in tight jeans and a crisp yellow shirt, approached her table. Chala stood up tentatively as Winnie broke into a wide smile.

'*Karibu*! Sit!' She shook Chala's hand and gestured at the waiter, who jumped immediately. 'Bring me a beer, man, and the lunch menu.' She used the same clipped 'man' that Chala would hear the whites, or *mzungus*, use. To Chala, it sounded like something out of a Sixties film. Despite the smile, Chala felt immediately in awe. Winnie's whole demeanour and mannerisms were more like those of a well-known politician than someone who ran a local charity.

Over time, Chala would discover that Winnie had actually campaigned as a local candidate for parliament. Scarred by a ruthless divorce, she had nevertheless been lucky to get away from a man who had beaten her, and vented her anger by rebelling against her country's macho culture. Although she'd never made it to parliament, she had established a network that would prove invaluable when she later decided to pour her energy into setting up a shelter for street kids on the outskirts of Naivasha. As she talked about the history of the shelter she mellowed.

'Look over there. You see those kids?' She pointed at the vegetable stall opposite them. Chala saw three boys in ragged clothing tapping at the window of a Toyota for money. The youngest couldn't have been more than five or six years old. Their tummies poked out through their shirts – a sign of hunger – and their eyes were bloodshot – a sign of the glue they sniffed to keep the hunger at bay.

'The glue causes brain damage, you know.' Winnie took a swig of her beer. 'There are more and more of these kids every day. We can only take so many ...' Her voice trailed off and Chala filled the space with a question.

'What makes them take to the street? Are they all orphans?'

'Here, you are classed as an orphan if you only have one parent living. Some have lost both parents, but many have a mother living who just cannot afford to feed all the mouths left behind when the father dies.'

'But the whole incidence of street kids is relatively new, isn't it? Why has it got so bad?'

'There's a one-word answer to that: Aids.'

Chala didn't know what to say. She felt suddenly intensely tired after her trip. Paul had gone with her to the airport, and saying goodbye had been achingly hard. They had already talked hesitantly around the rules governing the new space between them, Chala feeling that it was his right to decide what level of contact he wanted to maintain while she was away. When the moment of no return was finally upon them, Chala had fought against the tears and the doubt that she was doing the right thing. He had held her chin up to his face and said just two words before he turned away: 'Come back.'

'Do you want to rest this afternoon and go up tomorrow?' Winnie's question brought her to, as the brakes had done on the escarpment.

'Yes, if you don't mind. I think that would be best.' Winnie glanced at her sideways, perhaps wondering if she was up to the challenge, but Chala felt drained and didn't trust herself to meet fifty street kids today.

# CHAPTER 18

'*Jambo, habari yako?*' Chala wished she knew more Swahili. The boys were lined up in front of the main building, the smallest in front and looking slightly bewildered. She noticed the larger boys touching or patting them to reassure them. They were addressed in Swahili first by Winnie and then the on-site administrator, a man called Mwangi. A short introduction in English followed, telling them how lucky they were that this English lady had come to spend time with them. Chala squirmed and offered the only words she could in their common language.

She walked along the line, shaking hands with each boy and asking their name, wondering how long it would take her to learn them. Most lowered their eyes when she spoke directly to them, but a couple of boys stood out at this first meeting. One, a tall, lanky boy called Samuel, had lost one eye, but smiled at her with the one he had left. The other, one of the younger ones, a six-year-old boy called Julius, gave her the double handshake that Kenyans use for an informal greeting, causing a titter around the group. Chala warmed to the twinkle in his eye and his obvious sense of mischief.

At the end of the line were two dogs, also from the street, called Twiga and Chyulu. They lapped up her attention when she dropped down to stroke them, and a few boys laughed again when she tried to repeat their names. They clung to the presence of the staff, these dogs, and it came as a shock to Chala to realise later that this was because they were afraid of the boys. Habits of the street – and cruelty to animals was one of these – died hard, even in this haven.

Next came a tour of the shelter itself. Simple concrete buildings with corrugated tin roofs stood in a semicircle: classrooms, dormitories and a large all-purpose hall that functioned as a dining room and general social space, with a kitchen at one end. The property had been donated by a local landowner: ten acres that backed up against a ridge behind them, forty minutes' walk from town along a dirt road, with a distant view of the lake. Chala was impressed by the ethos of self-sufficiency around the project. The boys grew their own vegetables and bred rabbits, chickens and geese. There was even a cow that acted as a lawnmower on the football pitch, as well as supplying milk. As Mwangi led her through the buildings, she noticed that he used the bunch of keys strapped to his belt to open various rooms.

'You keep these locked all the time?' she asked him, not guessing why.

'Yes,' he answered matter-of-factly. 'Even the toilets must stay locked. You have to remember where the boys come from. It's better not to give them the temptation to steal or do harm to themselves.' It was a lesson she was to learn over and over again in the coming days.

Winnie wanted to set up a website, and one of Chala's jobs was to put together content. She and Mwangi would sit down with each boy in turn. With Mwangi putting the boys at ease and putting direct questions in Swahili that Chala felt unable to ask, she would uncover their stories. One boy found abandoned on the street at the age of three; another rescued from a mother who lived in the street herself and had gone mad; another who had spent three years in jail after a police sweep in an attempt to 'clean up the streets'. Some were newcomers and some had been here since the shelter opened three years ago. Some were fourteen or fifteen when they joined – these were the most difficult to keep from leaving, and occasionally a boy took flight again, unable to adapt to the unfamiliar security of the shelter. Julius had been found on the street by Mwangi, smoking a cigarette at the age of five. He had seven brothers and sisters, and an elder brother had persuaded him he would be less hungry on the street than he was at home. Samuel had been beaten repeatedly by the drunk uncle he had been sent to live with when his father died. When he lost his eye after the worst beating he had ever had, he escaped to the streets – at the age of eleven.

But this was all detail Chala would discover slowly through the interviews over the coming days. Now Mwangi led her into the hall, where all the boys had gathered on wooden benches. The occasional free-range chicken wandered across the concrete floor as Winnie addressed the boys. She was stern and headmistress-like, but clearly the matriarch in their lives. She would chastise, but she would also squeeze the cheeks of the little ones whenever they came near. Mwangi motioned Chala to sit on a bench at the back, next to the other staff members and Winnie. He then announced in formal English that the boys would sing a song to welcome her. On cue, the boys shuffled into position: a motley choir in their tatty clothes and bare feet or ill-fitting shoes. They sang the famous song played for tourists in Kenya's safari lodges, '*Jambo, jambo bwana …*' It sounded so out of place here, and Chala felt moved. She found herself thinking of Amanda and her voice, soulful and beautiful, at her wedding. How she would love to be able to share this with Amanda. And Paul. And Philip. She blinked back the tears. Her sense of fragility felt like a crime.

'Thank you so much.' Chala stood up after the song. 'Remind me how you say thank you in Swahili?' she asked Mwangi.

'*Asante sana.*'

'*Santi sana.*' She caught the smile on little Julius' face and knew that she had not pronounced it quite right.

# CHAPTER 19

'So, what's it like?' Paul's interest was genuine and Chala felt a wave of gratitude.

'I love it. I think the boys are starting to accept me and Winnie's hired me a moped to get up there. A bit hair-raising at first, but I've just about got the hang of it now. I've already got some great photos for the website …' Chala stopped and the pause stretched on the line between them.

'What about you? How's everything at home?' She wondered if Paul, too, would register the use of the word home. The open-endedness of the situation they were in made so many words loaded. She felt him tense.

'Yeah, everything's fine. I'm working on finishing a couple of new pieces for the exhibition next month and I've played a bit of cricket. You know John plays? Well, someone in the team had a skiing accident so they've roped me in. It's good fun, actually. I might have to find a woman to make the sandwiches when it's my turn, though!' He was trying to make light of their situation, but even at this distance Chala could sense the effort in his voice. She groped for something harmless.

'And Rudolph? Are you feeding him?'

'Hey, if I needed someone to nag me, I'd ask them to move in and keep the bed warm!' An edge had crept into the effort.

'Sorry, I didn't mean—' That word – the word he hated – so ready on her lips.

'He's fine.' Paul's voice cut through her hesitation. 'Let's face it,' – a soft laugh – 'nothing much changes in the life of a hamster.'

She softened, too. 'No, no I suppose it doesn't, really.' Another pause. 'But, you're ... OK?'

'Look, Che ...' His nickname stilled something in her. 'I think it's probably better if we don't try and do this on the phone. Is there an Internet café there?'

'Yes,' she said slowly. 'I think so.'

'Well, then let's keep it to emails for the time being, OK?'

'Of course, if ... if you prefer that, of course.'

'OK, speak soon then. I mean email soon.'

She looked deep into her beer after he had gone. They sounded like strangers and she hated herself for it. Would they be in the same place now if Bruce hadn't happened? If Philip hadn't died? Her stomach felt like a dangerous lake.

'Can I join you?' She jumped. It was Mick. A white Kenyan who made his living on cableway transport systems for the flower farms in the Rift Valley. He also chaired the Rotary Club that met every Wednesday, and had introduced himself briefly to her before the last meeting. Mick was probably in his early forties. After a lifetime of high-altitude sunshine, he had that weathered look of so many of the white Kenyans here, but he was attractive.

The memory of Bruce's hands flashed through her mind and she felt the underwater pull of the lake inside her.

'No strings, don't worry!' Mick had seen her discomfort. 'Tusker?'

She felt her redness deepen and cursed herself. 'Sure.' And, in the pause that followed, she added, 'Would you like one?'

'Yes, please.' He was mocking her English formality and she looked for a subject to take the focus off her.

'Tell me about the refuge project.' She knew some of the boys at the shelter had come from the project run by the Rotary Club so she jumped on this. 'What exactly does it do?'

He lit a cigarette and sat back in his chair, still looking at her with mischief in his eyes. 'It's basically a holding institution for abused children. You wouldn't believe the state of some of them when we take them in. It's a bit like looking after maltreated dogs. We nurse them back to some form of physical health and do our best to provide a supportive environment, but it's only temporary and then we have to rehome them. Some of your guys have come from there.'

'And how do they come to you in the first place?'

'The police often pick them up and bring them to us. But how about the shelter? How are you doing up there? Winnie says you're doing a great job.'

'I love it.' She felt herself start to redden again and he cut in.

'And outside the shelter, how's your social life?'

'Winnie's been very kind and I've been to her place a few times, but I'm happy to keep myself to myself, to be honest.' She felt lame.

'That's no excuse, girl. We need to get you out. A friend of mine, Tom, is having a party on Saturday. Why don't you come to that? Get a taste of Naivasha.'

'Thank you. That's very kind of you.' Oh God, a party.

'Good. That's settled then. Well,' he stood up and took her hand theatrically, 'my meeting beckons. I'll sort out a lift for you on

Saturday.' And he kissed her hand and withdrew, just as Winnie stepped onto the veranda.

'You want to watch him,' she said, deliberately loud enough for Mick to hear.

# CHAPTER 20

She knew something was wrong as soon as she saw Mwangi's face. The boys were in the classrooms, but the teachers were closeted in their tiny staff room, heads down and talking in low voices. Mwangi smiled at Chala as she entered the room and found a space to sit, but the smile was weak.

'Where's Fred?' He was one of the resident staff, teacher-cum-matron, the one who welcomed her with a cup of milky tea in the morning. She found it hard to follow Mwangi's answer, as if it hurt him to say it.

'They came in last night, looking for money. When they couldn't find any, they beat Fred badly.'

'They? Who are *they*? Is he all right? Does Winnie know?'

'Winnie took him to hospital this morning. We think it was a couple of boys from a gang in town. Maybe they had too much *pombe*. Maybe they had to do this nonsense so that the boss could let them into the gang.'

'But what about the *askari*?' On-site security consisted of one old night-watchman who did a bit of gardening during the day, too.

'He's OK. They tied him up and we found him still there this morning.'

The notion that a shelter for street kids could be targeted by petty criminals was shocking.

'Are the boys OK?'

'Yeah, they are OK. The little ones got a bit scared, but they are OK.' Many had seen worse. Violence played close to the surface of their lives.

Winnie came later to report on Fred's progress. They had slashed his arm with a *panga*, the machete blade seen all over Kenya. He had lost a lot of blood and had seventeen stitches, but he would be fine. He was thankful they hadn't touched his face.

Winnie told Mwangi not to worry. She would contract a security company to arrange proper armed security at night, at least for the next few weeks. Her voice was so firm, so full of certainty. Chala saw the lines relax on Mwangi's face. He had his own family and three children, and yet he carried the burden of these fifty street boys as if they, too, were his.

Later, at the hotel, Winnie sighed deep into her beer.

'You see why the website is important, Chala, why we need it to help raise money.' She looked vulnerable all of a sudden. 'We can't afford to pay for the security company for long. We need more money for things like this.'

Chala knew the boys only ate fresh meat once a week and the teachers' salaries seemed shockingly low to her, but they were the lucky ones. Migrant hopefuls flocked from all over upcountry Kenya to Naivasha, looking for work on the flower farms around the lake. One of the larger flower farms would employ around 5,000 people. That meant, with dependents, they were directly supporting a community of 30,000.

Chala had ridden out around the lake on her moped last Sunday. She had steered her way past donkeys and cows in the middle of the road, through a small rubbish-drenched town on South Lake Road with sprawling tin shacks and everything from vegetables to buckets and T-shirts laid out for sale in rows on plastic sheets in the dirt. A huge concrete church with a turquoise tin roof loomed over the makeshift housing around it, and gospel clapping boomed inside it. Late arrivals still crowded in: women dressed in shiny suits of red and gold, children dressed like dolls, little girls in frilly, pristine, white dresses with puffed sleeves and large bows around their waists. The power of the church was not just supernatural, Chala realised. It was also social.

She had gone past one flower farm after another. Endless lines of plastic greenhouses, hedged off by barbed wire draped in bougainvillea; long rows of concrete terraced housing with lines of coloured washing hanging in the bare yards in front of them. Most farms had their own community infrastructure – housing, schools, nurseries, clinics, football pitches, security. How little we know when we buy flowers at a supermarket in England, she thought, resolving to fill their house in Sussex with a regular supply of flowers from Kenya. She caught the pronoun again in her thoughts.

And then the road had climbed and Lake Naivasha spread out below her. Signs read '*Hatari!* Danger hippos at night' and 'Game corridor – animals have the right of way'. Chala had stopped to gaze at a herd of impala just beside the road and almost missed the giraffe on the other side, chewing at a thorn tree. A large warthog marched off into the distance, followed by half a dozen tiny babies, all with their tails in the air. She had stopped again to let a zebra cross the road and laughed at the nuance of a zebra crossing and thought of

Philip. Perhaps she would come back here with his ashes. Something in her still resisted letting them go, and yet it seemed wrong to keep them trapped in a box at the sidelines of her existence.

Winnie's voice brought her back to the present.

'What do you think?' She was asking about how to make the website work.

Chala focused intensely for a moment and then it hit her.

'Do we need permission to publish an individual profile, with a picture, of every single boy on the website?' She felt breathless.

Winnie laughed. 'Your world is different. No, we don't need permission. We are the guardians anyway.'

Chala was still a bit intimidated by Winnie, but the idea was bursting from her now. 'Then I think that's the way we can reach people. Make the boys real. Make people feel they're giving money to benefit individual human beings with a past and a future, rather than just a cause in a vacuum.' Winnie was smiling, and Chala didn't know whether it was at her naivety or her enthusiasm, but she continued.

'We'd have to build in an online payment facility, and we'd have to promote the site properly, of course, but this is the way we could make it different – the ability to sponsor an individual child, a bit like you can adopt an individual elephant through The David Sheldrick Wildlife Trust.'

'But everyone will want to adopt Humphrey.' He was the youngest, the little three-year-old mascot found abandoned at a police station, the one who was always put in the front row to welcome visitors.

'We can manage that through the website. There can be a quota for each boy, and people will have to choose from a menu of available children to sponsor, and the menu can be updated as quotas fill.'

Chala was excited now. 'We could give individual updates about what happens to each boy. Sponsors would know that their money was contributing directly to carpentry training for Simon or driving lessons for Kamau.'

'But things go wrong. These are street boys, their stories don't all have happy endings, you know.'

'Life goes wrong. That's part of the reality of it. People aren't buying a book about someone else's life, they're affecting that life, directly, with all the risks that go with that ...' Chala paused to look at Winnie's face. She was smiling again.

'I think we need to get you to Nairobi next week to meet Ken.' He worked for a national Internet provider and had recently married a cousin of Winnie's. He had agreed to build the website free of charge. 'Now, I think we both deserve another beer.'

Chala remembered the rush of joy she had felt as a child when Louise had finally wanted to play on her side in the netball team.

# CHAPTER 21

Saturday came and Chala half hoped the lift from Mick wouldn't materialise, but it did.

'Thought you might need a bit of moral support for the first time!' he said to her with mischief in his face.

'Oh God, is it going to be that bad?' Chala joked, relieved that she didn't need to walk into the party alone. 'I'm not very good at parties. I don't really like them very much.'

'Few drinks inside you, you'll be fine! Just watch the KCs!' 'What's a KC?' Chala asked.

Mick laughed from his stomach, but told her nothing. 'You'll find out soon enough.'

It all looked quite formal when they arrived – people standing around a drinks table in a garden – but as she walked into its fray she was quick to register how it differed from an English summer garden party. The garden was much larger than any she had been to in England, with papyrus and acacia trees and banks of cactus and bright orange lilies. There were women wearing flowing skirts and sandals, with matching pashmina shawls for the Kenyan winter. And men –

a good number of them anyway – stubbornly sporting sandals and short white shorts, oblivious to the evening chill in the air. As she approached the drinks table, Chala noticed that the 'bar fridge' was a two-metre black plastic water tank cut in half and brimming with beers on ice.

'Hey, Mick, where have you been?' A woman in cowboy boots approached them, completely ignoring Chala.

'Meet Chala.' Mick answered, and she warmed to him then. 'Chala, this is Donna.'

'Hi, how are you?' Donna gazed at Chala for a second as if she was her best friend and then cut her out completely, turning her attention wholly to Mick.

Chala stepped out of her comfort zone to approach the bar on her own and accepted the first beer that was put in her hand.

'You're new round here,' said the person who had put it there. He, too, was wearing sandals and shorts, she noticed. 'What do you think of us, then?' He couldn't have asked a more difficult question. She slugged back her beer and fired a question back in return. To her surprise, he responded immediately … and talked and talked. Chala's thoughts drifted to Paul. She missed him. Already. The way he would cheerfully crash into her space and her moments of reverie, the way he would sweep her out of them. But his anger – the dark lines on his face when he sank – no, it was a relief to get away from that. What would this 'space' be doing to him? Would it soften the anger? How *was* he?

She made an effort to tune in to what the man beside her was saying – something about a rhino charge.

'No, no, it's a car rally!' He laughed when she put her foot in it. 'It happens every year in an undisclosed location. You have to work out how to get from A to B in as little time as possible and over the shortest distance you can. That's why you need a car that can go off road.'

'And what's the point of it?' It was an honest question.

'What's the point? Man, it's serious fun for a start! Best beer you'll ever have is the one at the finish line.'

Chala wondered in an abstract sort of way what it would be like to be in a relationship with someone like this. She felt a rush of appreciation for Paul.

'And you raise money, too.'

'Oh, what does the money go on?'

'Re-fencing the Aberdares mostly, to keep the elephants inside the park. They need to keep the elephants on the mountains, I can tell you – last time I was there, I remember—'

'So, is this man behaving himself?' It was Mick.

He laughed back, 'What are you – her keeper?'

As the evening progressed, alcohol flowed and large ceramic pots with charcoal were lit to keep everyone warm. Trays of 'bitings' were carried round: samosas and spring rolls and cheese and olives. Laughter grew louder and some people started dancing. Chala was approached by a man with a laugh like Father Christmas who pinched her bottom but was so gentlemanly about it, it seemed churlish to react. She talked to a lady in her eighties with a cigarette in her hand and a couple of teenage girls whose mother and grandmother were also at the party. She met a Dutch vet, who had been here for two years and laughed gently at the vague bewilderment Chala shared with her. More and more people seemed to be drunk, and yet no one showed any signs of slowing down or leaving the party.

'Yeah, it goes like this,' said Femke. 'If you stay too long, the ones that are left will start taking their clothes off!'

'You're joking, aren't you? How are you getting back?'

She offered to drop Chala off on her way home and Chala was grateful. 'It's best not to do goodbyes to everyone. They will just make you stay. We can just slide away.'

'I feel like I'm starting to slide away already!' Chala wasn't used to drinking so much. 'Let me just go to the loo and I'll be with you.'

She sat on the loo feeling slightly dizzy and tried to focus on the postcards and photos plastered all around her. Immediately opposite her was a poster entitled, 'KCs, a lesser-known tribe of Kenya'. Aha, there it was again – KC. She forced herself to read on:

> 'They wear tight shorts, hand-knitted jumpers and frayed collars.
> They'd rather die than be thought of as scholars.
> You find them in small towns, muttering about tractor spares,
> Or roaming the country to fulfil one another's dares.
> They're allergic to political correctness and shoes,
> But not shooting or hunting or fishing or booze.
> You won't find the rights of women debated,
> But you will find that nearly all are related.
> They know everything to know about Kenyan genealogy,
> And quite a lot about canine and female biology.
> They love weddings and fun,
> And will travel miles and miles just to go to one.
> They don't do toy dogs, small cars or camp men,
> But they do a lot of stories that start with "I remember when ..."
> Their English is stuck in the Sixties and so are some of their ideals. Their
> favourite foods are all in Mother's homemade meals.
> They are good organisers and fair with their workers.
> It's a matter of pride not to be thought of as shirkers.

*You may think they do not deserve the rights that they keep,*
*But you cannot deny that their love for their country runs deep.'*

KC ... KC – and then it hit her and she was still giggling when she came out of the loo and bumped straight into Mick.

'Done something funny in there, have you?'

'I know what you are,' she laughed. 'A Kenya Cowboy!'

# CHAPTER 22

Her mind wandered beyond the breath, in awe of where she was. She let herself open her eyes for a moment to take in again the reality that swept away from them: an expanse of water, still as sand between mountains, shining in the light of early morning. Another of Kenya's amazing lakes. There was something infinitely serene about this one, a sense of space and oblivion.

After the two-and-a-half hour drive north from Naivasha, the short boat ride to the island with warm wind in their hair as they cut through the brown water had been exhilarating. There were crocodiles in the lake – they had seen one on the bank when they boarded the boat – and yet it didn't feel like a lake with secrets, not like Lake Chala all those years ago. They had spent the rest of the first day just relaxing and taking in the beauty of their surroundings, from their *bandas* – thatched bedrooms with no walls – which opened over the lake; from the infinity pool which seemed to merge with the lake, divided only by the turquoise colour of its own water; from the comfort of sofas in the shade of trees. An owl watched sleepily from a branch near the pool, as if on a mission to protect this small group of women.

It was Femke, on their way home from the party the previous week, who had persuaded Chala to join them for their yoga weekend on an island in Lake Baringo. Chala had been hesitant, not having done yoga before, not knowing anyone, not even sure that she could justify the indulgence and the extra day away from the shelter. 'Don't be so ridiculous.' Winnie had said. 'You need to see some of Kenya while you're here.'

But above all, it was the tiredness that had decided her. It was as if her energy literally ran out each day, so by the afternoons she felt heavy and weak. Grief and uncertainty, she reminded herself constantly, these are big things, bound to take their toll. Maybe the yoga would bring back some energy.

Philip's ashes still lay – patient and unassuming – beside her bed. She had thought of taking them with her to Baringo, but then decided against it, sensing she might not have the privacy she would need for the inevitable final ritual she needed to face.

She had taken to the yoga teacher immediately: a gentle, slim woman in her early forties called Jane, whose sense of humour dispelled the mystique of yoga and made it seem accessible at any level. All the same, Chala had been quiet that first evening and the first to go to bed.

She had woken in the middle of the night to strong wind that poured through the open sides of the *banda* and the sound of the lake like sea in a storm. She had pulled up the blanket and found it strangely comforting to feel the wind and even drops of rain on her face in the darkness. By morning the wind and rain had swept through, the sky was clear and the lake was utterly still. She had watched the sunrise from her bed, an egg-yolk sun climbing a mountain on the horizon and pouring weak, warm light across the water.

Jane's voice pierced her consciousness now, as they sat cross- legged on yoga mats on the stone floor of an empty *banda*, faces slightly tilted towards the view. It was a soft, yet strong, voice and, as she talked them through the meditation, Chala was reminded of Amanda.

'Recognise the thoughts that come to you,' Jane was saying. 'Name them if you like and then let them go like clouds in the sky. Don't follow them. Just come back to the breath ...'

Chala tried to concentrate on her breathing, tried to ignore the stiffness in the small of her back, wondered if she was trying too hard and conjured up behind closed eyelids a deliberate image of clouds in the sky.

'I am going to talk a little about each of the seven chakras in your body and I want you to follow my words at a distance. Allow them to float through you and feel the wheel of each chakra in your body.' Her voice was soothing. Chala tried to close her eyes deeper.

'Imagine a wheel at the base of your spine, spinning red energy. This is the first chakra, at the root of our being, grounding us to the earth. This chakra relates to our most primal needs. If it is balanced, we have a strong sense of the here and now and a will to live. We know what we want in life, we trust our relationships, we accept ourselves and our bodies as they are. If there is imbalance here, we feel unable to cope, life is unfair, we become the victim, de-personalised, lacking in energy and self-esteem.'

Is that my problem? Chala found herself thinking. When he gets angry with me Paul says I'm always the victim. And my lack of energy, is that what this is about? Philip was my anchor. I've lost my anchor ... And Paul? Chala felt a vague throbbing in her head and forced herself back to Jane's voice.

'Now feel the energy moving up from the earth beneath you,

through the red wheel at the base of your spine and into an orange wheel between your pubic bone and your navel. This is the sacral chakra, associated with our reproductive organs, our sexuality and creativity. If this chakra is balanced, we feel joy and pleasure in life, we can be independent and whole. If it is blocked, our sexual relationship with our partner may break down, we may suffer feelings of confusion, envy and lust.'

An image of Bruce naked above her shot through Chala. Is that what he was about? And yet it hadn't felt like lust either. It seemed to stand separately in her consciousness, parallel yet unconnected. An accident, she thought sourly – no, a mistake. Oh Paul … If he were here now, she realised, if she could open her eyes and see him in front of her, she would want him to wrap his arms around her, she would want to nestle into his neck and smell him.

'Now the energy is moving again, this time into yellow, inside your stomach at the solar plexus. Feel the wheel going round in your tummy. This chakra is associated with stamina, willpower and wellbeing. It is our true energy centre, close to the organs where we digest our food, the centre for our major emotions, our ambitions, our wants and desires. When it is in balance, we have a strong sense of personal identity, we like ourselves, we feel centred. When it is out of balance, we may suffer feelings of passivity, powerlessness, anxiety, guilt, lack of drive and willpower. We may become overly submissive to others, losing a sense of self, unable to process emotions, blaming ourselves for our failures.'

Chala felt as if someone had just punched her in the stomach. She wanted to cry. She felt as if Jane could see straight into the rotten core of her, as if she somehow knew what Chala had done as a little girl, as if she could see the guilt that lived inside her, on and on through each new lap of life's experience. She took a deep breath to steady herself. She shifted position, leaning against the wall to support her back. But the tears came anyway, soft and silent.

'And now, the wheel is moving again. The energy is climbing upwards from our solar plexus to a place just to the right of our heart. Here the colour is green. Our emotions have turned into love, tenderness and compassion, and unconditional love flows here. If this chakra is too open, we may become overly sensitive to others and drained by the outward flow of energy. If it is blocked, we may find that we have difficulty maintaining loving relationships; we may feel detached and removed, seeing only the bad things in other people; we may have difficulty expressing our emotions. Feel this green wheel turning near your heart and the energy pouring through.'

To Chala it seemed that her chest breathed wider as she concentrated on her heart. The tears still came, she felt them grow inside her and well up through her throat, and yet there was a sad sense of calm in them now, a recognition that, for all her faults, this chakra at least was not blocked. She saw Philip in her mind's eye and her whole being ached with unconditional love for him and all that he had been in her life. And then, suddenly, she felt constricted. Would Paul's love for her be unconditional enough to take her back?

'Feel your energy moving from the earth beneath you, up through the root chakra, through the colour red, into the orange of your sexual organs, up through the yellow solar plexus chakra, through the green heart and now up, up into your throat, into light indigo blue. This chakra is connected to our ability to express ourselves and communicate with others. If it is balanced, we are able to relate with quiet confidence to the world around us, we are able to express feelings and ideas clearly and listen sensitively to others. If it is out of balance we may find we have difficulty finding the right words, we may find ourselves hiding behind a quiet voice or simply unable to articulate a thought or feeling, or we may find ourselves becoming over-talkative, filling the space around us with little of value, avoiding confrontation with our inner selves.'

Chala felt an initial wave of relief, aware of her own ability as a listener, but then she thought of the beta blockers she took for public speaking, of the one she had taken for her own wedding. Was this to do with the throat chakra? Or a lack of confidence in the solar plexus? She thought of what Paul's reaction would be and laughed a sad, silent internal laugh. Forever analysing, trying to find explanations, labelling parts of her life like photos in an album. As if labels could change things, or make them go away.

She tuned back into the rhythm of her breathing and the silence that sat between the different wheels of Jane's journey through their bodies. She felt a shy wave of calm and thought of the ripples in the lake.

'Now the light blue energy is moving again,' Jane's voice floated over the lake, 'moving into a deep indigo purple in the centre of your forehead between your eyes. This is the brow chakra and it is connected to intuition and the power of vision in our mind. It's also the place where we frown and it has to do with concentration and mental fatigue. Feel it now, and if you find yourself frowning, relax and feel the purple energy smoothing out the lines in your forehead.'

Chala felt flustered and imagined a painter with a thick purple brush sweeping away the frown across her forehead. Jane's voice washed over them again.

'If this chakra is open our creative spirit flows freely, we can tap into our imagination and harness positivity in our lives. If it is blocked we may find we suffer from negative thoughts or poor concentration or fatigue. At the extreme end of the spectrum we may even lose the ability to distinguish between reality and fantasy. Feel this now, feel this purple wave of peace flow into your brow.'

Chala willed purple into her head and waited for the journey to continue.

'Now feel the wheel turning to a point right at the crown of your head: the centre of our spiritual being. The energy here is white. Feel the energy at the top of your head. If each of the other chakras is a string on a guitar, the crown chakra is the playing of a chord, combining all the notes together. When this chakra is blocked we may suffer from depression and feel trapped inside our bodies without any spiritual dimension. If it is too open, we can have difficulties relating to the real physical world around us. When it is balanced, we have a sense of peace and acceptance of our lives.'

Self-doubt gripped Chala. Her head hurt with the vision of these colours sweeping through her body. Dysfunctional. The word bubbled up inside her as she tried to hold back her tears. The tears stilled and she waited for Jane's voice, but there was only silence. Chala became aware, through closed eyes, of other people around her. She opened her eyes, slowly, and was shocked by what she saw.

Femke sat not far away, serenely upright, with sunshine lighting up the blond streaks in her hair. She was beautiful, Chala realised. Not in a head-turning sort of way, but in a way that grew as you spent time in her company. She exuded balance and warmth. She was one of those people who was just good to be around. And yet her face was also wet with tears. She, too, carried secret turmoil.

As she looked from face to face, Chala could see emotion on all of them. In that moment she wished for a camera, a camera to capture this for Paul to paint.

# CHAPTER 23

'So what did you think? Did you like the weekend?' Femke's voice was almost teasing, mischievous.

'Yes, I did, mostly. I've never done anything like that before.'

'What, sit with a bunch of women on a desert island and cry your head out?'

'Your heart or your eyes, not your head.' Chala laughed over her beer. 'Actually, I think you're right – head is a better description!'

'But it feels good, right? You feel better than before we went?'

'Yes, I think I do. I'm still tired, though.' Chala had been so exhausted the day they had got back, she'd slept for ten hours.

'You're not pregnant, are you?'

'Of course not!'

'Hey, why the "of course"? I thought maybe there was something with you and Mick?'

'You're joking! Anyway, for someone who spends her time expressing anal glands, you got pretty emotional too Miss Femke!' Chala loved Femke's accounts of her daily life as a vet.

'Yeah, even vets cry, you know.'

Chala longed suddenly, violently, to talk to Femke about Bruce. Would that be so wrong? Would it hurt to talk to someone about what she'd done? But she shrunk from another betrayal, searching instead for a safer intimacy. 'So, what was it that made *you* cry?'

'My boyfriend and I, we drove apart last year. I still miss him.'

'Oh.' Chala let the English slip pass. She hesitated. 'What happened?'

'Oh nothing special, really. He just couldn't do, how do you say, commitment?'

'Yes, commitment.' She thought of Paul. How does anyone do commitment?

'Hello, ladies! Another beer?' It was Mick, pulling up a chair before they could stop him. 'I'm not interrupting anything, am I?'

Femke and Chala made fleeting eye contact. Femke was the first to speak. 'I didn't think you KCs preoccupied about that sort of thing.'

He laughed as he sat down and turned to Femke. 'So how does a Dutch vet get a licence in Naivasha?'

'With great difficulty!' Femke had told Chala her story about the painstaking bureaucracy involved and the official letter issued by the Dutch embassy vouching for her qualifications and ability to operate as a 'vegetarian'. The Kenyan authorities hadn't noticed the mistake, and the letter was now framed on her wall.

Something about the way Femke blushed made Chala suddenly aware of an unexpected chemistry between her and Mick. After she finished her beer she excused herself, saying she'd heard the Internet was up.

She dodged potholes and mopeds and stepped into the bright green Internet café. '*Hujambo Mama Shelter!*' The owner greeted her warmly and she glowed at the nickname they had chosen for her. She smiled and sat down at the computer he waved her to. Nothing from Paul, but there was an email from Denise. They had already exchanged emails, mostly full of questions and answers about Kenya and the shelter. At last the message opened in front of her:

*Hi Chala*

*How is little Julius doing? How is the website coming along? And your yoga weekend? You know, I tried to do yoga once, but I guess a warehouse in London doesn't have quite the same spiritual pull as an island in the middle of a Kenyan lake!*

*Chala, I hope all this is helping you find a kind of peace. Perhaps I have no right to say this, but I hope you and Paul find a way back into your marriage and that I wasn't wrong to suggest you went on your own. It's good to hold on to what you've got. That was something I never learnt to do. Perhaps if I had, things would have turned out very differently, but perhaps not. Life has a funny way of creating its own stubborn path regardless, doesn't it? Have you seen the film 'Sliding Doors'? It makes me think of Philip sometimes!*

*Anyway, listen Chala, take no notice of me – it's late and I shouldn't be writing now – but when you come back, let's meet again, please. I need to talk to you about Philip. You have the right to understand.*

*Take care of yourself.*

*Denise*

Chala shifted on the bare seat. The tone of Denise's email was different this time, disconcerting. She sensed agitation between the lines – a new agitation. Was this something to do with Philip's letter? Denise had only mentioned the letter once, to say that she hadn't opened it yet, that she needed time to prepare herself. Chala had respected her privacy, avoiding any attempt to probe, but now she felt a butterfly twinge and wondered what her solar plexus chakra was trying to tell her.

*Sliding Doors*. Chala had seen the film with Paul shortly before she left. A light, safe romcom to take their mind off her imminent departure. She'd enjoyed Gwyneth Paltrow's role, her innocence, the way destiny worked out two parallel lives for her with essentially the same happy ending, but she had also squirmed at the exposure of deception, acutely aware, beside Paul, of the memory of Bruce inside her. And beyond the superficial romcom lurked a minefield that had haunted her all her life: the notion of destiny, predetermination versus free will, the extent to which we can exert control, the extent to which we are responsible, to blame for what happens to us and around us. Life without guilt – what would it feel like?

Over dinner Paul had surprised her: 'Everyone has a *Sliding Doors* moment in their life, don't you think?'

'That's a very female thing to say.' Chala felt defensive. 'What was yours, then?'

'I don't think I've had mine yet. What about you?'

'Does it have to be conscious?'

Paul tried to laugh. 'Trust you … No, something that happened when you were four does not count.'

'Well.' Chala felt herself hesitating, grappling with a ghost that would always be there between them if she kept her resolve. 'Well, I'm not sure I've had mine yet either.'

'I think you have.' Paul's smile was gone. 'Yours was the decision to go to Kenya.'

'Oh, don't say that, Paul.' She hated hurting him.

'Hey, don't worry. It's *Sliding Doors*, remember. It actually makes fuck-all difference in the long run.' He touched the side of her face and she wished she were a better person.

Chala realised she was staring at a blank screen saver. What did Denise mean when she said that the film made her think of Philip? Had she come to believe that they would have gone their separate ways regardless of the *accident*? But what about Emma? What would have happened to her if she'd lived?

She swallowed back the sense of self-loathing that always threatened to engulf her when she thought of Emma and began a slow email to Paul. She told him about the strange email from Denise and the moment she had yearned for him at the yoga, about her progress with the sponsor-a-child plan and about Kenya's election fever. She asked him about his painting and his cricket.

She longed to ask him if his anger would ever go away, if he thought it mattered; yearned to tell him about the notion of 'home' taking root inside her, but she knew she had no right.

Later, on the veranda at her hotel, Chala couldn't wash away a feeling of unease over Denise's email. She thought of the phone call with Philip before she had gone to Australia. Could this be another of those moments? What if Denise were in trouble? She picked up the phone and checked her credit. Yes there was enough ...

'Denise?'

'Chala, my goodness, are you OK?' She was obviously shocked to get the call.

'Yes, no, I'm fine. I was actually calling to see if *you* were OK.' There was a pause that felt too loaded and Chala filled it for her. 'I mean, I got your email and it just sounded, I don't know, you just sounded worried or upset and I wanted to make sure you were OK.'

Still Denise said nothing and Chala continued. 'Was it the letter? Did it stir things up for you too much?' She was using Paul's vocabulary.

'Oh Chala,' said Denise at last. 'Listen, I'm sorry about that email—'

'No, don't say sorry.' Paul's vocabulary again. 'I really appreciate what you said. It's just … I'm a bit worried about you.'

'I'm fine, honestly, I am … But yes, you're right. It was the letter …'

'What?' Chala began into the silence, but Denise cut her short.

'No, we can't do this on the phone. It won't be long before you get back. We'll meet then, when we can talk properly. Is that OK? And Chala,' she hesitated, 'how are you and Paul?'

'I don't know is the honest answer, but I think we'll be OK, I hope we'll be OK.' She dried up, wondering what was happening in Paul's head, sick of the inside of her own.

'Well, hope is a good thing anyway. You keep hold of that and take care.'

When she put the phone down, Chala breathed deeply. What could possibly be in the letter that had shaken Denise so badly?

# CHAPTER 24

There was some kind of traffic jam in the dusty centre of Naivasha. Chala edged to the middle of the road on her moped, wary of the narrow space between the vehicles and the risk of less cautious drivers behind her. She heard the reason before she saw it. The sound of drums and horns grew louder as the procession made its way along the main street, a loudspeaker booming to the people to let work continue, to vote for Kibaki. She glimpsed a wave of people, mostly men, brandishing flags and almost dancing along to the drums. People leant out of cars and trucks, whistling or making thumbs-up signs to show their approval. The atmosphere was almost one of carnival. Chala watched the procession pass and marvelled at it. We in the West, she thought, have forgotten to be passionate about our right to vote.

The elections were only a day away now. Winnie had warned that she should keep her head down – a certain amount of violence was always to be expected – and Femke had suggested that she stay with her over the weekend until the results were announced.

As the tail end of the procession straggled past and the sound of drums faded, vehicles pitched impatiently into motion through the dust. Chala had pulled her moped over to the side of the road and, as it spluttered finally into gear, she caught sight of someone in the corner of her eye, someone running who looked like Kamau, one of the oldest boys at the shelter. He'd been there four years now and there was still a shyness about him, a tendency to avoid eye contact. The long scar down the back of his head convinced her that it was him. The scar was a parting gift from his drunken father, a blow that had nearly killed him and forced him, at the age of eight, to take to the street.

'Kamau!' she shouted out as he ran ahead of her along the broken pavement. Other people turned their heads and looked at her, but he ran faster now. 'Kamau,' she shouted again, sure now that something was wrong. He wasn't far ahead, but the traffic was thick in front of her and she couldn't catch him up.

He turned his head and gave her a momentary look, frozen in time, before veering to the left and disappearing down an alley between two buildings. What she registered in the intense frown and sweat on his face was a look of pure anguish. She stopped the moped and looked down the alley he had fled into, but there was no sign of him.

When she finally arrived at the shelter, the tension reminded her of the time they had been broken into by a gang of thugs. Mwangi, Fred, Joshua and Simon were huddled in the staff room with Winnie, who was wringing her hands.

'Chala, come in, come in.' Chala had hesitated, feeling she was intruding. 'It's OK, you are one of us, sit down.' Winnie's voice was soft and strained. 'Tell her, Mwangi.'

Mwangi looked up at her with the face of an old man and then averted his eyes as he began to speak. 'Something happened with Julius and Kamau—'

'I just saw Kamau in Naivasha. I tried to stop him, but he just kept running.' She saw Mwangi tense. Her interruption hadn't made it any easier for him. 'Sorry, go on. What happened?'

'It was lunchtime and everyone was in the hall and then Fred saw that Kamau and Julius were not there. He went to look for them and found that one of the toilets was unlocked.'

'Why wasn't it locked? You know you need to keep them locked at all times, you know that.' Winnie waved her anger around the room in desperation and the men looked into their laps like schoolchildren.

Fred, the teacher-cum-matron, the one who bore the greatest responsibility for the boys' welfare, spoke into the silence. 'Mama, it was a mistake. You know it.'

'I'm sorry,' she softened. 'You are right. These things happen. How do we tell this story on your website?' She looked at Chala and there was a bitterness there that surprised her.

'What story? I still don't know what happened.'

'He was sodomised.'

Chala looked away as she processed the word. She fumbled for a response, still unbelieving. 'Julius? Little Julius? By Kamau? But—'

'But what? These are street kids, Chala. I told you to remember that.'

'But,' Chala could not let go of the 'but' – there had to be a 'but'. She thought of Kamau's face, the anguish in his eyes. Her mouth started to form words that didn't even begin to break the surface of the reality of what had happened. 'But Kamau has been here so long. He was doing so well. How could he do that? He looked so upset when I saw him.'

'That's because he knows he can never come back. He has written

155

his life.' It was Fred speaking now. Mwangi had sat back into his chair, tight-faced and powerless. Winnie was holding both hands together as if to force them to be still.

'But why did he do it?' Chala felt her own hands trembling. Why did people do such awful things to each other? Julius was their mascot, their little brother. They all loved and protected him. How could a boy who has suffered so much himself inflict such pain on someone he loves? How could a four-year-old kill her baby sister? She sensed Fred talking again.

'It surely happened to him when he was a little boy. It is the way of the street gangs. It happens to you when you join and later you will do it to other new boys. They carry these habits of the street inside them. Sometimes it is not easy to let them go.'

'It only needs one moment without God, one opportunity to tempt.' Mwangi was speaking again, all of them looking at Chala as if it was important she understood.

Chala nodded slowly. 'And Julius?' Her stomach was tight.

'He'll be OK. He is young and strong and he has food and love here. He'll be OK.' Winnie spoke for all of them, her back straight in her seat, quietly authoritative again.

Chala ached at the thought of the scars he would have to live with for the rest of his life. 'And what happens now?'

'You mean with Kamau?' Winnie asked.

'Yes.'

'We talked about whether to call the police.'

'The police?' Chala felt stupid and helpless at once. She hadn't even thought of this in terms of a crime.

'But that would be the end of him,' Winnie continued. 'He would spend the rest of his life in a prison, being abused for what he has done. God can decide what will happen to him now. We will not say anything. We have agreed.'

'But we are consigning him to the street for ever.' That 'but' again.

Winnie's eyes flashed at Chala, harder now. '*He* has consigned himself to the street. He can't come back here now, can he? What would *you* do?'

Chala registered the anger in Winnie's voice, but assumed the question was rhetorical. No one spoke. Then Chala realised they were all looking at her, expecting an answer. For a moment, she was back in the playground, a forgotten skipping rope around her ankles.

'You're right,' she said slowly. 'What else is there to do?'

When she got back to her room, she sat on the edge of the bed and pulled the small wooden box out of the bedside drawer. She placed it on the top of the table, hugged her knees and stared at it. She stared through memory after memory and rocked gently backwards and forwards.

Poor Kamau. His *Sliding Doors* moment. Would it always have ended the same way?

# CHAPTER 25

Chala was sick after breakfast. Whether it was the effect of the incident the day before, or nerves around what she was about to do, or just the oil the *mandazis* had been cooked in, she didn't stop to question. She brushed her teeth, took three deep breaths in front of the broken mirror and tucked the wooden box into her rucksack with a bottle of water. The bottom of the rucksack was already packed tight with clothes and a wash bag for her stay with Femke. But first she stopped by the Internet café. Yes, there was one unread email – from Paul. She checked that the rucksack was safe between her legs and waited for his words to open in front of her:

> *Hello Che.*
>
> *It was good to get your email. Not much to report here really. Yoga on a beautiful lake in the middle of nowhere takes a lot to beat … Summer came and went last week. Finished my hall of mirrors painting and may even have a buyer for it. Apart from that, the highlight of my week was a stunning cricket catch – so stunning in fact that I ended up in hospital in Brighton! Just a bit of embarrassing groin damage, nothing terminal!*

*Well, I thought it might be easier to write than talk on the phone, but I'm not sure it is …*
*Paul*

Chala sighed into the screen. 'Paul'. Just 'Paul'. Her fingers tapped their own words:

*Really happy to get your email. Going to be out of email contact over the next couple of days as I'll be staying at Femke's house – just a precaution in case there's any trouble around elections. Great news about the painting and hope you're fully recovered from your mishap!*

She stopped, feeling as if she were writing on a Facebook wall, and reached for an attempt at meaning.

*Paul, I know this is hard and I really really appreciate you giving me this space. I long to know how you really are and talk about how I feel, but I know it's not fair to do that. But I do miss you, a lot. Most of this is about Philip. I hope you know that. About just not knowing how to come to terms with him being gone and all the questions that I couldn't get out of my head. About needing to find a way to get beyond 'who I am', if that makes any sense. What I'm trying to say is that I think that what was happening between us was the price of all this, not the cause. But enough. I just hope that this 'space' is doing you some kind of good, too. Am off now to the lake with Philip's ashes. Another milestone. I will say goodbye again from you as well.*

She stopped again. The words 'I love you' ached at the tips of her fingers, but a judge inside hovered over them with a guillotine. 'Love, Che', she wrote.

She drove beyond Lake Naivasha and alongside the little lake that had been part of the main lake when water levels were higher. She left the tarmac behind and passed another tiny village with fruit stalls brimming with colour, goats and chickens in the middle of the road, and a pub called the Dusty Bum. Then the dirt road forked to the right, through the wide shade of sycamore trees, to the edge of the lake. This was common land, and the Maasai brought their cattle to drink here. At the other end of the green shore she could just make out a splash of red blankets and a group of dark, thin figures holding their sticks upright beside them as they sat and watched their cows drink.

She stopped her moped and sat on the rough grass, just a couple of feet in front of the water, with her rucksack beside her. Closing her eyes, she savoured the morning on her face, already warm. Quickly, and still aware of a mild nausea, she took out the box and cradled it in her hands. She heard Philip's quiet voice inside her head, gently mocking her.

'Come on, Chala, I'm already gone, you know that. Just open the box and get rid of those bloody ashes. You're an incurable romantic, just like your mother. I always told you that.'

Chala had pondered the idea of a pilgrimage to Mount Kenya to leave the ashes there, but Philip's sister's reticence to return to places of significance had held her back. It would have felt like an intrusion. When she came to Kenya she had assumed that she would visit the mountain and yet she'd done nothing to make it happen. Bizarrely, since her visit to Lake Baringo, it no longer felt necessary. And somehow, after all, it really did just feel right to cast Philip's ashes into an expanse of water, as he had – perhaps – cast himself out into the sea.

'Phiwip, I miss you,' she said out loud in the little girl's voice that had once been hers.

But Philip was gone, so what difference did it make where she left his ashes? Was it like praying – you did it just in case? But she didn't do that, Philip didn't do that, and yet all those years ago he had never scolded her for her superstitious terror of Rosie, her childhood doll, which had existed for her in a way that was more lifelike and terrifying than the memory of Emma.

'Chala, my sweet, let go. There is no world out here. Just stay with your own world and be present in it. Hold on to what you've got.'

'Why do you all keep saying that?'

Chala opened the box and concentrated on the ashes inside. 'But what if—'

'What if what?'

'I don't know, what if …'

Chala stood up slowly, holding the box open in front of her, wishing for a second that Paul was beside her. She looked at the gentle water lapping at the caked mud at the edge of the lake, looked around to make sure that she was alone, and paced slowly and deliberately to the water. She tipped the contents of the box into her open palm and closed her eyes. Then she spoke in a voice that reached across the water.

'Philip, I don't know if you chose to die, but I do know how you chose to live, and that is what I will keep with me for ever. Goodbye from me, goodbye from Paul … Rest well, wherever you are.'

And now she let the fine dust filter through her fingers. She watched it sprinkle onto the water and disappear. She bent over to scoop some of that water into her hands to rinse them, wiped them against her jeans and took one last long look across the Kenyan water, an image of Devon sea in her mind.

# CHAPTER 26

Femke opened the garden gate and beckoned her through a small stone-walled courtyard into the house.

'Where are the dogs?' Chala asked, kissing her on the cheek three times, Dutch fashion. The only other time she had been to Femke's house she had been jumped on by a gangly, chestnut-coloured whippet, with some kind of an Alsatian cross close behind.

'Kennel training,' Femke replied. 'They can come out in five minutes. Tea, or gin and tonic?'

'Actually, I think I'll start with tea.'

'Well, go and sit down on the veranda and I'll be there with my dogs and teapot in one minute.'

Chala sank into the sofa on the small area of decking that looked out over the garden. There were rock beds with cactus and papyrus and burning red flowers and swathes of orange nasturtiums along the edge of a thick green lawn.

'Do you think there'll be trouble tomorrow?' Chala asked as Femke appeared at the door with a tray loaded with tea and carrot cake.

'Mick says we just need to stay off the roads. If there's trouble that's always where it starts, but we'll be fine here.'

'Don't you ever get nervous living here on your own?' Chala admired Femke for the life she had built herself in Kenya.

'I did at first, but then I got accustomed. Anyway, I'm not on my own, there's the *askari* outside, and Esther and Joseph, my gardener and house girl, live in the staff quarters. And we've even got panic buttons now, with twenty-four hours armed response.'

Chala laughed.

'Why are you laughing?'

'I think you've been spending too much time with Mick. You've forgotten what that sounds like to people from Europe. I can't think of many people back home who would be reassured by the notion of panic buttons!'

'Oh, I forgot Tek Tek and Cheza!' She disappeared and came back with a stern look on her face aimed at Cheza, muttering in Dutch. The overgrown puppy looked up at her with a crinkled forehead and pleading eyes, while Tek Tek was released to say his hellos to Chala. He was a gorgeous, thick-haired dog, almost golden, with stand-up ears and a face that seemed to smile. Chala ruffled the mane around his neck and thought fondly of her old dog Rusty.

'So what's wrong with you, then?' Chala didn't know whether it was something to do with being Dutch or being a vet, but she was learning that her new friend liked to get straight to the point.

She told her about the awful incident at the shelter and about her private ritual by the lake. Femke's face softened as she spoke of Philip, but her first words when Chala finished were nothing to do with Philip.

'And you say you were sick this morning? Is that the first time?'

'Yes, I think so. Just nerves, I think. I feel fine now. Just a bit tired.'

'You know what I think?'

'What?'

'I think you're pregnant.'

'Don't be daft. It would be immaculate conception!' Chala tried quickly to calculate when she'd had her last period.

'When was your last period?'

'That's just what I'm trying to work out. I'm not very regular at the best of times and I've been a bit all over the place lately, what with Philip and ... everything.'

'So how long ago did you have it?'

Chala blushed, a wave of humiliation and fear sweeping up her throat. 'Well, I haven't had one since—' She stopped short, realisation pounding inside her. 'Not since before Philip died.'

'So you must be very late!' Femke looked triumphant and excited.

'But,' Chala began, echoing herself at the shelter the day before, 'but I thought it was just the stress that made me miss a period ...'

'Well, it's time to find out!' Femke jumped up and disappeared into the house.

'Where are you going?' Chala sounded alarmed.

'To the bathroom. I think I've got one.'

'One what?' Chala almost shouted the words.

'Here!' Femke emerged, brandishing a small box. 'Pregnancy test, but you should do the first one in the morning. You can do it tomorrow – on election day!'

\* \* \*

She removed the pee stick and stared at it as if it were an instrument of torture or divine judgement. She looked up at her reflection in the bathroom mirror and saw the little girl behind the curls and the grown-up skin. She could almost picture Rosie, pointing a finger at her. 'It's your punishment.' Chala blinked away the image and another jumped in to replace it: a woman telling her husband she was pregnant and being swept up into the air by him; the kind of joyous moment that was splashed across books about pregnancy and childbirth. Paul would never paint that moment, though. She saw the tears on her face in the mirror. This was the moment he would paint. Quickly, she put the stick to use. Election day in Kenya, the day that the die would be cast …

Quite soon, the first line appeared. She waited. Then another line began to appear, blurred at first, then sharper, unmistakable. She sank onto the bed, her mind swimming. Rosie was laughing at her. Chala wanted to call out for Philip. 'Make her go away, Phiwip.'

'Chala, are you OK?' Femke put her head around the door.

'Oh, what time is it?' She looked round the room, disconcerted.

'I think I must have fallen asleep. Sorry, Femke.'

'I waited for an hour, but then I felt preoccupied.' She hesitated, 'Did you … ?'

'Yes,' Chala took a deep breath. 'Yes. It's positive.'

Femke came over and sat beside her, noticing the stillness in her voice. 'Are you OK about it?'

'I don't know, I …' Chala took a deep breath. 'You know, Femke, I never wanted children. In fact, I always thought if I ever got pregnant by accident I would have an abortion.' She looked down, dreading the reaction her words might have, not knowing how she could possibly explain them.

'But why? Is it because you're not sure of your relationship with Paul?'

Femke's face was open, wanting to understand, but Chala felt powerless to cross the distance of who she was. How could someone who'd killed her baby sister possibly bring a baby into this world? She couldn't find words for this.

'I'm sorry. You're being absolutely brilliant and this is not what you bargained for when you asked me to stay!'

'Listen.' Femke had reverted to the strangely reassuring voice of medical authority. 'This is obviously very new for you. You need time to think and get accustomed. It's much too early for decisions yet.'

'Have you ever been pregnant, Femke?'

'No,' she looked sad and distant for a moment. 'I wanted to, but it didn't happen, and then I started to realise that he wasn't sure about it and then gradually I realised that it was me not a baby he was unsure of.'

'Oh gosh, I'm sorry.'

But Femke was suddenly chirpy again. 'Now come on. Get dressed and we'll háve breakfast – or how do you call it, lunch and breakfast – lekfast?'

'Brunch,' Chala laughed. 'And,' she paused, 'thank you, Femke.'

That night Chala dreamt she had to get to the polling booth to vote. She knew that the polling booth was in Brighton, but she had forgotten how to get there. She was going round and round in circles in the Lanes, aware that time was running out. Every time she asked anyone where the polling booth was, they just laughed at her. She was growing more and more frantic. Then a man shouted, 'It's over there, you idiot.' She followed his finger and saw a large post office on the other side of the road. The road was full of traffic going in all directions. Then suddenly it was a road in Naivasha, with *matatus* screeching past and motorbikes and donkeys and dust. Finally, she managed to get across and walked into the post office, but when she got inside, it wasn't a post office, it was a church, and so she walked through the echoing chapel and into a confessional. She was looking for the piece of paper to put a cross on the voting card, when suddenly the curtain opened.

In her sleep, Chala whimpered. In the dream, she tried to scream, but couldn't. Rosie, the cloth doll of her childhood nightmares, sat propped up on a counter behind the curtain. 'I know what you're thinking,' she said. Chala was unable to open her mouth. 'But if you do, it will be like killing Emma all over again.'

# CHAPTER 27

'Now, it's coming!' Giovanni had left a broken heart behind in Italy to reinvent himself in Kenya. He had initially set up a successful pizza bar on the coast, but it had attracted too many Italians and he had run away again – upcountry this time, where his incongruous fire-cooked pizzas had long since become part of the local landscape.

Today the pizza bar was packed, in tense anticipation of the delayed election result. Watchful Kenyan faces had hardened over the last three days, as the margin on candidate Odinga's apparent runaway victory kept closing, and still the counting stalled and the result failed to come. There had been road blocks between Naivasha and Nairobi, some cars had been burnt, and the embassies were advising people to avoid travelling, to stay away from the roads.

Chala closed her eyes for a second, breathing deeply over the new life inside her. She opened her eyes and took in the faces around her, glued to the large television screen that had been placed in the middle of the bar. Another painting for Paul – they might have been watching a particularly tense Wimbledon final: Kibaki, the favourite in this Kikuyu stronghold, facing match point against him by the unknown, unseeded player, Odinga. Raila Odinga was a member of the Luo tribe from western Kenya.

Femke sat, anchored nervously to the mobile on her lap. Even now, she kept glancing at it to make sure no new message had come in from her 'blockhead'.

'Your what?' Mick had almost wet himself when she'd first used the word.

'Don't you call it a blockhead, Chala?' She'd looked to Chala for support. 'The person who is your embassy contact, to tell you about the situation with the elections?'

Mick was sitting opposite them, and whenever Femke looked down at her phone, he frowned. Over the last three days he had popped in and out of the house, checking to see if his 'ladies-in- waiting' were OK, reassuring them that the occasional truck full of riot police in Nairobi was to be expected and needn't worry them in Naivasha. Once, he had offered to stay, looking straight at Femke when he said it, and she had blushed and said don't be silly.

Deuce ... and then advantage point Kibaki ...The head of the electoral commission stood up and cleared his throat. Kibaki – it was Kibaki after all – had won by a margin of less than 250,000 votes.

But the collective sigh of relief at Giovanni's pizza bar was short-lived. Voices and fists were suddenly raised on the screen and a flurry of jerky camera shots zoomed in on the head of the electoral commission being escorted out by security as people crowded in with angry accusations of rigging. For a moment there was silence in the pizza bar, and Chala caught the tight-jawed tension on the faces of white and black Kenyans alike. Then someone broke the ice.

'Whatever. Kibaki's in again. Reckon that calls for Tuskers all round, don't you think?'

'Sure. Ladies?' Mick turned to Femke and Chala.

'Um, no, not for me, actually.' The banter and bravado were exhausting.

'Neither me,' said Femke quickly, and Chala recognised the implicit gesture of support. 'I think we should get back, Chala, don't you?'

'Yeah, if we go back to your place now, I can probably get back to Naivasha before it gets dark, can't I?'

'Oh no, you don't.' Mick's voice was surprisingly sharp. He checked himself and continued more gently. 'It may not be over yet. You need to sit tight for the moment.'

* * *

Chala and Femke sat tight in front of Sky News in their living room and watched the burning slums of Kibera in Nairobi and angry young men shouting, 'No Raila, no peace.'

'You OK, Femke?' Chala asked as she made to go to bed.

'Yeah, it feels strange, no, just to see it on the television?'

'It does, yes …'

'But you, how are you feeling?' And she pointed at Chala's tummy.

'I'm OK. It's just …' – and the tears felt like a crime after what they had seen from the safety of their living room – 'I just don't know what to do.'

'Well, first you need to see a doctor as soon as the road is safe to Nairobi. Just one foot at a time.'

'Yes I know, I know. Thanks, Femke.'

But sleep refused to come. She tossed and turned on the tide of this new wave of life inside her. Images of fire in the Kenyan slums burnt holes in her own tiny drama, and Rosie loomed in judgement, remote and made of cloth. In a moment between sleep and wakefulness, the obvious and shocking realisation finally penetrated her defences: she was pregnant and she didn't know who the father was. She wanted it to be Paul. It could be Paul. But it could also be Bruce.

# CHAPTER 28

Femke snatched the phone off the table in front of them as it beeped the arrival of the latest message from 'the blockhead'.

'It is possible the head of the army and the police have resigned,' she translated. 'Don't panic. We keep you informed.'

'Bloody irresponsible!' Mick was there again to check on them. Today had been declared a last-minute public holiday. Just a precaution, Mick had assured them on the phone, but Femke's staff, Esther and Joseph, had come to work anyway, as most people in Naivasha had. 'We don't want this nonsense,' Esther had said simply to Femke by way of explanation. Femke was relieved she still had holiday left before her own return to work.

'What do you mean? Who is irresponsible?' Femke was glaring at Mick.

'I'm sorry, Femke. I know it's good to be kept in the picture, but they shouldn't be reporting idle rumours. That's the sure way to panic. All it does is feed your fear.'

'Sky can do that on its own.' Chala pointed at the screen as the latest breaking news headline swept into view and Femke snatched the remote to switch up the volume. The images of Kibera's skyline in flames were already familiar. A female reporter spoke in a voice fuelled by adrenalin of unprecedented outbreaks of violence in peaceful Kenya. New images flooded the screen of Kikuyu houses burnt to the ground and angry mobs smashing shop windows.

'Fucking woman, what does she know about Kenya?' Mick was shaking.

'She's only reporting what is happening.' Femke was defensive.

'She is sensationalising what is happening and that is a dangerous thing to do in this situation. It will only make things worse. Kenya is nervous, but these riots are not happening across the whole country. They are isolated incidents.'

Mick looked softly at Femke then and touched her lightly on the arm. 'I'm sorry, Femke. This must be very hard for you both. This is not your country.'

Chala realised suddenly how hard this must be for Mick, precisely because it *was* his country. The country he loved and had grown up in, suddenly torn apart and exposed to superficial media scrutiny and judgement. And if things got really bad, Chala and Femke could be on the next plane out. It wasn't so easy for Mick with his Kenyan passport.

Chala picked up her own phone, although the network had been jammed since the night before, and walked into the garden, leaving Femke and Mick inside. Tek Tek and Cheza lay fast asleep on the lawn, serenely oblivious. What would happen to them if there really was a need to leave suddenly? Chala doubted that embassies evacuated animals, but would it come to that? Mick seemed confident that it wouldn't. Perhaps she should at least register with the British High Commission when she got phone coverage back, though. Femke's anxious attachment to the Dutch embassy was sobering.

Chala sat down on the bench at the far end of the garden and watched vervet monkeys playing and laughing at the human drama around them. An unbidden narrative flashed into her mind: a pregnant woman miscarrying amidst the stress of evacuation. Instinctively, her hands moved to protect her stomach, a tug of conflicting emotions inside her.

Then she jumped as the phone sprang to life with a barrage of bleeps for all the missed calls and messages that had come in since post-election fever had hit international news. She seized the phone and looked at the names of those who had tried to contact her, momentarily wondering why Philip's name was not on the list. She was just about to open Paul's message when the phone rang and it was him.

'Che, are you OK?' The sound of concern in his voice was shocking; the echo of another conversation from England to Australia swam in her head.

'Hello Paul, I'm fine, it's absolutely fine where we are. We just need to sit tight until things calm down.' She talked and talked over the surface of what was happening, reassuring him as if she were a mother, gently stroking the secret life in her tummy. Slowly, he reacted to the apparent sureness in her voice and let her end the call.

By the time she roused herself to go back inside, Mick had gone and Femke was lying on the sofa massaging Tek Tek's ears.

'Did you tell him?'

'Who?' Chala was pleased to hear the feisty authority back in Femke's voice.

'That was Paul you spoke to, I think?'

'No.' She looked at her hands and imagined them on an old woman.

'It wasn't Paul?'

'No, I didn't tell him.' She looked up at her new friend. 'I can't, Femke, not yet. I need to see the doctor first and I can't tell him unless I'm sure about keeping it – it would be too cruel. He was the one who always wanted children, and I told him I would never have a baby.' She hesitated. 'I didn't think I could ever do it ... I still don't know if I can, and anyway we don't even know what is going to happen between us. I don't know what he feels about it all now.'

Even without the guilty secret that clung to her insides, it all seemed overpowering, but one foot at a time, as Femke said. First, she had to get to a doctor in Nairobi.

# CHAPTER 29

Chala sat in the afternoon shade of the garden. Light filtered through the acacia trees and she felt as if she was in a play with no lines. Her eyes dropped to the place where this new life was supposed to be and tired tears ran down her cheeks. I'm sorry, I'm sorry, I'm sorry. The words Paul hated, the words that had lived inside her since childhood. She didn't know if they were meant for Paul or the baby or even partly for Bruce, but they rocked over and over inside her like a mantra with no promise of comfort. Philip, where are you?

Femke had invited Chala to go with her to the blockhead's house just a few kilometres away around the lake – something about some paperwork from the Dutch embassy – but Chala had encouraged her to go on her own, thinking it would do her good to be surrounded by people speaking her own language for a couple of hours. That morning she'd found Femke huddled on the living room floor with her arms around Tek Tek's neck, sobbing.

'Femke, what's wrong?' Chala had knelt down beside her and patted Tek Tek.

'It's just … they are everything I've got. I'm frightened to leave them. I can't leave them behind if we have to go.' She had pulled herself up and wiped her face with her sleeve. 'You think I'm silly – silly Dutch vet.'

'Femke, I don't think you're silly at all. I was wondering the same thing about the dogs yesterday, but it's not going to come to that, Mick says—'

'I know what Mick says.' The Dutch accent was suddenly sharp in her voice. 'Mick says that because he has to.'

And then, when Chala had mentioned going to a doctor in Nairobi, the anger in her voice had been another shock.

'What is wrong with you? You are just like Mick. You refuse to believe what is happening. Listen, listen to this text.'

Chala had listened like a schoolgirl as Femke translated: 'More riots in Kibera. Schools closed in Nairobi. Armed GSU forces on many streets in Nairobi. Plans for protest rally with a million people. Avoid travelling. We keep you informed.'

Femke had hugged Chala hard as she left, pointing at her tummy and saying, 'You promise not to, how do you say, broodle?'

'Brood, yes, I promise not to brood,' she'd laughed. 'Go on, you silly Dutch vegetarian. I won't go anywhere.'

She looked around the small green garden now, spotting a vervet monkey with a handful of nasturtiums, marvelling at the existence of so many parallel worlds. What was Paul thinking? What was Paul feeling in his parallel world? They'd spoken again, her injecting all the calm she possibly could into her voice, so that he wouldn't worry about her, and feeling a fraud because the biggest turmoil in her was nothing to do with the Kenyan violence.

Later she and Femke sat cocooned again with the two dogs and the muted television screen in front of the fire. Femke had returned with a sense of resolution and a to-do list, which clearly gave her comfort. The blockhead had managed to get papers signed by the Dutch ambassador saying that they had the authorization of the Dutch embassy to travel. The papers offered no guarantees, but might help in a situation where road travel to Nairobi was impossible and individuals decided to act on their own and make a getaway cross-country through the Tanzanian border. Other Dutch members of the community there had all agreed to stay in contact over a potential convoy should they decide to take action. The to-do list was all about what to take, and ensuring they had sufficient supplies of fuel and so on. For Femke, it gave her a comforting sense of taking control of the situation before the last resort of an airlift, the knowledge above all that she could take her dogs with her.

Mick, on his round to check up on them, was predictably scathing. 'This isn't *Harry Potter*, for fuck's sake. Where do you think you're going to get the fuel you need? There *is* no fuel left in the petrol pumps in Naivasha. Oh, and do you know where one of the worst-hit areas is? Right on the bloody road that you tourists would be on in your gypsy caravan!'

The word 'tourist' visibly stung Femke. She had tried so hard to be accepted and build a life for herself here.

'Give her a break, Mick,' Chala intervened, and then more softly, 'Who wants a drink?' She went into the kitchen and poured two large whiskies and one very watered-down one. 'I think we could all do with this,' she said as she came back into the living room and then stopped dead. Mick and Femke were lost in a fairy- tale kiss right in front of her.

'Sorry.' Femke blushed a violent, endearing red, and Mick laughed slightly nervously and took a whisky off the tray that Chala was carrying. The familiar face of one of the reporters appeared on the TV screen and Femke jumped at the distraction and turned up the volume.

The reporter was standing at the charred site of a church in western Kenya, a church that had been full of women and children taking shelter when it was burnt down. The words 'cold-blooded' and 'massacre' were used over and over again, and the reporter gestured with her arms to highlight the horror of an account of a three-year-old child thrown back into the flames. On another channel another phrase was used for the first time – ethnic cleansing – against the backdrop of live footage of a man being slashed to death in Kibera. Raila Odinga was determined to proceed with the rally in the centre of Nairobi, despite the fact that Kibaki had declared it illegal. There were rumours that police had been ordered to shoot on sight. The spectre of a possible bloodbath that would set in motion a chain reaction of huge proportions loomed. Chala caught the tension on Mick's face as the Nairobi correspondent interviewed a mother in Kibera: 'If God wants me to die, I will die tomorrow. I will die for Raila.'

# CHAPTER 30

The first images on their TV screen looked like a science fiction film set in Nairobi the day after a deadly virus had wiped out its entire population. Cameras zoomed in on eerily empty streets in the city centre, over the shoulders of soldiers, a human barrier to prevent access. Femke placed two mugs of coffee on the table. The house, too, was quiet. There was no hum of Esther singing under her breath, no digging or chopping from the garden, no monkeys jumping on the tin roof. The whole of Kenya was holding its breath.

'How do you feel?' Femke asked. 'Weird.'

'Weird-tummy weird or weird-Kenya weird?'

Chala laughed despite herself. 'A bit of both, I think.' Her mobile bleeped another incoming message. 'It's from the Kenyan government,' she said, answering the expectant look on Femke's face. She read the text aloud. 'The Kenyan government warns you not to take part in any unlawful rallies.' She stared at the phone, alarmed by the intrusion. The TV screen still had the effect of distancing them, but suddenly the fingers of what was happening were reaching out and clawing into their lives.

'I got one, too, when I woke up.' Femke was trying to make it sound completely normal.

'From the Kenyan government?'

'No, from Safaricom.' She opened her message from the biggest mobile network in Kenya. 'Safaricom urges all Kenyans to stay peaceful.'

'Well, yours is a lot nicer.'

They refocused on the screen. An international reporter was tracking a small crowd of demonstrators waving orange flags and marching slowly along broken, muddy pavements towards the city centre.

'Hardly a million demonstrators, hey!' Mick's sudden appearance in the room startled even the dogs.

'Don't do that! I thought you weren't coming today.' Femke had jumped up and almost knocked over the coffee.

'Can't keep away.' He looked at her and she blushed. He loved that in her, it was so obvious.

'So, what do you think?' The edge of irritation, which Chala felt sure was to do with the fact that he kept making her blush, did nothing to hide the eagerness in Femke's voice, the attentiveness to Mick's opinion.

'I think we should bathe the dogs. Something to stop you clock-watching until the next headlines.'

They did. Cheza squirmed and whined, Tek Tek looked vaguely embarrassed and they all ended up soaked. Chala found herself laughing along with Mick and Femke, and then the laughter died inside her as she looked at them and thought, this baby should be theirs not mine. Instantly, the pronoun crashed down on her. Mine – not ours. Where was Paul? Was it simply that he wasn't there? Was it the doubt about whether it was actually his? Or was it something else, something worse? She got up and turned aside to hide the tears from Mick and Femke.

She moved quietly away with her mobile and sat on the veranda, staring at the acacia trees. Then she stared at the mobile. Her tears had dried and her face had a fixed look. She started to scroll through her phone contacts, then stopped. Would he answer if she called? What would she tell him? Did he have a right to know? What if *they* were the ones that were meant to be together? 'Yes, I felt it too.' She remembered his words, closed her eyes and saw his face, saw him looking at her … Perhaps he wouldn't answer. He could be anywhere in the world by now, somewhere his phone might not even work. He could even be in Africa. But what if he did answer? Her thumb hovered above his name and her heartbeat quickened. Was this her real *Sliding Doors* moment?

She let the phone drop as if it had burnt her.

# CHAPTER 31

'Your chests are bigger, I think,' said Femke over breakfast.

'Breasts, you mean breasts,' corrected Chala, but Femke caught the hint of pride in her voice.

'Did someone say breasts?' Mick was upon them out of nowhere.

'Not in your ears, they didn't.'

'*For*,' corrected Chala again lightly. 'For your ears.'

The release was palpable after the previous day's tension. They had waited with the rest of Kenya, the world watching, and clashes had broken the science-fiction stillness finally. Tear gas and rounds of blank ammunition were fired above crowds converging on the city centre. Outraged international media coverage leapt on images of screaming women choking on tear gas and waving white rags in the air.

But no one got beyond the army cordon. In the end the rally was simply not allowed to happen, and most of Kenya breathed a sigh of relief that the spectators in the West could not really understand. When Chala had spoken to Winnie that evening, she sounded tired but her words were pragmatic.

'White handkerchiefs are not the same in Africa as they are in your world,' she'd explained in the same tone that she used to talk about the reality of street kids. 'This rally would not have been peaceful. It is good that they stopped it.'

Today, the drive for normality was apparent everywhere, with shops reopening, businesses resuming, and – most strikingly – a local radio station banning all politicians from its airwaves. The press was switching its emphasis to the growing humanitarian crisis affecting all those who had fled their homes, turned into refugees overnight in their own country.

The road to Nairobi was open. Chala had resolved to go back to her hotel in Naivasha today and get to a doctor the next day. She held Femke close as they said goodbye, grateful yet inarticulate about the support and companionship she was going to miss. Mick came up behind, wrapping both of them in his comfortable embrace and telling Chala to call him if there was anything at all she needed. She pushed down the pedal on the moped, stifling the longing to have Paul by her side as Mick stood with Femke now, and sped off through the dust back to Naivasha.

'Mama Shelter, you are home,' were the first words she heard as she entered the hotel. 'Come, we have Coca-Cola again and Mama Winnie is waiting for you.' The familiar face of her favourite waiter positively beamed, and it was hard to imagine that elsewhere in Kenya people were beginning to suffer from malnutrition as a result of the last few days' events.

'Chala, *karibu*, come and drink to peace with me,' Winnie beckoned her.

'Is everyone at the shelter OK?' She thought of little Julius.

'Of course they are OK. Why shouldn't they be OK?' That angry edge in her voice again. 'Your Western press has been very irresponsible, you know, reporting as if the whole country is in chaos when the riots are only in pockets.' It was like listening to Mick without the swearing. Winnie sighed. 'This will cost the country dear. Our politicians have made a mess of things and your press has made it worse. Did you see the pictures of tourists running away? They were never in any danger, but now they will take time to come back again and we need them.'

Chala flinched from the use of the pronoun 'your' to talk about the Western media. No foreigner could ever belong here, she realised. If Femke married Mick and stayed for twenty years, she would still be 'the Dutch vet'. Perhaps there really was something in that whole business of the root chakra – feeling *grounded*. All her life she had struggled with the notion of belonging, assuming this was related at some level to what she had been capable of as a child and the way she had been ostracised at school. Yet Philip had helped her feel grounded, and without him she had moments when the world seemed to spiral out of control around her, moments that made her feel she was physically shrinking. Was it panic that drove Philip into the sea? Would his letter to Denise hold the answer? Oh God, how could she ever be a mother to this baby inside her? It was fantasy to think that she could bring up a child with someone she could not even be sure was the father.

'I'm sorry.' Winnie's words drew her up short, a dislocated echo. 'It must sound as if I'm blaming you, and I don't mean that at all. We are paying the price for our own politics, that is sure … Chala, are you OK?'

'Yes, I'm sorry. Yes, I'm fine – just a bit drained by it all.'

'Listen, Chala, these are not your problems and I'll understand if you want to go home straight away, now that the roads are open again.'

'No.' The determination in her own voice caught Chala by surprise. 'No, I want to see this through. It will only take a few more days to finish everything for the website and then I will go home.'

'Good girl.' Winnie's smile stretched across her face and Chala felt pleased out of all proportion.

She hesitated. 'But I need to see a doctor in Nairobi tomorrow. Nothing to worry about, just a check-up—'

'I can take you,' Winnie interrupted. 'I need to go, too. We'll leave early in the morning.'

\* \* \*

Chala forced herself to focus on the cappuccino in front of her, to lift it, to sip it, not to scream out and bang her arm against the table until it hurt. When the doctor had finally left no room for doubt and confirmed the pregnancy, she had felt as if someone had gripped her by the shoulders and was shaking her.

The taxi had taken her straight back to the shopping mall where Winnie had dropped her and she had gone straight into the Internet café there – quite unlike the broken-down green shack in Naivasha – and found out all she could about abortion. There was still time to undo this reality. Still time to *terminate*. But the word drilled a hole in her brain.

'Hold on to what you've got.' The phrase rang in her ears – in Philip's voice, in Denise's voice, in Amanda's voice, in Winnie's voice, Femke's, Mick's – until she started to feel dizzy with the effort of keeping everyone out. Only Paul was silent. Chala stared at the half-empty cup and thought of Denise; of how if Denise had been there now she might have been able to talk to her; of how Denise might have found a way of helping Chala's words come out and making them seem normal. How many suicides, she wondered, would never have happened if only the right person had been there at the right time? Had Philip really committed suicide? Could she have been the right person at the right time? She remembered his strange reaction when they had talked about abortion once. What right did he have to reject abortion if he had taken his own life away from her? What was in his letter to Denise?

The questions came and came, like playground kids around a skipping rope. What would she look like, this little piece of life? What made her so convinced it was a girl? What would she call her? Emma? What if it was a boy? Julius? She stared at the cappuccino.

And Rosie looked on from the recesses of her mind, a silent smirk on her face, made of cloth.

# CHAPTER 32

'Mama Shelter, you are stronger!' The gesture that accompanied Mwangi's words left no doubt about the euphemism.

'You mean fatter?' Chala wondered if her private reality was slipping slowly into public view. 'You know that we like to be thin in England. It is not good to tell a woman she's fatter!'

'But you are in Kenya, Mama. Here it is good for a woman to be big,' he quipped, repeating the gesture with his hands. Status and size went hand in hand. Chala assumed it had something to do with being well fed and what that represented. The boys at the shelter were all skinny and small for their age, testimony to the days when glue filled the cracks of hunger. Winnie's solidity won her authority and respect; women were meant to have flesh.

'Come, Mama, we have a new boy here. He is from Nairobi. He ran away when his father was killed in the nonsense.' He used the same term that Femke's staff had used to describe the recent strife.

'Josphat, *kuja*.' A small boy separated himself obediently from a cluster of boys collecting water and approached them, hanging his head. He looked about six years old. How on earth did he make the journey from Nairobi, and how had he ended up here? What had he seen before he fled? Mwangi would tell her everything in simple words in due course. Chala had learnt to be gentle at these meetings, to avoid seeking eye contact. She extended her hand.

'*Mimi ni Chala, unaitwa nani?*'

'Josphat.' The answer was barely audible, his hand limp. She longed to put her arms around him and hold him to her. '*Twende,* go and play with your friends.' She watched him flee to the safety of the group and saw Julius reach out and touch him briefly.

'Come, come and see our baby cow.' Mwangi was pleased that she was back, and Chala felt a warm wave over the tug of war inside her. At least she had not run away from the shelter before her job was done.

Later that day, she sat on the hotel veranda with her laptop and a conspicuous bottle of soda water to replace the cold beer habit that was so infectious here. She pored over the boys' names and tried to work out the logistics of how to make the sponsorship scheme work in practice. And yet the statistics dragged at her uncomfortably. Why did these fifty boys deserve to be trained up and supported by unknown donors in the West? A tiny handful of better-fed tummies in Kenya and a handful of rich donors feeling better about themselves – what would it actually solve? It wouldn't even touch the causes of the problem. She'd read somewhere that Kenya's population was forecast to grow by around thirty-five per cent in the next ten years. Everywhere you went you saw children, but only the well-fed middle classes bred less. For the poorest majority, large families were the norm, the only investment in the future they were able to make.

Chala's hand went to her stomach. Suddenly her ability to play God with the future existence of this seed of life felt wrong. The majority of people here could not afford the luxury of the choices she was dabbling in. People here dealt in consequence, not choice. She reached for her phone and dialled Paul's number, but when she heard the awkwardness in his voice, the moment died inside her. How could she possibly even begin to ask him to share her dilemma over whether to abort this baby? She needed to make this decision alone – she alone would have to live with the consequences of her act.

'Paul, I know this is difficult on the phone,' she said instead, 'but I will be finished here within a week ...'

Silence stretched on the line.

'So are you coming home?' She wished she could read his face as he said these words.

'If that's still OK with you, yes ... Yes, I would love to come home.' The word felt grounding. For a moment Chala forgot about the dilemma inside her and thought only of Paul and his arms around her.

# CHAPTER 33

A horn beeped and Chala looked up to see Winnie at the wheel of a pick-up loaded high with maize meal and fresh corn.

'Come on, Mama Shelter.' Winnie used the nickname with good-natured irony. 'Leave that laptop behind and get in.'

'So, what are we up to?' asked Chala as she climbed in, responding to the enthusiasm in Winnie's voice.

'We, my dear, are taking a shedload of *ugali* to the shelter. Have you seen what the *mhindi* has given us?' She gestured grandly at the brimming back of the pick-up and winked. Chala laughed. With a tiny variation, the same word in Swahili meant Indian or sweetcorn. Winnie was talking about an Indian who owned a small maize factory outside town.

'Well, it's good to see you smiling, girl.' Winnie looked pointedly at Chala.

'I feel good.' She had woken, well rested, with a sense of lightness this morning.

'Amen!' Winnie spoke with such emphasis she might have broken into song, and Chala laughed again.

It was a Sunday and the boys were lounging or playing on the grass. They jumped up and flocked to the pick up to see what Winnie had brought. Chala noticed little Josphat, taking his cue from Julius and running hard to keep up. Mwangi emerged from the staff room and organised the boys into a kind of conveyor belt to shift the bags of *ugali* to the kitchen. Julius dropped one and the boys chortled; then Josphat dropped a bag, as if to say 'me too'. In the distance below them silver light splintered through cloud cover onto the lake, oblivious.

Mwangi wanted a lift to Naivasha, so Chala squeezed into the middle on the way back. They took the usual shortcut down a pot-holed side road into the middle of town. As they joined the main road again, Chala was obscurely aware of more people and more noise than normal. It sounded like a distant football match. She turned to Winnie to ask what was going on, but the car suddenly leapt forward as Winnie stamped her foot on the accelerator. Chala tried to see what was happening as she and Mwangi lurched into each other, but all she could see were people running towards them. She tried to read the situation on Mwangi's face, but he, like Winnie, seemed frozen, despite the movement of their car.

Then time disintegrated into tiny, isolated particles, like shards of broken glass scattering in all directions. When Chala looked back on these moments, there was no fluidity in them; they were fragments, images burnt into her mind without any sense of chronology. Fire in the road and contorted faces. The flash of dark blades in the air. Women yanking tiny children by the hand through the dust. Their pick-up swerving and the shock on a man's face as the vehicle went over his foot. A tangle of bodies falling to the ground and the chaos of screams competing with a kind of pumping war cry. The stench of burning rubber.

Then the car was jolting and Chala felt herself being pulled down, her head thrust between Mwangi's legs. She was choking on dust and the vague smell of urine. She wanted to scream, to see what was happening, but he kept her head down close to his crotch and all she could feel was the lurch of the car and Mwangi's hand gripping the back of her neck. The pick-up seemed to jolt repeatedly and get heavier. She could hear a wailing sound that seemed to keep pace with them and grow and grow. She heard cracks in the air like fireworks. She felt the warm, yellow flush of fear between her legs.

When the vehicle jerked to a standstill, the wailing seemed to spill around them. At last Mwangi released his grip on her neck and she raised her head slowly, reluctant to leave the safety of his crotch behind and allow sight to complete the jigsaw of sound and smell. She tried to look at Winnie, but Winnie and Mwangi were already out of the vehicle. People seemed to be pouring off the back of the pick-up: women and children, crying and scattering all around them. She saw a pool of blood in the dust. Men in uniform were shouting and Winnie was waving her hands in the air. Chala realised that they were at the police station. She looked out through the windscreen into the face of a policeman just out of his teens and saw incomprehension in his eyes.

She shuffled across the wet patch on the seat, about to get out, when Mwangi appeared by the window.

'What—?' she started, surprised at the sound of her own voice, but he interrupted her.

'*Ngoja kidogo*. We are coming, just stay in the car, Mama.'

She waited and stared at the young policeman, resolute now, talking to the women and children huddled on the ground.

Then there was more screaming and people crowding at the gates of the police station and policemen shouting and blowing whistles and Mwangi and Winnie hurriedly approaching the pick-up.

'What—?' Chala heard herself again and was again interrupted, this time by Winnie.

'We need to leave now. We'll go to my house.' Mwangi jumped in beside Chala, and Winnie was already turning the key in the ignition as she pulled her bulk into position behind the wheel. She turned for a second and touched Chala on the arm. 'Don't worry, girl.'

And then the vehicle sped off, empty and rattling, out of the back entrance to the police station, along the cut-through to Winnie's house.

As soon as they got into the house, Winnie handed her a Kenyan sarong to take to the bathroom. Understanding, Chala changed out of her jeans, washed herself, and wrapped the kikoi around her waist. She looked briefly in disbelief at the face in the mirror, rubbed her stomach mechanically, and followed the sound of Winnie and Mwangi's voices onto the veranda.

'We are finished, Mama.' As Chala stepped into view, Winnie spoke over Mwangi's words, so that Chala was not even sure she had heard them right.

'Chala, *kuja*, sit and we will talk. Tusker for you.'

Chala apologised mentally, took the outstretched beer, gulped at it and looked at Winnie. Mwangi, too, seemed to implore Winnie with his eyes. Solve our problem, Mama, give us the answer.

'What is happening?' Chala broke the silence with the question that she had failed to finish in the pick-up.

'The police think it was the Mungiki revenging.' Mwangi could no longer bear the tension. He, too, needed to put words to what he had seen.

'Who are …'

'The Mungiki are a Kikuyu sect,' Winnie explained. 'A bunch of thugs who take oaths and are trained to hate and to kill.' Her voice was trembling and she took a swig of beer.

'But I don't understand.'

'You will never understand.' Winnie almost turned on her, and then softened. 'This is retaliation for all the Kikuyu that have been killed or chased away from their homes. Now it is the Luo tribe who are the targets. There are many Luo who come to Naivasha to work on the flower farms. Now these Mungiki thugs are working their nonsense.'

'But—' She didn't know how to finish her sentence. She still didn't know what she had seen – or hadn't seen.

Now she learnt in clipped sentences about the hackings, limbs slashed onto the ground, the brute madness of men fuelled by drugs and hatred and nothing to lose. She learnt that it was Luo women and children who had been thrown by their men into the back of the moving pick-up in a bid to get them away. Winnie had driven as if through a war zone, swerving down back streets to escape, her foot hard on the accelerator, the sound of shots close by.

Chala began to understand what Mwangi had done by thrusting her head between his legs. Every day he dealt with the damage wreaked by trauma. Despite his own fear, he had acted instinctively to protect her.

'Thank you, Mwangi,' she said between tears. 'You saved me from seeing.'

'You are a *mzungu*, Mama. You should not need to see everything we saw.' Chala registered the strange double standard she had come across before; the notion that white people were more fragile than black Africans and that a different set of rules applied. But Winnie cut through her thoughts and her voice was iron.

'*No one* should have to see those things.'

# CHAPTER 34

'Che. Che, are you OK? I saw Naivasha on the news. I thought all the troubles were over. What's happening?'

Chala paused to try and breathe calm into her voice. She mustn't let Paul hear her fear.

'Che?'

'It's OK, Paul, I'm in contact with the British High Commission. They're watching the situation, but they're not evacuating anyone yet. I'm at Winnie's house. It's safer to stay put than move around at the moment.' She paused again, willing her heart to slow down. 'There are roadblocks around the town and it's pretty chaotic, but they're not targeting whites or Kikuyu. I'm—' she gulped for air, 'fine.' She didn't mention that Winnie had faced a gang of thugs at her gate who warned her that if she was harbouring a Luo they would torch her house. Or that Winnie had made another journey to transport her own Luo cook to the safety of the police station. Unable to break up the violence, the police had opened the gates of the police station and the prison, turning them into makeshift refugee camps in the space of hours. Luo houses had been systematically targeted; crosses drawn overnight on buildings burnt to the ground the following day. Luo and Luhya men were being pulled out of cars and forced to strip to identify their tribe according to whether they were circumcised or not. Those whose penises betrayed them feared for their lives.

'Paul, don't watch the news, sweetheart. I'll call you again later.'

She rushed straight off the phone to the toilet, her body's response to the last twenty-four hours. Every time she opened her bowels, she looked irrationally for any sign of blood, as if the movement might dislodge the foetus.

Don't leave me now, stay with me. When she looked back at the previous day's events, she realised that her body had quite simply made the decision for her. It was the moment when she had wet herself in the pick-up – the flush of fear had been suddenly and irrevocably for the life of her unborn baby.

She looked at herself above the bathroom sink and saw the tightness beneath her eyes and the lack of sleep the previous night. Grief is grey, fear is yellow, she thought. You see it on people's skin. And yellow is the colour of the solar plexus, the place you feel real fear in your body, the colour of urine. Above her fear, she stroked the life she now knew she wanted to save.

When Femke phoned, she told her everything. 'I'm going to keep the baby, Femke.'

'Oh Chala, I'm very happy for you.'

There was an awkward pause. It felt wrong to talk about happiness in the current situation. And then Femke spoke again, ever direct.

'Have you told Paul?'

'No.' But there was an unfamiliar note of resolution in Chala's voice, a new confidence. 'No, I will be back in a few days. I want to tell him face to face.'

'And you and Paul, are you going to be OK?'

'I think so,' she said slowly. Suddenly, it seemed unimportant to try and measure whether they would make it as a couple. The bit that mattered was wanting to try. 'I want to hold on to what I've got,' she said, relieved to hear the words in her own mouth and not someone else's. The sadness in Denise hovered in her mind's eye. She would not add a life of regret to the sweet folly of Bruce.

'Will he want the baby, too? What if he doesn't?' Always ask the question.

'I think he will.' Chala chose her words carefully. 'And if he doesn't, then I will just have to accept the consequences. All I know is that I want to try and make it work.' She breathed deeply, changing the subject. 'But what about you? Are you OK, Femke?'

'Yes, I'm fine. I'm not the one who's in Naivasha.'

'And Mick, what does he say about what's happening?'

'He's angry with the international press again. All the talk about, how do you say, tribalisms?'

'Tribalism, yes.'

'These tribalisms are because of terror, not hatred under the skin. If someone puts a *panga* in your hand and threatens to kill your children if you don't use it, and if you are terrorised enough, you will use it.'

Chala pictured herself with a small girl by her side and what brute terror might make her capable of. 'Winnie thinks the same. She is convinced this was all orchestrated.'

'But who by?'

'God knows, but they say that these Mungiki have some very high-up connections.'

'You don't think the government are *letting* it happen, do you?'

'No, that feels a bit too conspiracy theory for me. I asked Winnie why they don't just bring in the army and crush the violence by force. She says they're scared of losing control. There are too many different tribes in the army, so it could get out of hand.'

'It is too complicated.'

'Yeah, it's no wonder the press just call it tribalism.' Talking about the situation in academic terms made it seem more manageable, kept the yellow tug at bay. Everyone everywhere had become an expert on Kenyan politics overnight. 'What about your blockhead?'

'They say to do nothing yet. We still have our letters if we need to go quickly with the dogs. Mick still says that's hippy shit.' She tried to laugh. 'Are you OK, though?'

It was the question that everyone kept asking.

'Yes, I'm OK. I just want this to be over. You know there are two boys up at the shelter who've had to go into hiding. David is Luo and Joshua is Kalenjin. Winnie says it's way too dangerous to have them here and so they're hiding in a house on the other side of the prison. And do you know what tribe the family is who are hiding them? Kikuyu! The tribe that are supposed to be their enemy. That says it all, don't you think?'

'Yeah, I know. I think Mick is nervous, though, in case this starts to spread around the lake. Everyone is watching and waiting. I don't know if I can stay here any more after this.'

'Don't think about that now.'

'Yeah, well, I'm just a silly Dutch vet full of hippy shit, right?'

'Something like that.' Chala hesitated. 'Femke? Thank you for being there for me. I don't know what I would have done if you hadn't been there.' She felt breathless again and swallowed the tears.

'Hey, you just look after the little one. Go and have a cup of tea.

That's your English solution to a crisis, isn't it? Go and have a nice cup of tea and I'll call you later.'

She left the comfort of conversation, made a cup of tea with a quiet smile and took it to the veranda to wait for Winnie's return. The house was eerily quiet without staff. Winnie had taken Mwangi back to the shelter, but had refused to take Chala with them. Everyone was protecting each other.

She watched a tiny hummingbird hovering and darting into the flowers of a frangipani tree. Shards of recent memory flashed at random in her head.

# CHAPTER 35

The bleep of an incoming text became a siren in her dream. Chala was having sex with someone with no face. Suddenly the siren sounded and they were locked together, naked, on a green hillside. They began to roll down the grass slope, over and over each other, moulding into each other. She could feel his lips and his breath, but still she couldn't see his face. Then there were men on horseback and suddenly people were firing at them. Chala stood up in her dream and someone aimed a rifle at her stomach. 'No!'

Her own scream jolted her awake. Her arms were clutched around her tummy and she looked at her unfamiliar surroundings in momentary childhood confusion, almost calling out for Philip. Then she stopped dead. The bullets of her dream were no longer in her dream. She fought an impulse to run to the toilet.

'Winnie,' she called, throwing a *kikoi* around herself. 'Where are you? What's happening?' All she could hear was the firework crash of bullets and distant shouting. She noticed the phone flashing beside her bed and grabbed it shakily. It was a message from the Dutch blockhead; Femke was translating and forwarding everything she received. 'The army is sending helicopters to stop the riots in Naivasha. Stay in your houses. We keep you informed.'

'Winnie!'

'I'm here. It's OK, girl.' Winnie appeared at her bedroom door as Chala was racing down the corridor. She, too, showed the dishevelled signs of a bad night's sleep.

'What time is it?' Chala felt disorientated, not knowing what questions to ask, grasping for detail that would make this normal.

'It's nearly midday.'

'What?'

'Yep, me too. I went back to bed to try and get some sleep after breakfast this morning.'

'What is—'

'It's OK. They are firing from helicopters to break up the riots.'

'Shooting people?' Chala could not process the information.

'No, they're just blanks, but all the same, you wouldn't want to be in that crowd at the moment.'

Chala wanted to curl up in a little ball. She sat down, not trusting her legs.

'Listen, girl.' Winnie was in charge again. 'It's good that they mean business. Then the cutting and burning will stop.'

Chala flinched from the implications of the word she had just used – cutting.

'But—' That impulse again, forever on her lips. 'I thought they were too scared to bring the army in. Why now?'

'Maybe they needed time to get the soldiers' relatives out first. They wouldn't fire if there were some of their own down there.'

'Oh God, what a mess. What do you think will happen?'

'The fighting will stop. The Mungiki will go back into their holes.

Some people's lives will be ruined and the rest will go back to normal. Life will go on as it always does.'

Chala wondered how she would ever be able to put this experience into words for people back home.

'And what about David and Joshua?' She remembered the Luo and Kalenjin boys from the shelter who were in hiding. 'What will happen to them?'

'Oh, they'll come out of hiding when everything's calmed down. They'll stay there for a while and then they'll go back to the shelter.'

Chala thought suddenly of Kamau and wondered what had become of him. 'Oh shit, I need to go to the toilet.' She jumped to answer the nervous call of her body again and disappeared with Winnie calling after her that she'd make some coffee.

There were messages on her phone from Paul and Amanda and Denise. They had seen images of chaos on the news as helicopters blasted over Naivasha. There was something absurdly surreal about the fact that people in England could actually see what was happening within her own earshot, when she herself could see nothing. Winnie didn't have satellite TV and she felt a peculiar sense of being locked in hiding, her head still metaphorically between Mwangi's legs.

She sent a variation of the same text back to everyone and joined Winnie on the veranda for coffee. The firing was sporadic now, but the helicopters still whirred noisily in and out of earshot. She started to ask Winnie a question about what had made her decide to go into politics, wanting to focus on something else, something from the past that could be nicely packaged up, something finished and safe, but Winnie didn't seem to hear her. She was looking intently towards the gate at the bottom of the short driveway up to the house.

'What is it?' Chala felt instantly breathless.

'I don't know,' she said slowly, and Chala heard the yellow fear creep into her voice.

Then the *askari* was shouting and someone was rattling the gate and she heard a man cry out.

'Go inside!' Winnie barked at her, as she began to stride towards the gate.

Chala hesitated for a second and then backed indoors, allowing the metaphorical hand to come down on her neck. She crouched down beside her bed, ready, if need be, to roll underneath it, and stared at the door. It's OK, it's OK, she said in her head to the little life inside her.

When she heard the footsteps, she strained to recognise the sound of Winnie's gait. Unsure of herself, she was about to slip under the bed, when the sound of Winnie's voice broke into her head.

'Hey girl, it's OK.' Chala wondered for a second if Winnie might have been forced to say those words by someone with a knife or a gun to her head, but she trusted the reassurance in Winnie's voice. She went to the voice and put her arms around Winnie and cried. Winnie, too, had tears in her eyes. She drew back from the embrace and pointed over at the wooden sofa in the corner of the veranda.

'This man needs a woman's help.'

'What?' Chala jumped.

'Come on, he is injured. We'll talk later.'

And together they washed and dressed the deep gash on his arm, holding the flesh together with a bandage until he could get the stitches he needed. Chala felt what a thousand nurses must have felt in war. It didn't matter what tribe he was from or what he believed in. He was a human being in distress – no more, no less. Later she would learn that he was the brother of Winnie's cook. His house had been burnt down and his wife and children had fled to the prison unharmed, but he had gone back in to help another brother with his family. Then a blank bullet had knocked him over and someone had slashed his arm with a *panga*. He had fled for help, seeking refuge at the house of the 'enemy', his sister's employer's house, the house of a Kikuyu, trusting in what he knew about her.

How deeply we act on trust when it matters, thought Chala again.

# CHAPTER 36

Mick turned up early the next morning and Chala was so pleased to see him she felt like crying.

'It's going to be OK,' he reassured her. Helicopters still circled intermittently overhead, though, and he had refused to bring Femke with him. Chala grilled him on what he had seen and what was going on around the lake. He said there were burnt patches on the tarmac where roadblocks had been set up, and there was a deathly hush around the empty market stalls that lined the road into town.

'It's still tense, but it's calm. The rumour mill is still running wild, though. Talk of an attack on the police station and the prison. Don't worry, it won't happen.' Chala remembered Mick saying nothing would ever happen in Naivasha, but she didn't remind him of that.

'How is Femke coping?' How quickly they had slid into being a couple, she thought, as she saw his face soften.

'She's OK.' The same line. 'We had a bit of a fright when the violence seemed to be spreading around the lake, but it'll all blow over now, I reckon. And then we've just got the after-effects to deal with. The flower farms are working together with the Kenyan Red Cross to put up a refugee camp for 10,000 people.'

'Good God, that many?'

'Yep, welcome to Africa.'

'But are these the same people that are at the police station and the prison at the moment?' Chala felt like a dumb schoolgirl, but she needed to understand.

'Yep, they are overflowing, and the police don't have any food to give them.'

'What about the Red Cross? Or some foreign aid agency?'

'The Red Cross is busy getting the camp sorted. Aid agencies are all focused on the western provinces. A few blanks from a helicopter is news, but 10,000 displaced people, hey, that's a throwaway line.'

'When did you get so cynical?'

'I think he was born that way.' Winnie joined them, bearing coffee. 'I don't like to agree with Mick – on principle – but this time he's dead right.'

'Winnie, *habari yako*?' He took her hands in his and Chala thought that Femke had found herself a pretty good Kenya Cowboy. 'How are the boys?'

'I haven't been up there since it all started. I dropped Mwangi at the police station when I took my cook, Emily, in on Monday and he managed to get back up there on foot. They're OK, but they're keeping their heads down.'

Chala thought of their ride in the pick-up with her own head down and shuddered.

After Mick had gone, Winnie announced that she was going to the shelter. 'There's still some tomatoes and onions in the fridge. You can make us something for lunch.'

'No, I want to come too.'

Winnie looked stern and was about to say something, but then paused. There was something new in Chala's voice. 'OK, girl. Come on, then.'

They drove along almost deserted streets, past burnt tyres and patches of rubble. Stray bits of evidence littered the side of the road: a mangled bicycle, a dead donkey, a discarded mattress. Chala tried to stop herself deducing what had happened, and yet it was a release to get out of the house, to see the world for real around her.

As they rounded the corner past the police station, she blanched at the scene they glimpsed through the wire. A swarm of people spread out on every free patch of dust between the station buildings and the wire enclosure. Women in rags breastfeeding babies and small children in the heat of the sun, giving whatever their bodies had left in them to give. Winnie saw it too and they drove past in silence. She stayed quiet for the rest of the journey, concentrating for signs of anything amiss on the road ahead of them, and Chala was relieved when they reached the shelter.

The boys flocked around them as usual and Mwangi and Fred beamed quietly, their matriarch back in the fold. Someone tapped Chala on the back of the leg and she turned round to catch Julius by the wrist. Josphat was laughing, in awe of his hero, but quickly lowered his eyes and went silent when Chala looked in his direction. After a few moments of conferring with Fred and Mwangi, Winnie nodded and clapped her hands.

'OK, boys,' she said in Swahili. 'Remember all those bags of *ugali* we brought up on Sunday? We've got work to do.'

Chala did her best to follow, but the Swahili was too fast. She pulled at Mwangi's elbow and whispered, 'What's she saying?'

'We are going to make food for the people at the police station.' His voice was as matter-of-fact as ever.

Chala felt a choking in the back of her throat. Her heart went out to these people. She didn't grasp the full tribal ramifications of the course of action Winnie had proposed, but she appreciated the irony of street kids preparing food for people who had themselves lost their homes overnight. She caught Winnie's eye and smiled.

# CHAPTER 37

Boys of all sizes stood at the tables lined up on the concrete floor, while others sweated over enormous vats in the kitchen. Some cut up the thick *ugali* into small white slabs, some put the chunks into plastic sandwich bags, others spooned soupy green mush made from local spinach into a second plastic bag. These were then tied together with the *ugali* plastic bag and the parcels piled high in woven baskets. The boys worked surprisingly quietly, making a thousand food parcels. Using the same maize meal as a base, they also cooked *uji*, a slippery, gooey porridge with sugar, which was poured into large black water containers and left to cool.

Winnie categorically refused to let any of the staff or Chala go with her. She dropped Chala back at her house and then disappeared in the laden pick-up. Chala waited, both nervous and dismayed that she had not been allowed to go with Winnie. If it was OK for Winnie, as a Kikuyu, to be seen feeding the Luo, then surely it would be no problem for a white girl? She lay down and tried to stroke peace into her tummy, but there was a restlessness bursting inside her. She opened her laptop to work on the website.

After a couple of hours she began to look obsessively at her watch and the compound gate. When the pick-up drew in finally, she jumped up to greet it, just as the boys always did at the shelter. Winnie's face was strained behind the smile as she climbed out.

'How did it go? What did the police say? How did you give out the food?' Chala wanted detail; she wanted to be able to visualise, grateful yet tired of being protected from seeing.

'It was hard, girl. There's no toilets there. Not enough clean water, not enough shelter and some people are getting sick. There wasn't anywhere near enough food to feed everyone. We just fed as many of the women and children as we could.'

'I want to come with you tomorrow.'

'I'm not sure if it's safe for you to come too.' She hesitated. 'The pick-up got stoned on the way back. It was a bit scary.'

'Oh God, be careful, Winnie. Maybe it's me who should be going in, not you. No one knows who I am, and I'm white. It might actually be safer.'

'Forget it!' Chala was crestfallen. 'Come on, girl, let's get some lunch. And a beer. I need a beer.'

'I'll get it, you stay here.' Chala jumped up.

As she handed out the beer glasses, Winnie looked at her hard. 'Should you be drinking that?'

'What?'

'I think you're going to be a mum, isn't that right, girl?'

'How on earth did you know?' But she was relieved that it was out in the open.

'I'm a woman and I'm African. I know a mother when I see one!' She laughed and raised her glass to Chala's. 'Here's to you, girl. You better be getting home to that man of yours pretty soon or he'll be sending me death threats.'

* * *

Chala was lying on the veranda between phone calls to the UK when Winnie's phone jumped into song on the table. Visibly drained, she had gone to try and get some sleep after lunch, forgetting her phone. It had already bleeped a number of incoming messages, and Chala had thought of taking it into Winnie, but then decided just to answer it.

'*Sema*,' she said to the unnamed number that had called. '*Utakufa, Mama, utakufa. Usirudi* police station.' Chala dropped the phone, unsure of whether she had really heard what she thought she'd heard.

At that moment, Winnie entered, stretching. 'Was that my phone? Hey, what's wrong, girl, you look like you've seen a ghost!'

'I might have got it wrong. It was someone speaking in Swahili, but I think he said that you will die if you go back to the police station. Winnie, what does this mean?'

Winnie picked up the phone, saying nothing, to check the number that had called. Number withheld. Chala watched her read through the various messages that had come in, watched her sit down slowly and stare at the garden, watched the yellow creep into her body language.

'Those messages, they're death threats, too, aren't they?' Chala already knew.

'They say that a Kikuyu who feeds Luos deserves to die.'

'Can't you call the police?'

'What can the police do?' She gritted her teeth. 'They are probably just empty threats, but there is one thing I don't like about this. They are using many different numbers – too many different numbers to be just one person making the same threat.'

'Winnie, listen.' Chala was sitting up straight like an eager schoolgirl in the front row. She heard the resolution in her own voice. 'You said there are white people there from a medical agency, right?'

'Yeah, there are two from France.'

'So, why don't I go in with the food? They won't worry about me, I'm just a *mzungu*.'

Winnie looked at her, thinking hard. She wasn't used to stepping back, but she also knew this was no game. 'But the car – they'll recognise the pick-up. You could still be in trouble.'

'So we get hold of another car. We can get one through Mick.'

'That would make sense,' she said slowly, 'but you don't have to do this.'

'I know that.' Chala chose her words carefully. 'I want to. I want to be part of this, too, and it makes sense, you know it does.'

'Make no mistake, girl, it is still a risk. This is Africa.' But she smiled at her as she had on that day that felt as if it belonged to another lifetime, when Chala had first enthused about the website and the sponsorship scheme.

But this time it was much bigger than the rush of approval. The sensation she had now was new: the feeling that she was doing something *right*.

# CHAPTER 38

'How are you? How are you?' The English words exploded around her in chorus as she stepped out of the rusty pick-up that Mick had had delivered early that morning. She smiled self-consciously and marched towards the building in pursuit of Odeaga, the policeman Winnie had instructed her to ask for. She was vaguely aware of a lifting of faces as she passed clusters of people sitting or lying on the ground, sometimes around tiny charcoal fires with a pot of water stewing tea or a few sad leaves of spinach. The shells of abandoned old cars had been converted into makeshift homes; she noticed one with a *kikoi* strung up like a curtain. People clung to the tiny line of shade provided by the station offices. The sticky stench of stale sweat clung to her skin and she caught sight of an open wound in a queue outside the French medical tent, festering with flies.

Odeaga turned out to be the same young policeman she had seen on the first day, the one with incomprehension in his eyes. Now he was business-like and efficient. He told her to park up at the far end of the driveway and, as she did, he rounded up women and children: children in one line, women and babies in the other. Children came running with cups in their hands, most of them old plastic water bottles with the top cut off, or other objects ingeniously converted to hold liquid. Odeaga called two more of his colleagues over to help. They handed out the butterfly bags of *ugali* and spinach to the women, while Chala and Odeaga poured *uji* for the children. Winnie had also bought 150 eggs, 200 bananas and a few kilos of tomatoes that morning. The boys had supplemented the egg count with around forty of their own from the chickens at the shelter, and all had been carefully hard-boiled. But Chala kept these supplies hidden for the moment, wanting to see how far the rest of the food would stretch. Odeaga told her that the road had opened today and a busload of women and children had departed for Kisumu, leaving Naivasha and any men they had left behind.

'What about food for the men?' she asked Odeaga as she slopped *uji* into outstretched cups, trying to keep the portions fair despite the wildly varying sizes of containers. Some of them hadn't eaten for four days.

'They are strong. They can wait.'

Pouring the porridge was awkward and took so much concentration that Chala hardly took in the faces in front of her. All she saw were arms and cups of different heights and sizes. Every now and again, Odeaga, ever watchful, would reprimand a child who had sneaked back into the queue for more and Chala would look up from her task and catch a child's eye.

The last container of porridge was empty at about the same time as the food parcels ran out in the women's queue. Chala looked up to take stock of the length of the lines before them. They seemed just as long as they had been when they started.

'Are these all new people? I mean, they haven't eaten already?'

'They are new,' Odeaga said simply.

So, they handed out the rest of the food, one tiny piece at a time: a banana to each child, an egg to each woman ... and then a tomato per person and then one tomato between two and then: '*Pole sana* – there's nothing left.' They turned away, some with a shrug, some in disgust, some just looking down at their feet.

The next day, Femke joined her.

'You don't have to do this, you know,' she had said on the phone, giving Femke a get-out clause, just as Winnie had done with her the day before. 'If you want you can bring the food to Winnie's, and I can take it from here.'

'No, I am coming.'

'What does Mick think?'

'I'm not his dog, you know.' Chala thought how Mick would laugh at the English nuance of what she'd just said. 'He says to be careful, though. None of the local organisations are willing to be seen taking sides. It's too dangerous. That's why he can't come, because of the Rotary Club.'

Half an hour later Femke was there and they held each other tight for a moment, before Winnie came up and took Femke by the hand. 'You are sure?'

'Yes, I am sure.'

'Good girls.' Winnie had gone early to supplement supplies and oversee the cooking operation at the shelter. 'But it would be good if you go in Femke's car today, so they don't see the same car going in and out.'

So they loaded up Femke's car and set off for the police station. Femke was quiet on the way and Chala understood why. They drove right up to the point that Odeaga had shown Chala the day before.

By the time they stepped out of the car, queues had already begun to form, children scurrying to find their cups. As they walked over to the building to find Odeaga, Chala caught the eye of a man crouched on the ground. His clothes were torn and his flesh hung loosely round his jaws. He had the haunted, wistful look that she had come to associate with hunger. She smiled softly, but he looked away from her in resignation. There were other men nearby, stretched out on the ground, apathetic from lack of food.

'Why don't the men go with their families on the buses?' Chala asked Odeaga, when they found him. Apparently some more buses had left early this morning and there seemed to be just a bit more space.

'They can't afford to go too. There will be no work when their families get home. The men need to wait and try to go back to their jobs here when they can.'

'But have they eaten anything at all?'

'There is water here.'

'Femke?'

'Yes.' Femke sounded hoarse, struggling with the sudden exposure to human suffering, used to dealing with animals.

'I think we should feed the men today. What do you think?' They both looked over at the queue of eager children and Femke nodded slowly. 'Odeaga?'

'Mama, I will do what you tell me.'

'OK, then we need two lines. One for the men and one for women with babies only.'

They held back, as Odeaga shouted orders. The police had emptied the garage and workshop area of vehicles and put in a TV, so Odeaga sent all the children and women there. Chala heard some women swearing at them as they walked away, but most went silently. Occasionally a woman shouted 'shame' at a man, as the men gathered uncertainly in line.

Chala felt Femke's presence beside her at the head of her line, handing out the *ugali* and spinach food packs with a shaky hand to women with babies strapped around their back or their middle. One woman's baby was swaddled in an old jumper and had the impossible pinkness of a newborn.

'*Ana mwezi ngapi?*' Femke asked the mother. 'Two days.'

Chala heard the exchange, heard Femke's shocked silence. She felt her own stomach twinge at the thought of giving birth in such circumstances and she forced her attention back to the men in her own line. A quick nod or downcast eyes, an occasional weak smile: the men were both grateful and embarrassed.

Femke's queue dried up before the food had run out and her body relaxed with the knowledge that at least all those mothers with babies had eaten today. Then they split the men into two lines and used up the rest of the bananas and the eggs and the carrots and the *uji*. There was nothing left for the women and children.

When they got back to Winnie's house, she handed them a cold drink and greeted Femke warmly with the double Kenyan handshake.

'We must be able to get more *mzungus* to help. There are loads of *mzungus* round the lake.' Femke wanted to talk to Mick, to call every *mzungu* in her phone, to make sure that they had enough to feed everyone.

Winnie smiled, but was firm. 'You know it is not a good thing for too many of you to be there, even if you are white. It will attract too much attention. It will bring trouble.'

Femke spoke to Mick and he agreed with Winnie. They

compromised by agreeing that anyone who was prepared to donate food could drop it at Femke's house, and that way at least they could increase their supplies.

The next day, Femke displayed her foodstuffs like jewellery to Winnie and Chala. Someone had brought three enormous crates of cucumbers. There were thirty loaves of bread, a whole stack of catering packs of biscuits, four extra containers of *uji*, a hundred extra eggs. Every child that day got at least a biscuit or a piece of bread.

As Femke prepared to get in the car, she nodded in the direction of Chala's tummy. 'How are you feeling? You look tired.'

'I think I am going to leave on Friday. The refugee camp will be open in the next few days and they won't need us any longer. I'm almost done with the website. I think I need to go home and tell Paul.'

'Goodness.' Femke was silent and Chala felt shy.

'What will you do? Will you stay?'

'Yeah, I think I will still stay after all. I want to set up a dog programme, to vaccinate all the street dogs against rabies.' She looked down suddenly and Chala saw that she was hiding tears. 'Ignore me, I'm just a silly Dutch vet, but I will miss you.'

Chala hugged her new friend and knew that it was going to be hard to leave.

# CHAPTER 39

There was a loud drum roll that went straight to the hairs on Chala's skin and in flooded the fifty-strong choir of street boys. They stepped into their positions with easy precision, the smallest at the front, tallest at the back. Even little Josphat looked sure of himself, next to Julius in the front row. And then the drums stopped abruptly and one of the boys in the middle sang a long note in a pristine voice that had yet to break. Someone else started a slow, rhythmic clapping and then everyone was singing and clapping a well-worn song. Julius clicked his fingers cockily and Simon clapped just a shade out of time.

Chala remembered the choking feeling she had had the very first time she'd come here and how long ago and how superficial that all felt now. She closed her eyes and savoured this moment.

After three songs, they shuffled into position on the benches and one of the older boys, Samson, received a nod from Mwangi. He stepped out theatrically and read from a sheet in front of him in self-conscious English. The ends of sentences ran into the beginning of the next. The effect was to make it sound like a poem and, Chala realised with a deep blush and a choking sensation, it was about her.

'Good friends are like stars. You do not always see them, but you know they are there. Be strong as you have always been. Let nothing shake you. We will all miss you.'

Then Sampson fell silent and Mwangi nodded again and Julius swaggered over and handed Chala a large flat object wrapped in shiny red paper.

'Shall I open it now?' Chala glanced at Winnie, sitting in the corner, for approval and Winnie just smiled. She opened it. It was a tray with photos of the boys varnished into the surface – the photos she had taken for the website, which Winnie must have had developed for the boys to use. She could not remember a time that a present had meant more to her.

She got up, hating to be the centre of attention, but realising that she must speak. She opened her mouth and began to say thank you in a voice that hid nothing of how deeply she had been moved, but someone interrupted her. It was Julius.

'*Kiswahili, Kiswahili!*' And suddenly there was a chorus of boys chanting for her to speak in Swahili. She told them in broken Swahili that they were like little brothers and that she would always remember them and loved talking with them. But she got the word 'talk' wrong in Swahili and said 'swim' instead and the boys chortled and chortled.

Chala looked at the faces of each one of the staff and let her eyes stop at Mwangi. He, too, was laughing.

\* \* \*

She breathed in the familiar sweaty warmth that had hit her the moment she had arrived at Nairobi airport and allowed the tears to fall unchecked. After the barbecue they had held in her honour, she had shaken each boy by the hand and then each member of staff. When it came to Mwangi she had lingered, wanting something momentous to leave him with. In the end she had told him simply that he was a good man. Then Winnie had dragged her away to her house, where she was allowed to shower before the guests arrived for the small farewell party that Winnie had organised. Mick made a speech and mocked the girl who hated parties and Femke gave her a necklace.

Winnie had insisted on accompanying her to the airport with her driver, even though it meant a 5.30 a.m. start, and had held her very tight before letting her go. 'Go have a baby, girl!' she had said in her best gospel voice.

As soon as she got through immigration, Chala headed straight for the Ladies'. She stood upright in the tiny cubicle, closed her eyes, took a deep breath and focused on somewhere beyond all the chakras in her body. She conjured up the sense of resolution around the decision to feed the refugees at the police station, how good that had felt inside her. She thought of Kamau and the chance he had thrown away in life because of an unlocked toilet door.

Then she walked to the café, ordered a coffee and sat down. Without touching the coffee, she took out her phone, scrolled down to the Bs and deleted a name. After a long pause, she drank her coffee and pondered the journey of the last few weeks of her life. The situation in Kenya was not yet resolved. As communities grappled with the newly displaced and hungry amongst them, politicians continued the stand-off and the estimated death toll was now up to a thousand.

But she was going home. Home to Paul. And she was leaving Kenya with a gift that no one had ever been able to give her before: a sense of self-worth, the irrefutable and unfamiliar sensation of having done something right. She stroked the gentle life inside her as if it were a metaphor or a promise. Her mother had conceived her by a Kenyan lake, Philip's ashes had been laid to rest in another of Kenya's lakes, and now she was leaving Kenya with her own child. Goodbye Kenya – a*sante sana.*

# PART THREE

# CHAPTER 40

Paul circled one of her breasts with his finger, and her nipple responded to the gentle tease of attention. He moved his finger in smaller and smaller circles and she felt the sweet current travel through her body. Still teasing, he traced the shape of each breast alternately, around and around the nipples, until she felt like dragging his head down onto her.

'You've put on weight, Che.'

She opened her mouth to speak, but he put a finger on it. 'I like it. I like the fullness of you. It's like having two women at once.' He tweaked a nipple then and she felt the spasm echo between her legs. 'I get the old one back and a new one too. I like it. I like what Kenya has done to you.'

They had talked endlessly about Kenya over dinner, a safe subject perhaps, a way of reaching across the distance between them, but it was such a relief for Chala to pour out the detail of what had happened, without the need to hide the fear she'd felt ... and a knot buried deep inside her began to unwind – slowly, tentatively, like a snail learning yoga.

Yet they had been shy of physical contact at first. Their hug at the airport had a quiet desperation about it. They had drawn back and looked into each other's faces for signs of what the other had become, but relief had got in the way.

'You're OK – thank God you're OK, Che,' he had kept saying. The frown was there, would always be there, but the relief was blatant in his eyes.

'And you're here. I'm so glad you're here,' she had softly acknowledged with tears in her own. She wanted to pull him towards her, pull his mouth into hers, yet she still felt that she didn't have the right to do this. She would show him she was there for him, but she would not pressure him. He had the right to decide when relief might give way to something else. She was nervous, too; nervous of him noticing the life inside her too soon, wanting space for them both to find each other first before she broke the news.

It wasn't until the end of dinner that he had reached over and touched her face. Now his mouth dropped at last to her nipple and he played her with his tongue, moving between one nipple and the other, burying his fingers in her wet warmth for him … and now, only now as he entered her, did his mouth meet hers.

She woke up from heavy sleep with his head resting against her shoulder. She looked at Paul, at the man she had married, the man she wanted to be the father of her child. His worry lines had softened with the peace of sleep, the frown of his mood swings folded gently back against itself. He looked contented, she thought, wondering briefly if Philip had had that look on him before the water swamped his flesh. She looked back at Paul and touched him ever so softly on the crease of his frown.

'I'm sorry, my love, for what I put you through.' But she said it inside herself, and it was a different kind of sorry, a sorry that opened horizons, a private acknowledgement of what he must have suffered and of her desire to be there for him in the same – ultimately unconditional – way he had managed to be there for her. 'I am stronger now, I need you less, but I love you more.' And the memory of a man who had given her unexpected pleasure on a night three months ago on the other side of the world seemed meaningless.

She thought of little Julius' ordeal at the shelter, of all the women and children who had lost their husbands or fathers in the 'nonsense' of Kenya, of the inevitable ease with which a human being will take up arms to protect his nearest and dearest, of the lengths to which terror or habit can drive a man. And the snail inside her doing yoga uncoiled in slow motion a tiny bit more. It didn't matter who the biological father really was. Her night with Bruce would remain behind a locked toilet door for ever. She would not burden Paul with a secret that could only hurt him. All her life she had lived with guilt and this would be her penance; one more piece of guilt, which she would suffer alone and in private, to give them a chance for a new beginning. Again, she thought of Julius and Kamau. It was a small price to pay.

She stroked her bare stomach under the sheets. This morning she would tell him about the baby. She moved her hand up to his temple again and gently leaned in to smell his hair and kiss him quietly on the forehead. She watched a slow, sleepy smile form on his face and he pulled her back into him with his eyes still closed.

# CHAPTER 41

'No thanks, I've had enough coffee.' She waved him away as he reached to refill their cups. 'So have you recovered?'

'From being abandoned by my wife after less than half the seven-year itch?'

The word sorry rushed into the can of worms that he'd just opened, but she squashed it back down and caught him smiling. 'No, not that,' she said in a deadpan voice. 'Your encounter with the cricket ball. I can't believe you had to go to hospital!'

Suddenly the frown was there, and Chala had that momentary familiar sensation of treading on eggshells in Paul's company, but now he was waving her away as if she were the one offering more coffee. 'Oh, that? Yeah, I'm over that.'

Chala took the hint and changed the subject, eager to hold on to the freshness between them. 'And what about that guy you were talking about, did he buy your hall of mirrors?'

'Yep!' Paul had a wide smile on his face again. 'Guess how much.'

'God, I have no idea.' She waited for Paul to tell her, but he was waiting for her to suggest a sum. What could a little-known artist possibly be paid for an unknown painting? 'I don't know, £100?'

'Is that all you think I'm worth?' She was about to object, but she saw the delight on his face. 'Up a bit.'

'£200?'

'Add a nought.' 'No, really?'

'No, not really.'

'Oh.' She stopped short. He was still smiling. 'Add another nought.'

'What? That's impossible! That's £20,000!'

'It's a kind of sponsorship thing, really. He's got loads of contacts in the art world. He's going to put on an exhibition and he gets twenty per cent of whatever we sell. I've been working madly ever since!' He pulled her over from her side of the table to sit on his lap. She sat with one leg either side of him, facing him – it was how they used to sit before they got married. 'It's my lucky break, Che. I know it is. This is my big chance.'

'That is truly brilliant.' She hugged him warmly, delighted that time was rewarding his courage at last.

'God, you're getting heavy.' He pushed her playfully off his lap and, unnoticed, she took a deep breath, but just as she was about to speak he grabbed her by the hand. 'Come on – want to see what I've been working on?'

She looked at him with momentary disbelief. She could only remember one other time he'd actually let her see an unfinished painting. He, too, she realised, had changed.

'Yeah, I know. Fuck it, come and have a look.' And she followed him downstairs into the basement.

He showed her two finished paintings and two he was working on.

He had never worked so quickly, never before started more than one painting at once. She reacted without self-consciousness in front of them all. The last one he showed her was still in its early stages and she could barely make out the detail around the one clear object in the foreground. It was a knife, a large African machete being wielded mid-air in a cloud of dust, yet the knife was shining and on it was the broken reflection of the face of a small child, eyes wide open in terror.

'My God,' Chala was awestruck. 'How could you produce something so powerful without even being there?'

'You like it?'

'It's incredible.' She looked away from the pain of the painting into his open face. 'You're incredible.'

'Come on, then, enough of this. Another coffee while we talk about what to do with £20,000?'

'And the money from the house.'

'Philip's house? You want to sell it? I thought you wanted to keep it for ever.'

'That was before I knew there was a way to have a new beginning. I want to move on, Paul ... with you ... and—'

'OK, don't go all hippy on me here. You might spoil the paintings.' He was laughing and pulling her towards him. 'But seriously,' he pulled back to look at her again, 'that's good, Che. You really have changed. I like the new you.'

Her hands were beginning to sweat. She needed that coffee. It was time to tell him.

'Fuck!'

Chala jumped. 'What?'

'You haven't even said hello to the kid yet!'

She almost jumped again.

'Rudolph first. Coffee second.'

They went upstairs and poked Rudolph out of his furry slumber and Chala found herself talking to Paul about getting a dog.

'A dog, a horse, a boat, a house in the sun – the possibilities are endless. Come on, coffee!'

They finally settled around the still breakfast-laden kitchen table and Chala allowed herself to float for a few moments longer in the bubble of Paul's enthusiasm. They talked about the money and the opportunity for Paul to turn his passion into a real living, about where they could choose to live if this happened, about the kind of work that Chala would like to get involved in. Without any formal transition they had passed from a night of tender yet slightly ambivalent reunion to talk about the one thing that indicated commitment as a couple: the future. After the last twenty-four hours, Chala felt sure that Paul would welcome the pregnancy with open arms. At last she gave life to the words that sweated in her hands.

'Paul.' Her hands gripped each other under the table. 'There is something else that affects our future together. Something I found out in Kenya, but I wanted to be certain about before I told you, and I wanted to tell you face to face.' She hesitated. 'I'm pregnant, Paul. I'm going to have a baby.'

The look on Paul's face would never leave her. She had expected confusion, surprise, shock, but also joy. She saw no delight in the wall of his face. He seemed to sink into himself and, when she searched his eyes, there was nothing but distance. He spoke, finally, and the words brought no relief.

'You're right.' His voice was flat. 'This does affect our future together.'

# CHAPTER 42

'Should you be eating that?' Paul pointed at the hot pepperoni on her takeaway pizza.

'I'm sure it won't do any harm.' She looked up and they made eye contact for what felt like the first time since she'd told him she was pregnant. He had spent most of the day away from her, out walking and in his studio, and she had waited in patient agony for him to make a move to speak to her. When he had surfaced and suggested they order a pizza, she had wanted to cry.

'I thought you always said you would have an abortion if you ever got pregnant.' It was an accusation.

'Yes, I know, I did.' She chose her words as if she were being tested. 'But you once said that I couldn't know how I would react unless it happened …You were right.'

Silence. She spoke again. 'That was why I didn't tell you straight away. I did think about abortion. It was only when I was in the middle of the riot that I suddenly knew for certain I wanted to keep it – that it suddenly seemed possible.'

'And me, what about my feelings? I'm not just a fucking hamster you can take out of its cage whenever you feel like it, you know.'

'I know, Paul.' She searched for words. 'But you always knew you wanted children. It didn't seem fair to put you through that if I wasn't going to have the baby. Especially in the situation we were in.'

'Fuck you.'

Chala flinched. 'What do you mean?'

'I mean,' his voice had returned to the cold, flat monotone, 'this is not about whether I want a baby or not. Of course I "want" a baby, you know that. You've always known that and yet you've always made me think that wasn't an option in any future we had together. I married you, knowing that. And now out of the blue, you swan in and present me with a fait accompli and expect me to jump up and down and clap my hands. Well, whatever you learnt in Kenya, Che, the world you left behind hasn't changed. It doesn't fucking work like that. How do I even know it's mine? How do I know you didn't fuck someone in Kenya?'

Chala looked at Paul now. She thought of the secret scar that Julius would have to carry through his life. Hers was nothing besides his. She spoke from a place deep inside her.

'You don't *know*, Paul. I did not fuck anyone in Kenya. I can say those words and you can choose whether to believe me or not, but you will never *know* what I have or haven't done.' She clawed for the essence of their wedding vows. 'More importantly, you don't need to *know*. The only things you need to know are that I love you and I want this baby with you – and to know whether you want a future with me and the baby in it.'

'You're right.' He took her hands in his, but the gesture felt sad and she froze inwardly. 'You had time to work that out and I need to do the same.'

'But …' The tears came quietly, inevitably, for all Chala's efforts. 'I know this must be a huge shock for you, but I thought you wanted me back.'

He looked at her, into her. 'But it's not just you any more. I need to work out what I really want. I'm going to go away for a bit, somewhere on my own. I won't be long. I just need a week or so to get my head around this. Can you do that for me? Let me have that?'

She looked for sarcasm in his face, but there was none. 'Yes,' she pulled strength into her voice from a new place inside her. 'Of course I can. You gave me space when I needed it and I will never forget that. Of course, you can have all the time you need to decide what you want.' She tried to look into his eyes, but he looked away from her and said nothing. She spoke again, finally, into the silence. 'I'll sleep in the spare room …' She got up, piled the half-eaten pizza onto a plate in the fridge, walked around the table and put her arms around Paul from behind, kissing his neck quickly and gently. 'I love you, Paul. I'll wait for you to call me.'

'OK.' He said it to the table in front of him, without looking round. His body was tense and she forced herself to walk away.

# CHAPTER 43

'Femke, how are you?'

'I'm good, but we miss you. Even Tek Tek and Cheza can't understand where you are!'

'I wish someone could tell me that!' Chala laughed. 'Gosh, it's good to hear from you. Have things settled down yet? What's going on now? Kenya has dropped completely out of the news here.'

'Here too, in a way. Everyone just wants to get back to normal. Kofi Annan is coming over to try and, how do you say, medium a solution.'

'Mediate ... and the IDP camp – is that still running?'

'Oh yes. I've been there with Mick a couple of times to drop off some clothes and blankets and stuff. It looks like it's been there for ever, like some kind of strange Arabian village with tents in the desert. But so many people have gone back to the western provinces.'

Chala smiled secretly at the speed with which Mick's name had come into the conversation. 'So, how are you and Mick, then?'

'He wants to take me to Tanzania for a long weekend.'

'Well, that's cool, isn't it?' She noticed the coy pause at the other end of the line – more than the usual time lag on an international call. 'It won't be the first time you've done a long weekend together!'

'His parents live there.'

'Wow,' Chala's laugh was warm, and she realised suddenly how much she missed Femke. 'Well done you, you've hooked a Kenya Cowboy!'

'*Pole pole*, we'll step one foot at a time.'

'Of course.' Chala left the English uncorrected this time. 'But anyway, I'm happy for you. That sounds good, wherever your feet are now.'

'You are laughing at me, you English bitch! Tell me, how are you?'

'Oh, no, let's not talk about me yet, tell me more about Naivasha. Have you seen Winnie? Do you know how they're doing at the shelter?'

'Yes, actually, we had a beer together in town yesterday. She's good, she looks tired and I think she misses you, but she's good. She said the two boys in hiding will wait one more week and then she's going to bring them back to the shelter.'

'Oh good, that's good.' Chala looked across at the present they'd given her, the wooden tray inlaid with photos of the shelter boys, now hanging on their kitchen wall. 'I wonder how little Julius is doing …'

'Enough, tell me about you. What did Paul say when you told him?'

'God, you're just as bad on the phone as you are in real life!' She took a deep breath, as she felt the inevitable sting of salt in her eyes and the twinge of panic where her baby lay. It was a completely different kind of feeling to the fear that had gripped her in the midst of the turmoil in Naivasha. That had been visceral and immediate; this was much gentler, more insidious, the anticipation of potential loss. She knew two things with certainty: she wanted the baby and she wanted Paul. She would do nothing to risk losing either of them, ever.

'Chala, what's wrong?'

'He's not sure what he wants. He's gone away – I don't even know where – to think about it all. He says I've had time to adjust, but he hasn't and he needs space to think.'

There was another pause and then Femke spoke. 'He's right, you know. It must be very hard for him. It is too sudden.'

'I should have told him before.'

'No, that's not what I'm saying. You had your reasons and now he has his. You need to be patient.'

'I know, I know.' At least Femke didn't know, would never know, the full extent of those reasons. And Paul, he must never know either. She would save him from that, whatever he decided.

'Sounds like you need a cup of tea.' The reference reminded her of all they had been through together in Kenya.

'Yes, I wish you were here to have one with me. I miss you.'

'Well, you can come and see me in Holland, when I go back for Christmas.'

'Sounds like a good plan. You know, there's someone else I'm going to see tomorrow. You remember me telling you about Denise? Well, I'm going to stay with her for a couple of days.'

'And the letter?'

'I think I'm finally going to find out what's in it. She says it's better she tells me face to face. I don't see what it could possibly say that makes any difference to anything, but I'm still nervous.'

'One foot at a time, Chala.'

'Yep, you're right, one foot at a time. Thanks for calling me.'

'I'll speak to you soon. Call me after you've seen Denise.'

'OK, and listen – good luck with your weekend in Tanzania.'

She sat with a coffee after the phone call – decaf, a new concession to the life growing inside her – and stared up at the tray of photos, trying to divert her attention to fund-raising ideas for the shelter. Waiting was hard. She and Paul had both done such very different types of waiting over the last couple of months, and now there was a new kind of waiting in the pit of her stomach. Perhaps this was more akin to what Paul had been through while she was away.

At least one of the pieces of waiting in her life would be over tomorrow. She drifted into a reverie about Philip, unaware that she was stroking her stomach again, soothing and protecting the life inside her from the waves outside. Would she ever know whether he had committed suicide? Her gut feeling was that he had, and yet at one level it didn't make sense. Why, after all these years, would he suddenly make such a decision? He had loved her like his own daughter, even if Denise had been unable to. She came full circle, as she always did, when she punished herself with this line of thinking. He was gone. She could never ask him.

But there was a letter. Perhaps the answer had been waiting quietly all this time.

# CHAPTER 44

Denise's house was a surprise. She had expected something quite
subdued and middle class, slightly arty perhaps, a Victorian ground-
floor flat with a terraced veranda into a shared garden, the feminine
touch of a woman who has long since got used to living alone evident
everywhere. But her first thought, as Denise showed her in, was about
what Paul would make of it. There was colour everywhere, dishevelled
and competing. The whole back wall of the living room was painted
a deep red, in violent contrast to the bright white around it, rich blue
cushions on a red leather sofa and a huge bunch of lilies in a long
black glass vase, placed strategically just in front of a mirror. Another
wall was covered by an enormous oil painting of a buffalo stampede.

'Your mother gave me that,' Denise said as she caught Chala staring
at it, 'after she first went out to Kenya. Beautiful, isn't it?'

'It is!' Chala focused on the painting. 'Paul would love your house!'

'Come on, I'll show you round and then I'll get us a drink.'

There was a nervousness in Denise; she seemed less in control than
she'd been the last time they'd met. Chala followed her, continuing
to marvel at the amount of colour everywhere, and suddenly it seemed

impossible that she and Philip could ever have stayed together. The only room that was subdued was the one at the back of the house, which she had converted into a surgery for her private speech therapy patients. It was comfortable and not overly clinical, with a sunlit view into the small green swathe of back garden, but there was no clue there to the passion of Denise's private personality.

Finally, they sat down with drinks in the living room. Denise filled the threat of silence with questions about the Kenyan crisis, and Chala found herself offering sound bite versions of what had really happened, impatient suddenly to travel back in time.

'The letter,' she said finally, after Denise had served their second drink, without remarking on Chala's opting for just tonic. 'What did it say?'

Denise's face tightened. 'I will tell you what it said, of course I will, but we have time. This is hard for both of us, I know. Do you mind if we take it a bit slowly?'

'One foot at a time?'

'What?' Denise looked at her quizzically.

'Just something my Dutch friend Femke says.' She hesitated, sensitive to Denise's need to delay the moment, but other questions flowed in front of the door that Denise was afraid to unlock. 'What I don't understand is why you wanted to see me last time, if you hadn't even read the letter then. I mean, I can understand why you couldn't bear to be with me after the accident' – the habitual flinch – 'but then why did you want to see me again at the funeral? Why did you want to even re-establish contact?'

'I don't know.'

It was not the answer she had expected. Chala waited patiently for more.

'It wasn't your fault. It's just that I couldn't see you without seeing Emma. I just couldn't cope, couldn't get beyond it, and I think I blamed Philip, for not being in the room when it happened, for not being able to stop it, for not being able to stop me feeling the way I did. He just withdrew into himself. We weren't helping each other get through the situation, and he was fiercely protective of you, and you, you started to become part of the battleground of ghosts between us. Do you remember that doll you had?'

'Rosie?'

'Yes. I wanted to kill that doll, get rid of it. I was sure it was making your nightmares worse, but Philip wouldn't have it, said you were too vulnerable to deal with another disappearance. God knows who was right, but I started to realise that I was going to lose my sanity if I stayed. I just had to get away.'

'OK,' Chala said slowly. 'I understand all of that, but why did you want to re-establish contact when Philip died?'

'Maybe it was partly guilt. When I started to get stronger again, I felt guilty about the way I'd abandoned you – you and Philip. The whole thing was an accident – a terrible accident – but we should have been able to help each other and move on over time, together. I couldn't do that. I have never remarried, never had another child …'

Realisation struck Chala: Denise had never moved on sufficiently to create a new life with another child in it. She looked at Denise and saw pain in the lines that had given away nothing at the funeral.

'And then, when Philip died, I just thought what a waste … and the only way that I could avoid burning up with regret was to reach out to you.'

Chala touched her gently on the arm. 'Didn't you ever want to get back with Philip?'

'Sometimes, but I was never sure enough, or never had guts enough. I always thought he was the weak one. In fact, I know now how weak he was—' She said this with a splash of vehemence that made Chala look up.

'Why did you think he was weak?' Chala asked, defensive.

'He was always so ... so passive. Always sitting on the fence. He would never defend anything or anyone.'

'What do you mean? I know he hated confrontation and he was non-judgmental to the extreme, but I always loved that about him.'

'Yes, I know, I loved that too, but ...' Denise looked uncomfortable. 'It's hard to think of specific examples that don't sound petty. You must know what it's like, living with someone day in, day out. The differences between you are what attract you at the beginning and then, with time, they are exactly what frustrate you. Eventually, if you're lucky, you get to a place where you just accept the differences ... and I think, if the accident hadn't happened, we would have done that too.'

She trailed off, but Chala was still desperate to understand. 'Yes, I see all that – in theory – but I still don't really get it.' Never presume to know the secrets of a marriage, she remembered Philip saying to her once.

'You know Philip was engaged to someone else when we met – did he ever tell you that?'

'Yes, I knew that. She was a bit of a nutcase, wasn't she?'

'He *allowed* her to be.' Even after all these years, this was clearly still a sore point for Denise. 'We were madly attracted to each other – although there was no physical contact between us, Philip was a stickler over that – but he took ages to break it up. The first time he broached the subject with her, she all but threatened suicide. Did he ever tell you that?'

'Really? No, he never mentioned that.'

'Well, she didn't exactly say it, but she insinuated it – even in my company once at a party, she said that she would fall apart if he ever left her. It was a weird thing to say in a social context, but I saw the way she checked to make sure that Philip had heard it. She was saying it for effect and he fell for it every time. It drove me mad. It was so obvious they were no good for each other, and as we became friends he told me he wasn't sure he loved her enough to marry her, but still he didn't have the guts to leave her.'

'So what happened in the end?'

'Someone else appeared on the scene and swept her off her feet and she was the one to break it up.'

'Poor Philip.'

'Not at all. He was relieved to be free and that's when we were allowed to happen, but if I'd got fed up of hanging around I'm not sure he'd have ever come after me. He just took what life gave him. Even after the whole wretched thing happened with Emma, he never fought for me, never tried to make contact or come after me. Sometimes I wanted to shake him and say life doesn't have to be only what comes along. I wanted him to take life by the horns, not just take whatever it happened to throw at him. I'm sure he lost touch with loads of our friends after I left. I was the one who would organise the parties. He would never make the effort on his own. I bet he never sent a single Christmas card ever again.'

Chala remembered the lack of ritual around Christmas in their house with fondness; she had grown up with a proud sense of Philip's lack of convention. It was disconcerting to hear such a different interpretation of all this now.

'I must sound harsh.' Denise reacted to Chala's quietness. 'Truth be told, we were as bad as each other. Neither of us had the guts to bridge the distance I allowed to grow between us. Neither of us ever tried to go back. Ha!' Denise's laugh was hollow. 'I never thought of it like that. He was the one who was too weak to run away from his engagement and then I was the one who was too weak to stay in our marriage.'

'No, I think what you did took a lot of guts.' Chala had made a mental step backwards, trying to understand what had happened between them. 'You made a clean break. That made it easier for everyone to move on. You forced yourself to build a life and you discovered something that you love, and a way of caring for people around you.'

'The wrong people.'

'Now you sound like me!' Chala managed a weak smile and continued. 'On the rare occasions that I could ever get Philip to talk about the past, he told me that it was better that you kept what you had between you intact. That your relationship never had time to sour enough to scar the memory of what you'd had together.'

'Gosh, your mother would have hated that – much too cynical.'

'Or not. You could argue it was deeply romantic at some level. He loved you, you know.'

'Don't you think he ever blamed me for leaving?'

'No, I think he blamed himself. I don't know why he always seemed to blame himself so much.'

Denise got up sharply and walked over to the window. Chala waited for her to come back and sit down again, but she started to speak, with her back to Chala, still staring out the window. 'The letter … it was written not long after I left—'

Then the phone rang and Denise moved away from the window to pick it up and her voice transformed itself into cool professionalism.

'Listen,' she said as she put the phone down afterwards. 'Let's leave the letter until tomorrow. Can you bear that? Let's have supper and talk about the weather for a bit, shall we?' She smiled warmly, and Chala, exhausted already, found herself breathing out and joining in.

'OK, the weather it is, for now.'

# CHAPTER 45

But the weather didn't last long. Chala was just returning from the loo, between courses, when she caught Denise scanning her quizzically.

'Yes, I'm pregnant.' She almost wanted to laugh, desperate to share this news with someone who could take it at face value.

'Are you pleased?' Denise gave nothing away, however.

'I wasn't at first, but now I am. Now it feels right to have it.'

'And Paul?'

Chala searched for words and both women made eye contact. 'Is it his?' asked Denise quietly.

'I think so.' Chala's response was barely audible. But Denise spoke quickly. 'Do you love Paul?'

'Yes.' Chala felt emotion welling at the back of her throat again.

'Do you want to have your baby with him?'

'Yes.'

'Then it's his.' There was the tiniest pause and then Denise spoke again so quickly that Chala would wonder later if she'd recalled the conversation accurately. 'So how did he react? I take it you didn't tell him until you got back?'

It was uncanny how perceptive Denise was about her. It made Chala imagine this was what it might be like to have your own mother.

'No, I didn't tell him until the day after I got back and now he's gone away to think about it all. He was shocked and angry, I think, that I didn't tell him while I was still in Kenya. And I always said I never wanted children, but then it felt different, when I actually got pregnant. I—' Chala swallowed. 'I couldn't kill it.'

'Chala—' Denise had reached across the table and pulled Chala's hand towards her, looking straight at her, and Chala wanted to curl up and hide from the intensity in her. 'If you love him, stand by him and by your decision. It will be for the best, trust me.'

Silence. But eventually Denise filled it comfortably. 'Right, time for some very rich, cheeky chocolate mousse – perfect for pregnant women – and now I understand why you've been refusing my alcohol all evening!'

As she disappeared into the kitchen, Chala realised, gratefully, that the conversation that might have developed between them had been allowed to drop. Even now she almost doubted what had actually been said. At some obscure level, it was almost as if Denise was enabling Chala to do what she herself had failed to do: to turn the clock back, to pick up the pieces and rescue her future with Paul.

'He'll come back, I'm sure of it.' Denise was back, spooning thick dark chocolate into their bowls.

'What makes you so sure?'

'I don't know him, and I suppose I don't really know you either, although I feel I do, but I could see it in the way he looked at you at the funeral. He adores you, it's obvious, and he cares about you. He cared enough to risk losing you by letting you go to Kenya. He won't want to lose you now. He strikes me as very different from Philip.'

'In what way?' Chala was intrigued.

'Philip would never fight for anything. It strikes me that Paul will.'

'Philip fought for me,' were the words that went through Chala's mind, but she didn't voice them. 'I hope you're right,' was all she said.

That night, Chala dreamed about a buttercup-yellow room and in it her own little baby girl lay sleeping peacefully in a cot. Beside her, perched on the tiny pillow at the head of the cot, sat a cloth doll called Rosie, who kept watch to make sure that nothing ever happened to her charge, never for a second closing her eyes.

# CHAPTER 46

Fried bananas and honey, fresh croissants and the smell of coffee, talk of the weather again and the previous night's sleep and the day's innocuous headlines – there was nothing left to delay the moment that both women were dreading.

'Do you want me to tell you what it says or do you just want to read it?' Denise looked as though she had slept very badly indeed. 'Oh God,' she continued, not waiting for Chala to reply, 'I hope I'm doing the right thing, sharing this with you. There are some things best left alone and this may be one of them. I'm beginning to question my motivation. I thought you had a right to know, but now I'm not so sure that it isn't just me wanting to share my burden. Chala, are you sure you want to know?'

It was the most tortuous speech Chala had ever heard Denise make. She laughed with false bravado. 'After a build-up like that I couldn't say no, even if I wanted to!' But she continued more gently when Denise failed to respond to her attempt at humour. 'Yes, Denise, I do want to know what's in that letter.' She paused. 'Nothing in it can change the way I feel about Philip.'

Denise poured herself a coffee from the caffeinated pot and another decaf for Chala, pulled out the envelope and placed it on the table. 'I think it's probably best if you just read it yourself. I'll be in the living room. Give me a shout when you're ready.'

Chala found herself staring at the envelope, much as she had looked at the pee stick in Naivasha, delaying the moment of no return. Then, too, a woman who cared had been waiting in another room. Pregnant or not pregnant? What could this letter possibly hold that could surprise or upset her? She picked up the envelope and smelled it for some sign of Philip. Then, feeling silly, she turned it over, opened the flap, pulled out the letter and started to read.

*My dearest Denise,*

*How did the pain that came into our lives lodge so firmly between us? In a way I suppose I should feel grateful that you left, because by leaving you have taken away the easy option. Does it shock you that I actually thought about suicide? Suicide is for cowards, I hear you say. Or for those brave enough to accept the consequences of their actions, I might argue.*

*Now that you've gone I cannot leave Chala and I'm not even sure I would have had the guts to leave her anyway. Perhaps if I thought she would have made you happy, filled the space of Emma, but you drew back from us both, as if there were some kind of awful collusion between us. Poor Chala, she is the innocent victim of this mess.*

*I know you already blame me and yet you don't even know what really happened. When I am strong enough, I will give you this letter so that you know the whole truth. I can't do that yet. There is too much of me that still hopes you will come back. I don't know how it got this far. It all happened so quickly and then suddenly there was this historical truth out there and we all used the word 'accident' to cover up the details, and*

*Chala was so little, a part of me thought it wouldn't matter. But I am eaten alive by what nobody knows. I want you to know, but I want you to forgive me. Can you do that? Can you forgive me? Can you give us another chance? Give Chala a chance?*

*If I think your answer could be yes – or when I am strong enough to deal with the possibility that your answer may never be yes – then, only then, will I give you this letter. And then you will know that Emma was already dead and that Chala never had anything to do with what happened.*

*I checked upstairs before I left the house. I know you told me never to leave her alone, but I thought it wouldn't matter. I was only going round to the corner shop to buy loo roll. She seemed fine, but when I got back she wasn't. I didn't realise anything was wrong until Chala was already in the cot. I don't know how long it was before you came into the room. I was in a state of shock and you were so convinced by the version of events that you thought you'd seen. There were so many people around – doctors, police – and I can't remember any of it clearly. You seemed to do all the talking and I let you.*

*By the time I came to and realised what I had allowed to happen, it was too late. By then it would have looked too weird, too suspicious. And then there was the inquest and I was scared they might think I had done something to her. All the time a child was responsible, no one was guilty, it was just an accident, but if it was an adult, it might have been something else. I was too scared to open that door. I still am. Scared. And guilty. And sorry.*

*If you ever read this it will be because I have reached a stronger place. If ever you want to come back, I am here for you, for you and for Chala, and I will stand by her now as best I can.*

*Philip*

Chala drew her knees up onto the chair and put her arms around them, as if she needed the physical sense of her own body, as if its physicality were the only thing she could rely on right now. She closed her eyes, remembered the way she had seemed to float away from herself in a hotel room in Australia. She needed to stay inside her body now. She forced herself back to the words, read the letter again. The wheel of her brain moved slowly.

Cot death. Very little was known about it then. Now everybody knew about it, avoided putting their babies in certain positions. Her mind was working in slow motion, a rational piece of it trying to calculate what age she might have been when the notion of cot death became normal.

She felt peculiarly hollow, almost lethargic. So, it was a ... real accident after all. A tiny real accident that created a lifetime of guilt in a little girl. It wasn't Chala who'd killed Emma. Her hand moved to the life in her tummy. Paul, she wanted to cry out. Paul, imagine if I'd killed this baby. For nothing. She felt two emotions surge inside her, emotions that didn't fit naturally in the same space: relief and a mute bitterness. Suddenly, memories were swimming through her: the endless nightmares about Rosie, the taunting at school, the dryness of her eyes when they rescued the fox at the side of the road, the fraudulent calm in her step on her wedding day, the rotten core of her being that had made it possible to sleep with someone else and had made it seem impossible that she could ever be a mother ...

This rotten, dysfunctional core was a *mistake*? She didn't know how to process what this meant. And yet Denise had believed it was her ... and Philip had allowed the world to think that was true. Philip, why didn't you tell me? The bitterness gave way to a powerless sense of empathy. She was not the only one who had carried guilt in the core of her being because of this tiny, genuine accident.

She looked up, confused by a noise at the door, to see Denise walk in and sit down at the table.

'You've read it? You understand now that it wasn't you?'

She looked at Denise with incomprehension on her face. And she saw the pain in Denise's own face.

'Oh God, you must feel terrible. No wonder it had such an impact on you.' She understood suddenly how this revelation must have played havoc with Denise's own sense of self. Like a painter returning to a tired old canvas, in one swift movement the letter had splashed paint over the top of Chala's guilt and painted a new, red gash of guilt in Denise's own life. It was Denise's interpretation of events that had allowed a child to grow up thinking it was all her fault. 'Denise, don't blame yourself. There's been too much blame, too much guilt already.' She reached out and put an unsteady hand on Denise's arm.

Denise spoke quietly. 'I felt consumed by guilt when I read the letter. I'm so sorry, Chala, for my part in all this. I couldn't tell you by phone or email.'

'Denise, don't. I understand.'

At a rational level, she did understand, but emotionally the letter had been too much to take in. You couldn't paint away your entire sense of self with just one stroke of a brush, could you? You couldn't paint over a lifetime with just a few words, could you?

That little girl in the playground – she remembered the incomprehension, the utter bewilderment she'd felt in the face of Louise's revelation; the life she had spent since, trying to make sense of it, come to terms with it. And Philip? His secret guilt. She felt as if she were in her namesake lake all over again, a sickly cloying of dark water all around her.

# CHAPTER 47

Daytime sleep had left her feeling drugged and heavy. Exhausted and unsteady, she had gone to lie down after the conversation with Denise and fallen asleep on top of the bed. Still fully clothed, she felt now as if her whole body were creased. She tiptoed into the bathroom and splashed cold water over her face to try and reduce the puffiness around her eyes. She went back into her room and sat in the artificial darkness on the side of her bed, looking at her feet. One foot at a time, Femke always said. Which foot now?

She walked over to the window and pulled the thick, green curtain back slightly to see what kind of day was left. It was a hazy autumn afternoon and copper-coloured leaves sprinkled the pavement. A school memory surfaced. Amanda was off sick and a shy new girl called Betty had asked if she could sit beside her. Chala had felt pleased and flattered and proud, but then in the break she had seen Louise pulling Betty aside in the corridor and whispering something in her ear. Betty never sat beside her again.

Oh Philip, how could you have let that happen? How could you have stood on the sidelines of my growing up like that? Who would

I have been if I'd grown up without that kind of stigma? I understand why it was too hard to say anything at the time, I do, but later? Why didn't you tell me later?

'I will never lie to you, little baby,' she spoke softly to her tummy.

But then she sank back down on the bed again, the irony crashing around her. There would be a secret between her and her baby. If she could never tell Paul she was unsure who the father really was, then she couldn't tell anyone else either, she could never tell her own child. Like Philip, she would carry the burden of a secret guilt to her grave. The irony, she thought again: a lifetime of misplaced guilt, replaced by another, new, self-inflicted guilt. She would never get away from it. If she had not grown up defined by guilt, if the rot had never taken root, would she have been capable of that night with Bruce? And if that night hadn't happened, would there be a baby now?

She ached for the little girl she'd been; she ached for Philip. If only he had told her. She would have been able to reassure him, tell him she forgave him, perhaps saved him from taking his life ... if that is what he did.

A noise at the door made her jump. It was Denise, asking awkwardly if she would like a cup of tea. Her face looked old. Chala tried to find a spark of the anger she'd felt towards Denise before they met again at the funeral. After all, it was Denise's interpretation of events that had been taken at face value, her version of what she thought she'd seen that Philip had colluded with, and if she hadn't run away Philip might have found the strength to bring it all out into the open. But she could find no anger inside her for Denise. And when she thought of Philip there was just a soft, open wound that she didn't know how to dress. She wanted desperately to talk to Paul, to process this new reality with him, to hand it to him like a present: here – I'm not a bad person after all.

He would have sat her on his lap, looked into her eyes and said it didn't make any difference to how much he loved her, but he would have rejoiced too, helped her focus on the positive.

'Chala, are you ready to come downstairs for a cup of tea?' Denise spoke again, almost in a whisper, and Chala found herself thinking of Winnie. Go girl, go and get yourself a cup of tea – and be strong for that woman. She needs you now. She could almost hear Winnie's voice; the rich, deep, gospel tone of her words.

'Yep, I'm coming. I'll be down in a sec.' She looked into the pain on Denise's face. 'Thanks, Denise.'

'Do you think he did it, then?' They were on their third cup of tea and Chala was stretched out on the red leather sofa.

'I honestly don't know. I don't suppose we'll ever know.'

'I was so sure he did, you know, when I got back from Australia. I kept remembering this conversation we'd had when I was about fifteen, about the way we'd all do it if we had to. I knew how he'd do it. I said he'd just walk into the sea and he said, yes, that would be a good way to go.'

'Maybe that was just a coincidence, something you seized on in your reconstruction of events.'

The word reconstruction struck a chord for Chala. She thought of all the reconstructions that had played in her head over the years as she'd tried to create a version of her childhood act that made it possible to live with herself. But the reality of what she'd done, what she'd been capable of at such a tender age, had seeped into every pore of her being – and yet it had all been based on a lie, an untruth allowed to turn into reality. She wanted to reach back to the little girl she had been at school, reach out and tell her classmate Betty it was OK, it was OK to sit next to her.

'I just wish Philip had told me,' she said quietly.

'I told you he was weak. That's just something we have to accept.'

'But he wasn't weak for me,' she objected gently, still unable to accept any criticism of Philip. 'At least he stayed, at least he didn't give up or run away, at least he tried to protect me.' She was thinking of Philip, but she realised that the words sounded like a recrimination. 'I'm sorry,' she said quickly, groping for solidity. 'I didn't mean that the way it sounded. I completely understand why you left, it's just that—'

'You're right, though.' It was said simply and it was disarming.

'No, no, that's not what I meant. It's just, oh God, I don't know ... I wish I could talk to Philip,' she finished lamely, up against the wall of his non-being. Denise said nothing, but her face was soft in sympathy.

'You know,' Chala spoke as if she were thinking aloud, 'I'm actually less sure now that he committed suicide than I was before I read the letter. I mean, if he contemplated it all those years ago and didn't do it, why would he do it now? And if he had chosen to do it, surely he would have wanted to make things right by sending that letter or a version of it to us both?'

'Maybe that's what he did.'

'You mean by allowing it to be found in the attic?' Chala thought of what Philip had said on the phone about sorting out the old boxes in the attic before she had gone to Australia. No, if he had wanted to sort them out for that reason, surely he would have taken the letter out – and either destroyed it or written another letter to go with it after so many years. 'You know, I think he did try and tell me a couple of times. I can remember him being really awkward and trying to put something into words, but I felt bad about it, and I thought it wasn't fair and it must be too painful for him dredging it all up, and I put my arms around him and said it didn't matter.' If only she had the power to turn back the clock and have that conversation again.

'I think something like that happened once with me, too. Early on, after it happened, but I was so angry with him I never let him finish. I thought he was just trying to make excuses about not being there.'

'Oh God, it must have been so awful for you.' Chala felt another rush of sympathy for this woman who had lost her baby and her husband and her sense of self in a single wave of destiny.

Denise smiled very gently, almost wistfully, and then changed the subject. 'How do you think Paul will react?'

Chala felt the dark water around her. 'You mean about Philip?' It was easier to focus on Philip. 'I don't know. I think he'll be hugely disappointed, and angry, but …' She couldn't hold back the rest, couldn't stop the tears coming. 'I don't know how to measure anything any more. I don't even know if Paul will come back. I don't know how to stop "being me" just because I suddenly discover that I didn't need to go through all that, don't need to be the way I am …'

'Oh Chala, don't.' Denise too was groping for solidity. 'Think of the baby, think of Kenya, of what you did there.'

Chala saw Julius laughing, the frozen pain in Kamau's face, the tiny swaddled baby born at a police station in the aftermath of the riots, the hungry shame of the men she had fed. She stroked the promise of life in her tummy. Hold on to what you've got. And suddenly she was reaching out to Denise and both women sank into the female warmth of each other's arms.

# CHAPTER 48

Upstairs in the yellow room, Emma is sleeping soundly. She is lying on her back and her face is flushed from the warm, late afternoon sunshine that streams through the slats in her cot. Downstairs, her four-year-old sister is hugging a rag doll called Rosie as she sits curled up on the sofa in front of the television. Philip has told her not to move. He has just nipped out to get something. He won't be long, not long at all. Chala is a good girl. She sits and she doesn't move, not an inch. 'Now you sit still, Rosie. We have to wait for Phiwip.'

The front door opens and Philip enters the room, smiling and congratulating Chala for being such a good girl. He dumps a bag of loo rolls on the table and beckons her to him. 'Come on, my sweet. Let's go and get Emma for her supper.'

'Can Rosie come too?'

'Of course she can. Come on, then.'

Chala holds Rosie around her hip as best she can, imitating the way she sees Neece and Phiwip holding little Emma. She follows two large feet up the stairs. As they walk into the yellow room, the atmosphere is very still. They approach the cot, where Emma is lying, still fast asleep, and Chala tugs at Philip's arm. 'Up, up,' she says. 'Put me up.' This is the game they always play. Chala gets lifted into the cot and then she lies back beside her little sister and plays at being another baby, while Denise or Philip change Emma's nappy.

Philip sweeps Chala up and drops her gently into the cot, but then he stops dead. There is something odd about him. He looks as if he is playing musical statues and the music has stopped and he is stuck in a funny position. Chala wriggles down beside her sister, but Emma also seems to be stuck in a funny position. Chala grabs the pillow and tries to play peek-a-boo.

Philip has fallen on his knees by the side of the cot, as if he can no longer stand, and still he makes no movement, just stares. Chala's little mind doesn't understand. She covers Emma's face with the pillow, trying to make her take her turn at peeky-boo.

At this moment, Denise walks into the room – no one has heard her come back – asking where everyone is, but her question dies in the moment that it takes to register that all is not right in the yellow room. She takes in the scene in front of her: Philip on his knees in front of the cot, the frozen shock on his face, the sight of Chala bent over Emma, holding a pillow over her face – and the silence, the terrifying silence, from under the pillow.

In a split second which will last the rest of her life she races to the cot and snatches Emma from under the pillow. She shakes her gently, she puts her cheek against Emma's little cheek and her flesh knows that the flesh next to it is dead. Then she screams, and screams, and screams …

Chala starts crying, and Philip slumps further into a heap on the floor, and a doll called Rosie stares at them all with unblinking black-cloth eyes.

\* \* \*

Chala watched this new reconstruction like a film in her head and knew that it made more sense than any of the other versions ever had. She wished it were a memory chip she could simply insert to erase the vision that had haunted her all her life. And yet this new knowledge was powerful, validating, a new resource to draw on every time she faced the habit of her own being.

She stroked the bump beneath her jumper and looked at Paul in the wedding photo on their mantelpiece. She had been back home for two days now. She and Denise had talked twice on the phone and she had also spoken to Femke and Amanda. The call with Amanda had been hard, with so much to tell and one thing she could never tell. Amanda had said she would find someone to help out with the kids and come and visit immediately, but Chala had said with the directness of true friendship that she wanted to be alone and have time to come to terms with it all before Paul made contact with her.

He had not called her, and she had no idea what was going on or where he was. It made her feel full and empty at once. Full with the knowledge of her baby and the urge for them to move on together – away from the murky history of her past – and empty with the ache of his absence and the uncertainty of what would happen.

She wanted desperately to share this new reality with him, but she also feared his reaction when she told him about Philip. Paul, too, had suffered the consequences of Philip's guilty silence, living with Chala's demons, and she was worried about how he would judge Philip. The memories of what she had half-seen in Naivasha were a constant salutary reminder of what human beings are capable of, and she wondered often what had become of Kamau, banished from the protection of the shelter after one moment of weakness. His scar, in many ways, would be worse than Julius'. She simply couldn't find it in her to blame Philip for colluding with the version of events that had been accepted in a world before cot death had even been properly understood.

Chala sighed deeply and got up, responding to the frequent urge to pee. She went through the motions mechanically, her thoughts still buffeting between memories of childhood and Kenya and Paul and Philip.

And then she screamed.

# CHAPTER 49

The blood was unmistakable: small dark spots on her knickers.

'No. This isn't happening. This can't happen.' She crouched down over herself, still sitting on the toilet seat with her knickers round her knees. 'Paul, Paul, Paul …'

Shaking, she wiped herself and inspected how much blood there was. It was like the beginning of a period. She stood up unsteadily, patting her tummy, putting a panty liner into her knickers and pulling up her jeans, all the while crooning aloud to herself. 'It's going to be OK. It has to be OK. Don't worry, little one, don't leave me now. Oh Paul, Paul come back …'

She found the number and called. The nurse was business-like. 'You need to go to bed immediately and rest. Bleeding can be quite normal, but you can't afford to take any chances. Plenty of fluids and bed rest is what you need. Call us back in twenty-four hours and we'll see how you are and maybe ask you in for a scan, but right now just rest.'

Chala walked in painful slow motion to the kitchen, collected a bottle of water, a carton of orange juice, a packet of digestive biscuits and the cordless phone, and moved slowly upstairs. She left the curtains open, desperate to avoid any suggestion of darkness, undressed down to her T-shirt and knickers, avoiding the temptation to check her panty liner already, and climbed into bed. She picked up one of the unread books on the bedside table and got to the third page before she realised she had no idea what the book was about. She forced herself to reread the opening sentence. 'John was not the person Lucy had married.' She put the book down, too apathetic to find out who John and Lucy were, unconcerned about their private drama.

No more loss, no more loss, please, no more loss. It was like a wave beneath the surface, an ironic reaffirmation of the karma that was still deep inside her, despite the recent discovery that her childhood guilt was misplaced. But the new mother in her kicked in over the top of this wave. She breathed deeply, willing calm into the physical environment around her baby, projecting comfort and reassurance beyond her fear.

What if Paul came back and the baby was gone? Would he be pleased or disappointed? Inhale, exhale, concentrate now on the baby, just the baby now, just the baby ... Slowly, slowly, her mother's body rescued her with woozy sleep.

When the phone rang, it came from far away and it rang and rang before she came to and picked it up from the bedside table.

'Hello?' Her voice was full of sleep.

'Che? Were you asleep?'

'Paul?' My God, Paul. 'Paul, how are you?'

'I'm good.' There was the fraction of a pause which seemed to last for ever. 'Listen, I want to come home. Is that still what you want?'

'Yes, yes, please come.' The snail doing yoga had just learnt to do a backward flip.

'OK, I'll be there later today. Are you all right?'

'Yes. Yes, I'm fine. Paul? I'm sure it's nothing to worry about, but I've started bleeding. The nurse told me I needed to rest, that's why I'm in bed—'

'I'm coming now. Don't move.'

Was it just coincidence? Chala lay back against the pillow and smiled through her tears. He had called at exactly the right moment. He wanted her back, he was coming 'home' – the euphemism they had used while she'd been in Kenya was still there – he was coming back to her. Only one other thing mattered now: the little life inside her, the last vital piece in the jigsaw of home.

# CHAPTER 50

She heard the door open downstairs and then nothing until he was suddenly in the room. Paul looked at her for a moment before either of them spoke and Chala took in the bags under his eyes and the ever-present frown.

'Che, are you OK?' He sat on the edge of the bed and pulled her gently towards him. 'Tell me what happened.'

She spoke slowly to keep herself in check. 'It started about five hours ago. It could be nothing ... or it could mean I'm going to lose it.'

'Shh-shh,' Paul reached beneath the duvet and placed a hand gently on her stomach. It was the first time he had done that and she looked straight at him. 'Has the bleeding stopped?'

'No, it's not very strong, but it hasn't stopped yet. I checked just after your call.'

'Oh Che, try not to worry.' He didn't tell her it would all be OK, but his next words were momentous. 'We're in this together now.'

She pulled him closer and they held each other and she wondered if it was too much to ask to be spared two losses in one go, if it was more than she deserved. And then she remembered that she wasn't responsible for baby Emma's death. It wasn't her fault.

'Is that all you've eaten?' Paul pointed at the open packet of digestives.

'Yep.'

'Right, then I'm going to make something decent for that baby of yours.'

'Ours.' She said it almost in a whisper.

'Ours.' Paul said it quickly and got up and disappeared downstairs.

She waited quietly, a newfound calm inside her – together, they were in this together now. He returned after a while carrying a tray with two plates of spaghetti and salad, and went back down to bring up two glasses and a bottle of red wine.

'But I can't drink, Paul.'

'One glass will do you good. It'll relax you, and that's just what you need right now.' That unequivocal optimism she loved in him. 'Here's to us.' Paul looked relieved, and she recognised that feeling of relief, of having chosen to do the right thing.

'To all of us.' It was a silent prayer to a God she didn't believe in. 'Thank you, Paul. I love you.'

They ate awkwardly, concentrating on not making a mess, propped up on the bed and pausing between mouthfuls to reach over to the bedside tables for their wine. Afterwards, Paul cleared the trays and returned with two mugs of hot chocolate. He stretched out beside Chala under the duvet and stroked her hair.

'I missed you, you know. I was angry with you, but I missed you too. A couple of times I wanted to phone, but I wasn't ready.'

'Where did you go?' The question was gentle, an easy way into a subject that she had no idea how to broach.

'I booked myself in to a cruddy B & B on the seafront in Hove. Can you believe it? The one we used to run past, with old people behind the windows, sipping tea.' Paul was laughing mildly at what was already a memory. 'It felt a bit like an institution.' He laughed again. 'But I hardly spent any time there – too many old dears wanting to talk to me!'

'So,' Chala hesitated, wanting to know more, wanting to understand, but also wary. 'Was it just too much too quickly? I mean the shock of me being pregnant after everything that had happened and not saying anything to you from Kenya? I'm sorry I didn't tell you, I really am. It just felt too big to do on the phone or by email and I didn't think it was fair to tell you unless I was sure I wanted to keep it.'

Rosie was there, shaking her head suddenly. Maybe you won't be able to keep it now. Maybe it's too late … She grappled with the ghost of her resolve, yearning for the painter to wash away one more gash of guilt.

'Paul?' The ghost moved round and round inside her. She looked at his face, at the tiredness beneath his eyes. In her mind's eye, she saw the look of concentration on Philip's face all those years ago, when he had tried and failed to tell her his own secret.

'What?' There was an edge in Paul's voice, and he stopped stroking her suddenly.

'What I said before about what matters, when you asked how you could even know if the baby was yours …' She floundered.

'Look,' he interrupted. 'I had to go through it all in my own head, everything it meant – you going away, you coming back, the baby. There's been so much—'

'Shit … I know.'

'Yeah, so much shit in the past few months and it all came to a head with your little bombshell.' He stopped and Chala opened her mouth to speak, but he cut in again. 'Listen, I feel a bit like I've been to hell and back, but I *am* back and that's what's important. I don't want to talk about it anymore. All that matters now is the future.' And he started stroking her hair again, as if it helped him concentrate. 'And the present,' he said then, still stroking and looking straight at her.

She waggled a finger at him gently. 'Bed rest means no exercise,' she smiled and put a hand to his face. In the distance of her childhood, she could see Rusty, rolling on the ground, and Philip released from a moment that might have changed their lives. Philip had started to try and tell her something and she had felt sorry for him, misunderstanding his anguish, and changed the subject. He had wanted to tell her his secret, she could see that now. She thought of Paul's painting, his hall of mirrors, and the events in her own life felt like mirrors receding backwards.

'Just my luck!' Paul laughed her back to the present and pulled her to him. She stroked his face and her eyes thanked his for ever. 'So, what about you? How have you been?' Paul dropped her gently back against the pillow.

'Very focused on the past.' And she told him about meeting Denise and Philip's letter with its strange revelation after so many years.

'Jesus, Che!' She looked at his face. She knew he was grappling with what it meant, rewinding the story of their lives together, rewinding the story of who she was, trying to catch the ball that had been thrown at him from nowhere. 'So, you grew up thinking it was you for fucking nothing,' he said slowly.

And she took a deep breath and braced herself for the reaction against Philip, for the anger to start, but it didn't come.

271

'Well,' he spoke in a way that was uncharacteristically measured, and she wondered whether he was just tempering his words for the situation or whether the time apart had changed him. 'I guess we can't be too hard on Philip. Who knows what Pandora's box he might have unleashed if he'd come clean all the way back then? He might not have had the chance to be there for you at all. And anyway,' he looked as though he was speaking from somewhere far away, 'he must have paid the price, living with a skeleton like that all those years.'

'But why do you think he didn't say anything later, when I was older? I think he tried to once or twice when I was still a teenager, but even if he couldn't then, why not later, when I had grown up?'

'What would be the point in that? After so long. He probably only thought it would do more damage.'

'Yes, I know, that's kind of what I thought too.' Chala was oblivious to the irony of their exchange, her faculties numbed by the strange mixture of relief and dread that swam inside her.

'Try not to worry, Che.' He said it again and she smiled weakly, acknowledging his understanding of her, his sensitivity to the edge that accompanied the joy of their reunion. He didn't say it would all be fine.

But he was there, with her, the three of them together ...

# CHAPTER 51

Despite Paul's presence beside her, Chala slept badly that night. She woke up time and time again, dreaming of waterfalls and storms and pools of blood – and each time she put her hand between her legs to test for the telltale sign, she could feel only a slight moistness. She forced herself to refrain from unnecessary trips to the bathroom to scrutinise the sanitary towel she had put on before she went to sleep.

When she woke up and saw with relief that light was pouring through the chink in the curtains, Paul was still fast asleep beside her. She was desperate for the loo and yet now that it was here she wanted to delay the moment of truth, the proof on her sanitary towel of whether the danger was over or not. The feeling was becoming familiar: first the pregnancy test, then the letter, now this. But this time was different; this time there was no female friend in the next room, but a man in her bed who had chosen a future with her.

'Paul,' she shook him very gently.

'What?!' He jumped out of sleep into total irritated wakefulness and then realised where he was and said more slowly, 'What is it?'

'I need to go to the bathroom to check. I thought you would want to be awake when I did it.'

'Oh yes, yes, of course. Do you want me to come with you?'

'No, you wait here. I'll be back in a minute.'

She was back quickly. Paul looked expectantly at her, reminding her momentarily of Femke's dog, Tek Tek.

'No blood.' She had tears streaming down her face, still afraid to hope for too much.

'No blood!' He looked happy. 'Is it twenty-four hours yet? What do we do now?'

'Just about. I think we ring the nurse.'

* * *

'You know I wasn't sure how I'd feel if you lost it. I mean I know you would have been devastated, but I didn't really know how *I'd* feel. Now I *know* that I want it too.'

'Oh Paul, that means so much to me.' But Rosie still lurked on the sidelines of her consciousness. 'It's not over yet, though. I'm so scared to hope. Let's wait and see what the scan says.' Chala moved with deliberate, careful steps as if she might break.

They followed the nurse into a room full of apparatus and Chala went behind a curtain to put on the green cotton robe, while the nurse attempted small talk with a monosyllabic Paul. By the time Chala was in position, the doctor was with them, talking them through the procedure, trying to calm their nerves with the coolness of her voice. Chala reached out for Paul. He took her hand in his and she noticed he was sweating. Both of them watched the weird, slippery black and white screen as the doctor moved across Chala's bare stomach. She tried desperately to breathe normally. I'm sorry, I'm sorry, I'm sorry. The quiet, unnecessary mantra she had grown up with washed against the surface of her consciousness now as she waited and waited for the doctor to speak. At last she did and Paul's hand tightened round Chala's.

'I think it's going to be OK. Looks to me like you've got a perfectly healthy little baby growing in there.'

For once, the artist in Paul was totally absent. There were unashamed tears in his eyes as he squeezed Chala's hand again.

'Do you want to know the sex?'

'Paul?'

'I do if you do.'

'I do.' She said it through tears, laughing at the echo of their wedding vows.

'It's a girl,' the doctor told them.

'But of course,' Paul laughed.

'I knew it. I knew it.' They were both laughing now.

'What do you want to call it – I mean her? Do you know already?' It didn't occur to Paul that it might still be a little early to speak of names; it just didn't fit into his worldview.

'I don't know, I—'

'Do you want to call her Emma?' Neither of them noticed that the doctor had quietly slipped away.

Chala thought hard for a second, appreciating Paul's gesture. 'No,' she said at last. 'No, not Emma. I want her to have her own name and her own fresh chance in life. Something vivid and colourful, for the daughter of a painter.'

'Violet? Rose? Amber?' he said playfully.

'Fuck off!' she laughed back.

'How about Indigo?' More serious now.

'Maybe. I'm not sure. Everyone would call her Indi, wouldn't they? Actually, that's nice. I like it. Let's just call her Indi. What do you think?'

'Indi it is.'

Paul stroked her face with his free hand and kissed her on the lips and Chala felt as if she were flying – away from her past, away from the yellow room, into a blue sky.

On the horizon of her being, her observer sat, looking a little like a cloth doll with unblinking eyes, quietly nonchalant and waiting for her future.

# EPILOGUE

He felt the heavy ache behind his eyes before he opened them. Then a thought struck him and he opened them quickly and forced himself to focus on the bed beside him. There was no one there. Thank God for that. He knew through the pain that it would have solved nothing.

Paul pulled himself slowly to a sitting position, measuring the strength of his hangover, feeling the rasp at the back of his throat. Vague images of a woman in his arms in a dingy salsa bar played in his head, breasts demanding his attention through flimsy cloth that could not hide her nipples. He had no recollection of how he'd got back, how he'd become separated from her. When he had seen her at the bar he had thought she was pretty – that he remembered – but when he got close the thick smear of too much lipstick had kept drawing his attention, vaguely disgusting him. He had wanted to wipe it off – that, too, he remembered – but it had stayed there in all its smudgy redness and the lure of her breasts on the dance floor was not enough to make it go away. In the end, it was probably her lipstick that had stopped him bringing her back. A sobering thought.

He looked at his watch and realised with more relief that it was too late for breakfast at the B & B. At least he'd be saved from the solicitous looks of the old dears here who seemed to think that he had been sent from heaven for them to mother, but, Jesus, he needed a serious fried breakfast now. Walter's Café, he thought. Walter's Café will save me. He forced himself to brave the lukewarm shower and cold water on his face before taking on the already wintry sea air.

We are never more aware of oxygen in the air than when we're hungover, he thought. It was good to be hungover once in a while, something rare these days, something that reminded him of the heady early days of college, when he had been able to forget briefly the interminable pressure from his parents. He had succumbed, of course, like so many others, to their version of who he should be, following their instincts in his choice of career, even believing for a while that he fitted into the box they had bought for him. It was Chala who had broken the box into tiny pieces around him. She believed in him in a way that no one ever had before – in the artist cowering behind the lawyer.

He moved slowly up the hill from the beach towards Walter's Café and his thoughts dipped sluggishly back to the time he had first seen her. The fiery hair, the slight mismatch of her clothing, the coy flash of her eyes – physically, he had loved her instantly, wanted to place her on a cliff and paint her from every angle. But he had been wary at first. Because he was recently out of a relationship with a control freak and because of what he had learnt first from Claire and then Dan. 'She's trouble, that one. You can't grow up with what happened to her and be OK. There's darkness in her, it's written all over her.'

Maybe now he was paying the price. And yet he loved the darkness in her – that too had drawn him in. She didn't just attract him, she interested him, at a level that no other girl had done. Of course his parents didn't really go for her – she wasn't ambitious enough for a start.

They tried to hide it, but he could tell anyway and the knowledge was a sour taste in his mouth, until it eventually grew into the sweet taste of rebellion and he chucked in his job. She the pessimist and he the optimist, and yet she was the one who had given him the strength to be optimistic about turning his passion for art into his life.

And now, just when it really looked as though it might turn into not just his life but also a living, she had shaken him to the core.

'The works, please.'

'Black pudding too?'

'Yep, everything you've got.' He needed strength. He watched the waitress' bottom as she walked away from the table and felt grateful again that he had not slept with the girl in the lipstick last night. He took out his phone and registered with a mix of relief and disappointment that there were no messages or missed calls from Chala. He was surprised that she had stuck to her word about waiting for him to call.

Why didn't he really go away somewhere, call Dan, anyone, to take him away from this self-inflicted sentence? Not Dan, he could not have stood the told-you-so sympathy. Of all the people he might have spoken to – and there weren't many, he realised in a flash of loneliness – the one he had felt most tempted to call in the first couple of days was Amanda. She knew Chala so well it would have been so easy to sit and talk to her, but he realised there would have been an uncomfortable edge of revenge in it too, and the bottom line was he couldn't tell anyone until he'd worked out what to do, and then, depending on which way he decided to go, he might never be able to tell anyone anyway.

'Here you are – that should sort you out!' The waitress smirked as she laid the plate down in front of him.

He smiled back at her, grateful and greedy to start. The mental swirl in his head relaxed as he fed the dulling ache behind his eyes. Then came coffee and he smiled again as if he had been brought a piece of heaven.

'Heavy night, then?' She laughed and her open mouth showed a perfect line of small white teeth.

No lipstick, he thought. And then, what the hell am I thinking? Yet, she didn't move, waiting for him to speak. There was no one else left in the café and the owner or manager sat crumpled behind a newspaper in the far corner by the till.

'Would you ever have a baby with a man knowing it wasn't his? Without even telling him?' He looked her straight in the eyes. The look of shock was momentary and settled itself into thoughtfulness.

'It depends,' she said finally. 'I might.'

'Thanks for your honesty.' He looked at her long and hard.

Then she took a risk and he admired her for it. 'I'm off when you've finished. Do you want to do something?'

He looked at her again and she held his look, but he knew it was impossible. 'In another life,' he said, and she nodded and moved away slowly with a smile.

In another life, he thought with stubborn irony, he would have been part of that statistic. Yeah, he had surfed the Internet like a sick child on the first night and come across a statistic that he had found staggering: one in twenty-five men believed a child was theirs when it wasn't. But how many would knowingly have a child that wasn't theirs? And what tiny proportion would choose to have a child that wasn't theirs *in secret*? This was the choice that he couldn't yet quite believe he was contemplating.

He backed out of Walter's Café with one last smile for the waitress and headed again for the open space of the beach. By now the first Saturday post-lunch dog-walkers were out with their little plastic bags. He walked and then sat and then walked again. He tried to think about cricket or football, but she had forced him into the thick black world of her own inner existence. Damn her. Who had she fucked? What had she been wearing? Did she come? The questions jabbed at him, catching him by surprise again and again, and he reeled, repelled by the detail that his brain painted for him against his will.

He walked over the pebbles, then sat down again and stared at the sea. He was glad he hadn't blown it before it was too late, hadn't confronted Chala when she broke the news. Some deep sense of privacy and self-protection had kicked in straight away and hardened him, made him cold and distant. He had not processed this new reality yet, but he knew one thing – ignorance of the detail was the one thing that gave them a chance, gave him a chance.

He sank back against the pebbles, closing his eyes, feeling the weak sunshine on his eyelids. He pictured the waitress wistfully and tried to undress her in his mind – more an exercise in distraction than anything else – but the moment he took off her clothes, she turned into Chala.

In another life … He clung to the theme, as if it would hold some great revelation that would make his choice easier. In another life he would not have been hit in the balls by a cricket ball and accidentally discovered he had a genetic testicular abnormality that impeded the production of sperm. In another life his wife would have been by his side in A & E and shared the discovery, not off on some soul-searching, grief-stricken mission in another country. In another life he would have told her anyway on the phone or in an email, but he had needed to come to terms with it himself. He had wanted to tell her face to face if, or when, she came home. The irony struck again – just as she had waited to tell him face to face about being pregnant.

Before the cricket accident, he had always hoped and believed that she would get over her aversion to having a baby one day. There was no rush. It was a private dream he had taken for granted, an unspecified vision of a future together. The cricket ball had knocked him sideways – ha! All of a sudden he was the one who would stop them having children and now, just as suddenly, that had sort of been given back to him. He looked at the sea and saw an opportunity to cheat destiny and bring up a child with the woman he loved – if he could just let go of one irrevocable fact.

He started walking again, not knowing where he would go next, following his feet along the coastline, until he eventually found himself in the centre of Brighton on a busy Saturday afternoon. He wandered into a bookshop and dipped in and out of back covers in the science fiction and the crime sections until he felt bored and restless.

'Are you looking for anything in particular?' A male this time, not a female, with or without lipstick, tempting him to get back at the woman he loved.

'No, not really.' Then a thought struck him. 'Do you have a copy of Kahlil Gibran's book?'

'You mean *The Prophet*?'

'Yeah, that's the one.'

He paid for it and then ordered a coffee and unwrapped the book, feeling vaguely self-conscious and feminine. But he wanted to find the words again, the words he had spoken at their wedding without truly thinking about them. He had been swept along by her choice and yet she had come back to them time and time again – they really meant something to her – and now he wanted to find out what they really said. *Spaces in their togetherness* – that was the sound bite that had stuck and it sounded OK, but what did it really mean? Did it mean she had a right to fuck someone without telling him? Did it mean he had a right to consign her to unforgiven guilt for ever by not telling her about his own infertility? Hadn't there already been enough guilt in her life? Did space really mean deception? Does the end justify the means?

Fuck! He flicked through the pages and found the passage. He looked around briefly, self-conscious again, and then started reading against the mental backdrop of a cliff in Devon overlooking the sea.

*Love one another, but make not a bond of love:*
*Let it rather be a moving sea between the shores of your souls.*
*Fill each other's cup but drink not from one cup.*
*Give one another your bread but eat not from the same loaf.*
*Sing and dance together and be joyous, but let each one of you*
*be alone,*
*Even as the strings of a lute are alone though they quiver*
*with the same music.*

*Give your hearts, but not into each other's keeping.*
*For only the hand of Life can contain your hearts.*
*And stand together yet not too near together:*
*For the pillars of the temple stand apart,*
*And the oak tree and the cypress grow not in each other's shadow.*

Paul looked up slowly and stared indiscriminately at the book stacks beyond the coffee tables. His eyes stung. If Chala were sitting opposite him now, he would have told her that he must still be hungover, but she would have seen through him. She would have known that he was moved.

It felt like a wave, a slow, powerful revelation between the lines of what he had just read. *She did not know who the father was.* She knew it could be someone else's, but she also thought it could be his. She would have tortured herself over whether to tell him or not. If she had decided not to tell him, it was because what had happened was too meaningless to put their relationship at risk and because emotionally her commitment was to his baby. Her words had already said as much.

Paul's head felt suddenly very clear. If he had slept with the lipstick woman, it would have meant nothing. If he trusted Chala, he must trust the strength of her decision and decide upon his own with equal strength.

Then why not be strong enough to bring it all out into the open and just deal with it and move on? Paul saw his own hall of mirrors painting in his head. The mirrors he had opened up inside himself bounced back at him and he knew that their message was true. Because you are not, they said simply. Not strong enough for that. Not strong enough to confront the details that would seem to confer meaning where there wasn't any, not strong enough to unravel the private inner space of their lives in an attempt to make them more connected. Spaces in their togetherness. Yes. They had a chance this way, a real chance …

Paul finished his coffee and walked into the street again, half-expecting the world to have changed around him. He could feel the decision gaining ground inside him. It was not yet made and yet he felt it pulling at him. The light was beginning to fail slowly in the sky, but he wanted to return to the sea.

It was a soft grey-blue now, and calm in the late afternoon light. Did you really just walk into the sea, you old bastard? He realised with a pang that he would have liked to talk to Philip more than anyone. He would have valued Philip's opinion. He felt sure – suddenly and obscurely – that Philip would have understood the decision he was taking himself towards.

And as he stared and stared at the great expanse of sea in front of him, he understood that his decision was made. There would be secrets in their togetherness. Their lives would be like a painting, something beautiful with unexpected shadows; their lives would be like life.

THE INSPIRATION BEHIND

# YELLOW ROOM

Yellow is the colour of the third chakra, associated with our sense of self-worth, the place where guilt and secrets dwell. Why are we so fascinated by secrets? Why do we *have* secrets? Whether they are born of fear or shame, denial or the urge to protect or avoid hurting another, so often they create pain and guilt. We pay a price for the things we keep bottled inside us, and sometimes the bottle bursts. At one level, *Yellow Room* is a book about the power of secrets to run our lives. Philip carries a secret to his grave and we will never know whether it drove him there. Chala wants to believe that Paul is the father of her child but knows he may not be. Unbeknown to her, Paul knows that he can't be. So now they both carry secrets inside them. Are these like the nurturing 'spaces in togetherness' of their marriage vows? Or is there another, more sinister, future waiting for them? Secrets are often bound up with relationships and how we define their boundaries, often connected to our sense of who we are and how we are seen by the world. In the widest sense of the word, they can be about the things we bury or hide from ourselves. Secrets are a clue to our sense of personal identity if we listen to them.

*Yellow Room* was born from a very simple idea: what would it be like to grow up with your identity shaped by something that happened in your childhood and then discover that it never happened? Your whole sense of who you are, moulded by the guilt associated with something horrific you thought you did at the age of four – which you only find out years later was not your fault after all.

What is this thing called 'I' that burns at the centre of our haphazard path through the maze of life? This is a question that haunts me and my writing. Nature versus nurture: we are the sum of our genes and we are the sum of our experiences. We may also be influenced by inherited or collective memory if we believe in certain ideas about morphic resonance across the boundaries of time and geography. We acknowledge that the world we live in is transient and ever-changing. Yet we carry our stubborn belief that some kind of unique essence of 'me' exists through the various twists and turns of our own life. We use phrases like 'I'm not feeling myself' or 'I want to find myself' or 'It's not me' or 'I am at one with myself' as if there is only one identity living inside us.

And yet I often feel we are like a house that looks pretty much the same on the outside but with a whole bunch of different residents who take turns to look out the window or stoke the fireplace. A house inhabited, not by a hermit who gets up and goes to bed at the same time every day, but by a committee of different personas and alter egos constantly chuntering away and making decisions about how to present 'me' to me. The committee is never idle; some items appear on the agenda again and again, some are always new. Whatever challenges this wonderful committee faces – be they personality traits caused by unchangeable genes or big life events that threaten the very foundations of the house – their task is always the same: turn it all into a story, a story that is cohesive and convincing – the story of me.

In *Yellow Room* I wanted to explore how a perceived reality can shape a person, and what happens when the goalposts of that perception shift. I also wanted to explore the relationship between the internal world of our own inner stage and the external world, and how this affects who we are and who we can become.

Enter Kenya. Chala's experiences here – the orphanage, the post-election violence, the landscape, the people – all of this interacts with and impacts on the way she views her own personal drama and, ultimately, the decision she makes to keep her baby. Kenya is not just a setting; Kenya plays a role in the story of who she is and who she becomes. The inspiration for what I write about Kenya is based on personal experience, although it does not purport to be factual. There are details like the month of the elections which I have taken the liberty of changing.

I lived on a farm in Africa. A flower farm in a valley overlooking Lake Naivasha. Actually, Karen Blixen's old weekend house still sits there, unfenced, and protected by hippos at night. My father is buried in the bush nearby, and my mother still lives in a log cabin close to the lake. I grew up with Kenya in my blood, although it wasn't until 2005 that I went to live there. The farm where my husband worked was about half an hour along a potholed road from Naivasha, a Kikuyu town in the Rift Valley, which was one of the areas hit by the post-election violence of 2007–2008.

About 1,200 people were killed and over 500,000 displaced in the aftermath of the disputed elections. I kept a diary during the days that followed the elections. As events unfolded, with the burning of Kikuyu slums in Nairobi and the killing of Kikuyus in the Luo stronghold of western Kenya, the tension and horror were tangible. What struck me forcefully was how little normal Kenyans wanted what was happening. The 'tribalism' referred to so glibly in the media felt like something that was being deliberately stoked, not a spontaneous reaction to the political stand-off between the Kikuyu and Luo candidates, Kibaki and Odinga. Then, just when things appeared to be calming down (and after my diary), violence flared in Naivasha: revenge against the Luo (and associated tribes) who had attacked members of the Kikuyu tribe elsewhere in Kenya. I use the word 'flare', but it felt orchestrated. The Mungiki militia were brought in on trucks.

Recently, the case against current president Uhuru Kenyatta, subsequently accused, among others, of inciting ethnic violence to help secure the victory of Kibaki, was dropped at the International Criminal Court, amidst controversy surrounding alleged intimidation of witnesses …

The orphanage in *Yellow Room* is also rooted in reality, inspired by a project run by an amazing woman who has since died of cancer. Although I have changed the characters for the purposes of the novel, the awe and respect I have for the people involved is real, the shelter really did prepare food for the displaced who took refuge at the police station, and some of the boys there have since become Facebook friends. What I admired most about this project was the fact that it was based not simply on charity but on creating self-sufficiency and self-respect. I have made a personal pledge to donate ten per cent of whatever I earn from *Yellow Room* to this or similar projects in Kenya.

Secrets. The boys of Naivasha's orphanage will have their own secrets, some too deep to ever share. Kenya has its secrets; maybe time will uncover the truths we do not know, and maybe it won't. As individuals, I believe we all harbour areas of turmoil within us that are either consciously or unconsciously hidden to various degrees. Secrets are like scars that heal over a wound which never quite disappears.

# ACKNOWLEDGEMENTS

I was once told that the hardest thing to write would be the acknowledgements. It's true. It's impossible to name all the friends and family who help to make a book possible ... but I would like to say thank you to those who have played a special role for *Yellow Room*. Mum for being a pillar of support and inspiration. Bull, who gave me the peace and strength to keep going. My agent and friend, Broo, whose sensitivity, candour and dedication eased the growing pains and created a better book. Deeker, Andy, Nicola, Nella, James, Tom, Celia, Es, Amanda and Amanda for their feedback and encouragement. Paul for being part of the journey and a delight to work or share wine with, Lisa and Sean for their editorial input, and the team at Cutting Edge Press for publishing the first edition. David, Broo (again) and Rebecca at The Dome Press for giving the book a second life and publishing the new edition. Jem for the lovely new cover; Amanda, Aidan, Mark, Jackie and Anne for their quotes; Jackie and Anne again, Nellie, Victoria, Book Geek, (Being) Anne, Claire and indeed anyone else who has reviewed and given space to the book on their blogs. Of all those who provided inspiration on the way, I'd like to make special mention of just a few. My Dutch friend Mac, a sister of Femke's in real life. Debbie, who founded Naivasha Children's Shelter and poured heart and soul into it until the day she died. Joseph, Paul, Francis and David who were shining lights; Peter, Bernard and every single boy from the shelter I had the privilege to meet while I lived in Naivasha. Caroline, Joyce and Fred for helping prepare food for the refugees in my back garden and for teaching me so much about Kenya and being Kenyan. June and Hans for making it possible to be there in the first place. My father, who died before the book was finished, but lives on in me and my writing.